The Charming Spy

Book 2 in The Seductive Spies Series

By
Cheri Champagne

Jacket design and illustrations by Deana Holmes
Editing by Forrest Driskel (Pandamoon Publishing), Dayna Reidenouer, and Amanda Bidnall
Sensitivity Read by Jenna Beacom

ISBN: 978-1-7777443-3-5

Dedication

For every person that yearns for more.

The Charming Spy

Prologue

The Rookery, London, October 1801

Bramwell Stevens tightened his grip on his younger sister's hand as he staggered along the ragged cobblestoned street in St. Giles. Night had long since fallen, the gin hovels full to near bursting, and pockmarked harlots lounged against building walls, lifting their tattered skirts to any man with a coin.

Did that truly just happen? Will someone notice? Could it have been a dream? Good God, what will we do now? A litany of distressing thoughts wandered through his mind as they walked. *It was all a horrible nightmare, surely…* The hard cobblestone beneath his feet and the chill bite to the air told him otherwise.

The air was cold and stank of drink and vomit, the scent almost overpowered by the acrid odour of piss and rotted flesh.

Crooked buildings towered high above them, dark and intimidating. What lurked within was likely soiled in sin.

A plump woman with deeply rouged cheeks and two missing front teeth sauntered toward them. "Gimme a penny, love, an' ye can satisfy your young urges… an' for another ha'penny, th' lassie can watch."

Bram cringed and pulled his sister closer to his side as they continued to walk past. "I ain't interested," he grunted.

The lightskirt shouted blasphemous curses at him as they hurried away. He led his sister down an adjoining street, hoping to find a safe place to bed down for the night. The only light to be seen came from the cloud-covered moon hanging mockingly in the sky and dim candlelight flickering in the windows of passing buildings.

He suppressed a shiver.

A pistol went off in the distance, followed by a hollow scream, and Bram's hair stood on end, gooseflesh puckering his skin. Little Yvette tightened her grip on his hand, a garbled whimper lodged in her throat.

"I wanna go home," she whispered in her high, childish voice.

Bram's lips tightened into a grim line, the blood draining from his face. He was far too young for this responsibility but, tonight, he had been forced swiftly into manhood. Yvette was now under his protection, and his alone.

"We ain't goin' home," he returned. The image of two bodies slumped on the floor of Mama's bedchamber rose to his mind's eye. One was bloodied and broken beyond recognition, and the other stiff with a neck twisted at an unnatural angle. The image would be branded on his soul forevermore, of that he was absolutely certain.

His stomach lurched, threatening to cast up his accounts, but he swallowed them down. He'd not have food for Lord knew how long… Whatever was in his gut could very well mean life or death.

"We ain't got no home now, Yvie. We gotta make our own way."

A sob rose in her throat. "I want Mama."

His heart flipped, and unshed tears clogged his throat. "I do too," he croaked.

He could never go back now. He could never let Yvie see what had happened.

A group of men staggered out of a building, and one fell on his arse while the others roared with drunken laughter. The man who guarded the door shouted obscenities before telling the men they weren't to return to the establishment.

The hairs on the back of Bram's neck stood on end, and his gut knotted with unease.

Ballocks. He prayed they wouldn't see Yvie. She was a young thing, but some bastards didn't care about that, only about their own scurrilous needs. She was a bonny lass, and he was gaunt and lanky, his sixteen-year-old body still growing into that of a man's. He could never take on a group of men to defend her honour, whether said men were foxed or not.

Before they could be sighted, Bram led his sister in a sharp turn into an alley, the blackness enveloping them instantly.

"Bram." Yvette's soft whisper echoed off the leaning walls of the close. "I don't wanna be here."

"I know. Hush now, Yvie," Bram whispered back.

His eyes had widened in the darkness, his heart drumming wildly in his chest as they stepped hesitantly forward. Awareness prickled along his skin, tightening his shoulders. There was not a sound, no movement in the surrounding obscurity. But Bram could feel it: the unmistakable presence of another person.

They halted in their tracks, Bram's arm lowering to his sister's trembling shoulders, pulling her close against him. He had to choose among the evils: continue on and risk whatever it was that lay ahead, stand in the darkness and wait out any danger, or put Yvie at risk with the drunken men.

He could never risk Yvie. Despite the unknown dangers of the close, Bram made his decision. He gripped his sister's hands and, pulling her behind him, placed her hands on his hips, ensuring that she held the material of his short coat in her small fists.

"Stay with me," he whispered almost inaudibly.

As cautiously as he could, he inched through the close, his sister directly on his heels.

Bram kept his ears trained, listening intently for any sign of movement around them. The end was near. The blackness fell away up ahead, where the narrow alley opened onto the next street.

We will make it.

The whoosh of fabric alerted him, but it wasn't from where he'd expected. His gaze rose to the rooftops and followed a dark, caped figure that threw itself gracefully over the edge of the building to cling against the wall of the close.

Bram's breath stilled in his throat as his feet stopped. *The caped figure cannot see us,* he assured himself. *Can they?*

His eyes widened ever further in an attempt to see the figure in the dark. Only the gentle scraping of the person descending the wall told him where they were. *Dear God.* The person had be an agile animal to lower themselves from four stories up and not fall dead on the cobblestones.

The soft *clomp* of boots touching the ground echoed around them as the mysteriously shrouded person reached the bottom.

"It is perilous for a young man and a little girl to be out in St. Giles…most particularly at night," the disembodied, silken voice of the person in black called through the cold air.

Yvette's grip on Bram's coat tightened, and he felt her press herself against his legs and arse, her head at the small of his back. He wanted to reassure her. He wanted to tell her that he'd protect her with his own life, if it came to it. But he daren't show weakness to the caped pursuer.

His stomach knotted with fearful nerves, but a flash of bravery and determination squared his shoulders. Bram pulled his hands into fists and lifted them, ready to strike should the mysterious personage come near.

"There is no telling what horrors could happen to one so young in the darkness of night…" the voice continued, masculine and cultured, as it slowly advanced. Bram was now certain the caped figure was a man and, damn, even an aristocrat with his fancy speech.

A low chuckle floated across the darkness. "It is fortunate, then, lad and lassie, that you happened across *me*."

Bram's brows drew together in confusion and wariness.

"For I shan't harm you," the man continued. "As a matter of fact, I intend to teach you."

There was silence for a moment while Bram puzzled through the man's words. *Teach?* Why the devil would anyone want to teach two orphaned children in St. Giles?

Then it came to him. Damn if he'd submit and become somebody's pickpocket, chimney sweep, or, God forbid, brothel boy. And he damned well wouldn't let it happen to Yvie.

A shudder wracked his narrow frame at the disturbing thought, his fists tightening further.

"We'll not be nobody's—"

"I believe you've misunderstood me," the voice cut over him. "There is a school in Northampton that I believe would be mutually beneficial for you and its master."

Bram licked his dry lips, wariness hardening each beat of his heart. "Why would a toff wanna teach a nobody like me?" His eyes narrowed. "Wot's in it fer ye?"

"Why, there's quite a lot in it for me, young lad. I would be teaching you to work for me."

Bram's suspicion heightened. "We won't work in no brothel," he asserted, "and we ain't gonna be no pickpockets or chimney sweeps."

Another soft chuckle echoed around him. "I wouldn't dream of it." The man heaved a light sigh. "Indeed, what I have to teach is rather more interesting than that. More dangerous as well."

Bram waited for the man in black to continue, his suspicion melting into grudging curiosity.

"At the school, we teach maths, sciences, history, Latin, Greek, French…" His voice trailed off, and Bram could swear the man smiled. "We also teach cryptology, infiltration, espionage, reconnaissance, sabotage, weapons usage… The list is rather long, actually. But rest assured, it would be a very thorough education."

"Blimey," Bram breathed.

He could feel Yvette shifting behind him, trying to look around him at the man who spoke. But he knew that she could see nothing.

The cloaked man cleared his throat. "Unfortunately, this offer will be for you only. Your sister may reside in the school with you and receive a basic education, but she is yet too young for our other topics."

An unearthly cackle rose up in the street behind them, and Bram tensed. Yvie pressed herself further against him.

Nerves fluttered in Bram's stomach as he thought about his next question. "Who do ye spy fer?"

"Why, for England, of course," was his smooth reply.

There was something about the man that compelled Bram to believe him. Relief hit him full in the chest, and he relaxed his fighting stance, his arms falling to his sides.

"Why me?" He licked his cracked lips once more. "Why would ye choose t' teach *me*?"

The man was silent for several moments before he finally spoke. "I feel…compelled to help you. I have a son about your age." Bram heard him shrug. "I also believe that you would suit our group quite nicely. You show bravery, courage, and an admirable protectiveness for your sister. What more reason could a spymaster need?"

Bram grudgingly nodded. "Wot's yer name?" he grunted.

There was a brief moment of silence before the caped man spoke. "My name is Lord Theophilus Samuels, Viscount Leeds."

"Cor," Bram whispered. He had been correct in thinking the caped man was of the gentry.

He scrunched his face in thought. He and Yvette were currently without a home. If he rejected this offer, they would sleep upon the hard ground with danger lapping constantly at their heels for possibly the remainder of their lives. If they didn't become beggars or other unsavoury things, they could very well die of starvation.

He could not allow that to happen to Yvie. He could not allow her to live such an existence, short though it would be. He wanted her to live long and one day get married and have children of her own. If accepting this man's offer of an education and becoming a spy could give her a better life, then he would damned well do it.

"Aye," he said, his voice becoming stronger. "I accept yer offer."

* * *

Bram's feet ached something fierce. They must have walked clean across London. He and Yvie had never before ventured this far from home. The buildings were unsoiled in these parts, though slightly dusted with coal smoke. The straight cobblestoned streets were lit with oil lamps; proper carriages rolled down the thoroughfare carrying toffs to their balls, the opera, or other such things; and it didn't stink of death.

Bram rather liked it.

Yvette had begun dragging her heels. A shiver wracked her small frame, and her mouth gaped in a yawn.

Would that we could find a safe place to bed down for the night.

"Here we are." His lordship gestured toward the double doors of a building obscenely large to Bram's eye. He'd never been to the part of London where the toffs lived.

The building was tall and wide, with intricate carvings around the door. Every window glowed brightly with candlelight.

Yvie tugged on his hand, and he went willingly into the grand townhouse. Bram gaped. The foyer was bright with a white marble floor and staircase. The walls were a matching white and trimmed with rich gilt tones. The wide staircase had a tasteful carmine runner going up the length of its centre, which complemented the red trinkets about the space.

"Good evening, Chips." Lord Leeds addressed his butler.

Chips, who was surely not past his twentieth year, bowed properly to his master. "Your lordship."

"Have hot baths brought up to the rose room and the yellow room, if you will. Our guests will journey with us to Brampton on the morrow."

"Of course, your lordship." The butler bowed once more, then spun to stride purposefully toward the rear of the foyer and down a wide corridor.

"Father?" A crackling, youthful voice echoed in the grand space.

Bram looked up to see a finely dressed youth crest the top of the stairs. He could not have been much older than Bram himself. This must be the son Lord Leeds had mentioned.

"Father, I cannot find my sparring—oh!" He halted mid-step on the stairs, his astute blue gaze travelling over Bram and Yvie.

The lad continued to the bottom step, his heels clicking on the marble floor, then lowered in a perfunctory bow. "My pardon for interrupting. Good evening."

"Christian," Lord Leeds intoned, "this is Mr. Bramwell Stevens and Miss Yvette Stevens. They will accompany us to Brampton on the morrow. Young Mr. Stevens will be attending school with you."

How had the man known their full names? Bram hadn't told him, had he?

A strange, fervent light entered Christian's cobalt eyes at the news.

The moment passed quickly as his lordship spoke. "Mr. and Miss Stevens, this is my son and heir apparent, Master Christian Samuels."

"It is a pleasure to make your acquaintance, Miss Stevens." He nodded at Yvie before extending his hand to Bram. "A pleasure."

Bram accepted his hand and shook it. Master Christian Samuels' eyes glittered over their linked hands.

"Welcome, Stevens." He lowered his voice, the impact full of meaning. "Tomorrow shall be the dawn of your grand, lifelong adventure."

Chapter 1

Eastbourne, mid-May 1815

Predawn light shone dimly through the dingy fourth-floor window of Sir Bramwell Stevens' shared servant's bedchamber. He sat upon his narrow cot, watching the dust motes dance along the air as he tossed aside the threadbare counterpane.

He had been working as a footman in the household of Algernon Chaisty, the Marquess of Hale, for nearly a fortnight, and he had yet to find any irrefutable evidence of his lordship's nefarious, traitorous activity. Bram had nary a doubt of the man's guilt; not only was it in the way the man spoke of Prinny—His Majesty, the Prince—his views on politics, the secretive late-night meetings with disguised fellows, and the hushed whispers, but his superiors had also garnered irrefutable bruit from other agents in undercover posts. Rumour— and even witness testimony—however, was different from evidence. The man was undeniably a spy for Bonaparte; Bram simply couldn't prove it.

He shook his head, a lock of nearly black hair falling across his forehead. Assignments had never before taken him so long to complete. Most traitors had some bit of evidence or another hiding in a locked drawer, strongbox, a loose floorboard, or the like. Lord Hale certainly knew how to cover his proverbial tracks.

Brushing the hair away from his eyes, Bram rose and padded on bared feet to the cracked earthenware washbasin and pitcher sitting mournfully in the corner of the cramped room. The tall chest of drawers on which they rested had been formerly used in one of the guest bedchambers but had been broken by a past guest and subsequently sent to the servants' wing.

With a glance over his shoulder to ensure that he did not wake his slumbering roommate and fellow footman, Stewart Davies, Bram poured a dram of water into the washbasin, then gathered his shaving supplies from the locked box under his cot.

He looked into the fractured looking glass, which hung just at his eye level, gazing into his own gilt-coloured eyes. He worked up a lather in the shaving cream over his broad jaw and unfashionably tanned cheeks. He spared no expense when it came to his shaving supplies. Not many footmen were able to afford such luxuries, but then again, Lord Hale was not his only employer, and Bram could not abide a rough shave.

The faint fragrance of sandalwood floated up to tease his nose, and he grinned. He slid the blade from atop the chest of drawers and flipped it expertly between his nimble fingers before placing the blade against his cheek and sliding it down with a *snick*.

Bram was accustomed to the role of footman. He'd played the proverbial game in countless households under countless names. This was the first role, however, that he loathed enough to consider requesting reassignment. And it was for that precise reason that Bram remained. He would not allow this blackguard to continue on as he was.

Finishing his shave, Bram wiped at the remaining suds on his smooth cheeks and jaw with a worn towel, completed his ablutions, retrieved his livery from the small standing wardrobe that he and Davies shared, and began to dress. Within moments, he was fastening the last of the clashing copper buttons of his odious green livery and settling the voluminous white powdered wig atop his head. Damned nuisance of a thing.

Bram left the room, ensuring that his shining, high-heeled shoes did not wake Davies as he strode across the floor. The halls were nearly deserted at this hour, but a few maids scurried about in their duties and a select few footmen like himself made preparations for being called upon by their masters.

He trotted down the narrow servants' stairs, taking two steps at a time, the *clip-clack* of his heels echoing around him. The cook was in the kitchens, fixing the first meal of the day, and the scent of freshly baked sweet rolls wafted up to Bram; his mouth watered, and his stomach growled.

Slowing to a walk, he rambled into the kitchens. Then halted.

The room was filled with a cloud of white powder. Three red-faced maids ran hither and yon with pots in each hand while one scullery maid stood sobbing in the corner and two footmen laughed uproariously from their position next to the doors leading to the breakfast room. Mrs. Patel shouted at the lot of them, her normally rosy round cheeks now a blotched red and her short curling hair sticking out at all angles from beneath her mobcap.

"Get that pest out of here!" the cook shouted. "Lord knows what 'is lordship will do if 'e finds out about this! Lucy, Helga! Over that way!"

Bram watched as a pigeon fluttered over a mound of dough, another plume of flour rising into the air. The maids scrambled to catch it with their pots.

"Harriet! Behind you!" One of them pointed.

The small scullery maid let out a high-pitched screech and swatted at her head, her cap falling to the floor and the hair beneath it flying in all directions.

This would get them nowhere.

Bram hurried to the larder and found a mostly empty sack of potatoes. He dumped the remainder into a nearby basket then jogged back into the fray. Quick as a flash, he located the beastie, brushed past the squealing maids brandishing pots, and captured the pigeon in the sack.

"Oh!" Mrs. Patel pressed one thick hand to her large, flour-covered bosom, releasing a relieved, gusty sigh. "You've saved me, Smithe!"

He sent her a wink and a grin, even while his nerves grated at her use of his pseudonym. "I'd do anything, madam, for one of your sweet rolls."

"You rascal." She scowled reproachfully, but the quirk of her cheeks belied the action.

The bag in his hands flapped about, so he turned on his heel, taking the beastie outside to release it.

When he returned to the kitchens, the weeping scullery maid had gathered herself enough to begin sweeping the floor, while the other maids wiped other surfaces and prepared the boiling water for the master's morning tea.

Bram cleaned his hands on a cloth before palming one of the sweet buns from the tall worktable.

Mrs. Patel opened her mouth to protest, but Bram swooped in and pressed a quick buss to her red cheek and quit the kitchens before she could utter a sound.

He tossed the warm roll back and forth between his hands before taking a big bite. Sweet warmth burst over his tongue, and he filled his lungs with a grateful breath. He hadn't lied to the woman: her rolls were sodding delicious.

Mrs. Patel's echoing voice followed him down the corridor as she barked orders to the kitchen maids. Huffing a quiet laugh, he popped the last of his small morning meal into his mouth, sucked the sweetness off his fingertips, then retrieved the white footman gloves from his coat pocket and slipped them on.

Swallowing the final bite of his pilfered treat, Bram opened the panel concealed in the grand foyer wall that hid the servants' passage, slipped through, and quietly closed it behind him.

The foyer was grand indeed, if one were wont to use any word other than "repugnant" to describe it. Tall, wide columns wrapped entirely in gilt stood in each corner of the space, while an enormous round table sporting a hideous arrangement of ill-combined flowers rested in its centre. The ceiling and doorways were outlined in gilt, the checked floor was gilt-flecked with cream and green, and each surface was shined to reflect the flickering lights of the garish chandelier hanging above the table. The room veritably reeked of ostentation. And poor taste.

Straightening his wig and tugging stiffly on his coat, Bram resumed his customary morning post against the far-right wall, staring invariably at the hideous bouquet.

After having been in residence for a sennight, Bram knew his way through the majority of the corridors. The foyer held grand doors to his left and right; the front entry to his left, and the right opened onto the courtyard. The corridor to the family wing was at the back of the space and to the right, while the guest chambers and other gathering rooms were down the corridor to the left.

He blinked, stiffening his spine.

Light footfalls came from the direction of the guest wing and the faint scent of oranges reached him. That scent could only belong to one woman: Miss Rose Wilkinson. She and her sister, Miss Violet Wilkinson, were Lord and Lady Hale's nieces, and now permanent— if reluctant—houseguests. She came through the foyer every morning before the others in the house had awoken. Even the butler, Garrott—bloody awful name for a man; he should have changed it ages ago—had yet to rise.

Despite having been in residence for so short a time, Bram found himself becoming increasingly intrigued by the young woman each time he set eyes on her. She held herself boldly, yet also shyly. She was a paradox in the form of a handsome female.

And there she came. Her shining blonde hair was tucked beneath a tightly knotted, wide-rimmed black bonnet. She wore a modest, high-necked black bombazine day dress, but the drab material did nothing to disguise the lithe curves beneath. She was tall and slender with a bosom just large enough to fit in a man's hands but not so large as to spill out of them…

He shook himself internally. He should not be thinking of her in such terms.

Miss Rose strode quietly into the large space, sliding on her black kid gloves, then glanced up, skidding to a halt at the sight of him.

Her warm brown eyes darted warily around the foyer, her lips curving inward to worry them between her teeth.

Something in his stomach tugged at the sight. Was she fearful of him? She'd seen him standing there every morning since he'd been given the position, but perhaps she took time to become comfortable with new acquaintances? Or, perhaps, *men*?

His inner thoughts turned dark as he realised what must be the cause of her reticence. Her uncle. The man didn't hide his cruelty; could his abuse of his nieces have caused a mistrust of men in general?

Bram cleared his throat.

"Would you care for your pelisse, Miss Wilkinson?"

Ignoring him, she slowly walked toward the courtyard door, her deep, coffee-coloured eyes fixed directly ahead and her gloved fingers fidgeting with the small onyx pendant at her neck.

Bram stepped forward and opened the door for her. Her startled gaze met his on a gasp. Her expression reminded him of a frightened deer, frozen in both shock and terror, hoping that it had not been sighted.

Anger and dismay raced through his gut, but he easily hid the emotions from his expression. Would that he could erase whatever trauma had caused her to be so skittish. Instead, he grinned in an effort to ease her worries.

"Thank you," she said dully before she scurried out the door.

Bramwell cursed inwardly as he resumed his post. Miss Rose Wilkinson was a curious mouse. What did she do on her morning jaunts? Where did she go? How could he ease her fears around him? She rarely spoke in his presence and, when she did, it was always so softly uttered he had to struggle to hear her.

Hell, but he was intrigued.

He grinned before he caught himself and carefully pasted a bland expression on his face. Such were easy enough things to learn, after all. A footman, however, knew better than to trouble himself with what the master and his family or guests were doing.

It was a good thing, then, that Bramwell was not truly a footman…but a spy.

Chapter 2

Twining her finger around the silver chain at her neck in her habitual nervous habit, Rose Wilkinson hurried through the courtyard of Willow Hall. She glanced over her shoulder toward the door, but the footman had already closed it behind her.

Rose had once been kindly and sociable with everyone, servants and noblemen alike. But that had been before the fever had gone through their village in Ramsgate two years past and had taken the lives of Mama, Papa, and her younger sister Helen. Orphaned, Rose and Violet had been forced into the home of their aunt and uncle.

A shiver of dread crawled down her spine, and she shook it off, pushing thoughts of her unfortunate circumstance and the Handsome Footman far from her mind.

The morning light was still dim, but over the furthermost hill just beyond the gardens was a tiny burst of sunlight. Sunrise was but moments away. A light, cool, mid-May wind tugged at her skirts and the dull black ribbon hanging from the knot beneath her chin.

She and her twin sister, Violet, should have been out of mourning now, but not only did they lack the funds to replenish their wardrobe, but her ladyship and his lordship would not abide such a flagrant overshadowing of their daughter. Rose suspected that her aunt and uncle intended to keep their impoverished relations in black bombazine for the remainder of their lives. It was fitting, she supposed…a life in mourning.

Rose's maudlin thoughts forced her feet into an unladylike trot as she hurried along the garden path. The ever-brightening morning light lent an almost blue glow to the early-blooming flowers of the garden; the pinks turned a pleasing mauve and the yellows a soft bluish white.

Passing the tall willow trees—after which the estate had been named—and several rows of shrubbery, Rose glided effortlessly down the path toward the grand, smooth stone wall that surrounded the estate's massive gardens. And to the wrought-iron gate hidden along it.

With her gloved hands wrapped tightly around the iron, she shoved, forcing the gate to open, the vibrations of its motion trembling up her arms.

A tumultuous smile broke across her lips as she gazed over the fields into the far-off horizon. She closed her eyes, filling her lungs with a deep breath of brief independence.

The familiar wetness of a dog's snout bumped her hand, followed by the hot roughness of a tongue. Rose turned to smile into Dog's warm brown eyes. She rubbed her hands over his shaggy black-, grey-, and brown-spotted white fur, scratching him behind the ears as his tongue lolled happily from the side of his mouth.

"Good boy, Dog," she said, knowing that her voice pleased him. "Yes, that's a good spot, isn't it?"

It was on Rose's second sojourn out of doors after she'd come to live at Willow Hall that she'd found him: a little scruffy slip of a thing, half-starved and in dire need of love. Rather like herself. On her behalf, Violet had inquired about his ownership to the nearby homes, and, to Rose's pleasure, he'd become hers. With the help of the stable hands, she'd built a wooden structure from broken slats and hid it within the bushes behind the gardens' wall. She provided food and water daily, and yet, still, she dearly wished that he could live indoors with her.

Blinking away yet more maudlin musings, she slid a slice of beef from last evening's dinner from a pouch tied beneath her skirts and handed it to her companion. He eagerly ate the morsel.

With one last pat and his responding wet kiss to her cheek, she rose from her crouched position. "Are you ready, Dog?"

He blinked up at her.

"Let's go!" She picked up her skirts past her knees and ran.

Chilled wind blew at the tendrils of hair that had escaped her bonnet, the ribbons dangling beneath her chin. The black material of her skirts flapped gaily in the wind behind her as she pumped her legs faster. Her heart thundered in her chest, and the muscles in her arms and legs burned along with her heaving lungs.

Unbridled joy followed her as she tore across the land. Here, in the open meadows, she was able to release her pain and fill her heart with blissful freedom. Just her, Dog, and the land.

Countless minutes passed while she ran over the grassy fields. It was when she felt a gentle tugging at her skirts that she slowed to a stop. Lungs heaving, she bent over, her hands resting on her knees. Dog rolled to his back at her feet, and she laughed, scratching her fingers along his belly.

"Thank you for reminding me of the time, Dog."

She mustn't return to Willow Hall too late or there would be the devil to pay.

She straightened, sweat trickling down her temple and between the shallow valley between her breasts, but she ignored both.

"Come, Dog." She scratched him behind his ears. "It is time to return."

Alternating between walking and jogging, Rose led Dog back through the tall grass over the fields.

Worrying the pendant at her throat, her thoughts wandered as she walked. Every morning for a sennight, the Handsome Footman had offered her his charming, rakish smile that never failed to make his golden eyes glimmer with some underlying mirth. And every morning, she wished that she could be a part of the joke.

He awoke in her a deep, burgeoning desire that she had not felt since the tragic loss of her fiancé, Peter Jones, who'd perished in battle just before the fever that had so changed her life.

Dog's nose purposefully nudged her hand, and she became suddenly alert. Her gaze flicked toward the garden's wall. They had come upon it sooner than she had expected.

A willow branch moved on the other side, and Rose lowered to a crouch, her heart abruptly in her throat. Was it her aunt? One of her cousins? Lord, but just the thought set a nauseating spin to her stomach. If they found her with Dog, they would surely take him away. She waited for several heart-thundering moments, but no one emerged through the opened gate.

Had it, perhaps, been a bird? She sighed in relief.

Turning to scratch Dog behind the ears, she whispered, "I shall see you tomorrow."

Rose determinately ignored the disappointed pang to her stomach as she entered Willow Hall to find that the Handsome Footman had been replaced by the butler, Garrott, at the door.

Pushing that disquieting feeling aside, she hurried into the wing of guest rooms and rushed down the hall toward the stairs leading to the upper guest bedchambers.

Lord and Lady Hale declined to allow Rose and Violet to stay in the family wing, or to step foot into any of the familial rooms. Rose could not bring herself to be disappointed, however, though she mightily missed playing on the pianoforte.

Careful to not be seen in her running attire—for Lord knew her aunt would have much to say about the condition of her tattered and mud-splattered skirts—Rose sped into her shared bedchamber. Quickly washing the saltiness from her skin and changing into a more suitable black bombazine day dress, she fixed the knot of hair at the Crown of her head and quit the room.

The hall of guest bedchambers was dark, but then, Lord and Lady Hale were unlikely to look fondly on the "unnecessary" expense of candles for their unwanted permanent houseguests.

Lord Hale had never given a reason, of course, as to why Rose and Violet's presence was so detestable to the Chaistys, and Rose had never been brave enough to inquire.

Her heart thumped in fear as she reached the morning room and saw her sister, aunt, and cousins already breaking their fasts. She had hoped that they would remain abed or take a tray in their rooms as they were wont to do. Alas, her misfortune was evident in the rigid set to the Chaistys' spines and the disapproval upon their brows.

Rose watched as her aunt's lips curled back in a sneer. "It is about time you game gown, girl. The food has all be gone cold." She paused to consider the words. Mayhap her aunt hadn't meant *game gown*, but *came down*. The words themselves were not so terrible, nor the nature in which she'd said them. It was the look of pure hatred on her aunt's features that put ice in Rose's heart.

Her cousin, Lord Americus Chaisty, both the heir to the title of Marquess of Hale and the current Baron of Bristol, gestured to the empty chair beside him. Rose turned her gaze on him. "Do have a seed, cousin." His disturbingly lustful gaze swept her from head to toe before his tongue darted out to lick the corner of his mouth. "I have reserved the place beside me…"

A chill travelled down her spine as Rose stepped warily into the room, the drab brown and green wall hangings coordinated with the hideously matching rug beneath the table. Two large windows brought morning light into the adequately sized room, but the sunbeams failed to brighten her mood.

Something rumbled through her chest, but she ignored it as she reached the sideboard.

She selected a plate and gazed at the food beneath the covered dishes. As pleasing as the scent of fresh fruit was, Rose's appetite had suddenly fled. She selected a piece of stale toast, a spoon of coddled eggs, and a generous helping of fruit. Far be it from her to deny her body the nourishment it needed.

She turned to place her plate on the smooth oak tabletop, but halted. Her aunt gazed at her with pure ire, the severe grey knot at the base of her neck pulling tightly at her stern eyebrows. The fierce gaze lighting her dull blue eyes did nothing pleasant to her pinched features; the deep lines around her lips gave her the perpetual appearance of someone eating something sour.

Lady Uriana Chaisty, her overindulged cousin, gazed disdainfully down her long nose at Rose. "What is the *matter* with you?"

Rose glanced hopefully at Violet. Her sister's dark blue eyes were concerned as she tried to signal with her fingers. Regrettably, Rose missed the signal entirely as Lord Bristol suddenly stood before her, his black eyes burning with stark hunger and fury.

He clamped his hand on her jaw, his long, slender, aristocratic fingers digging deeply into her cheeks, the force of his grip making her lips purse. "I asked you"—she flinched as he spat a detestable word—"where you hat gone this morning. I saw you wandering through the garden from mig lishbiber window."

His livid gaze whipped toward Violet. "Shut up, woman."

Rose looked into his black eyes and was struck, not for the first time, by how much he resembled his father, both in temperament and in appearance. His dark brown hair was wavy but cropped short; he was slender of build and stood only slightly taller than Rose.

"I apologise, my lord," she said softly, through the painful pinching of her mouth. "My thoughts were elsewhere." She swallowed nervously, her stomach buzzing with trepidation. Would he hit her as his father would? "I-I went for a walk."

His sneer turned into an expression of geniality, though it failed to reach his menacing eyes. He slowly released her, only to grip her hand in his. "You would be wise…"

He turned to glance over his shoulder as Lord Hale entered the morning room.

Taking advantage of his distraction, Rose slipped from her cousin's punishing grip and curtseyed to the room. "Please excuse me."

She rounded Lord Bristol, avoiding the stares of the others and the pitying glance she knew her sister must be giving her, and strode toward the door. Her fingers played with the onyx pendant hanging from the silver chain around her neck; she hoped no one would halt her retreat.

Then she saw him, and her heart froze. The Handsome Footman stood stony-faced in the corner of the room, his lips a thin line and his jaw clenched.

She briefly closed her suddenly stinging eyes before speeding from the room. Her humiliation was complete.

* * *

Bramwell wondered if one could lose one's teeth if they clenched their jaw too tightly. For he was certain that his teeth were perilously close to being ground to dust.

His heart slammed in his chest. He'd been forced to suppress the instinct to step in, to block Lord Bristol's access to Miss Wilkinson, to shove the man away and… Images of his mother, her skin purple with bruises, flashed through his mind, and he clenched his fists.

But Bram couldn't help. As much as he wished to follow the distraught young lady from the room after teaching Lord Bristol the much-needed lesson not to abuse those with less power than he, Bram was on assignment. The outcome of the war with Bonaparte and the lives of countless men and women depended on his silence and constant vigil. He must remain in character, and a footman was loyal to his master.

Lord Bristol let out a vile laugh as he returned to his seat at the table and Lord Hale sat at its head.

"Very good, my boy," his lordship lauded. "You must teach them their place at every opportunity. Mustn't allow them to become complacent." Hale tapped the side of his narrow nose.

"Something is odd about her," Lady Hale grumbled as she brought her teacup to her puckered lips.

"Mmm." Lady Uriana nodded in agreement. "She's soft in the head, I'm absolutely certain."

Miss Violet Wilkinson dropped her fork to the table with a clatter before she rose, her chair scraping dully against the rug at her feet. She leaned forward, her palms on the table, as she addressed the group.

"My sister is not soft in the head," she growled.

"Mind yourself, girl," Lord Hale rumbled ominously. "Know where your next meal comes from." He flipped his knife over in his fingers and Miss Wilkinson's gaze followed the movement.

Bram watched as she banked the burning fire of hatred in her deep blue eyes before she pushed away from the table. "Pardon me," she said. "I have lost my appetite." She fled from the room.

"Deserves to be put in her place, that one," Lord Bristol mumbled menacingly.

"If you're going to take your cousins on, son, you had best be careful." Lady Hale shovelled a forkful of kipper into her mouth and spoke around it. "Wouldn't want a bunch of bastards running around the house."

Bram clenched his jaw ever harder, the cringe-worthy grinding echoing loudly in his ears.

Lord Hale leaned forward with one elbow on the table's surface as he pointed his fork in warning at his son. "You are not to tup your cousins, son. I have plans for them."

"But—"

"No exceptions." Bristol groaned, and Hale continued in a low voice, "You know their worth. Do not damage the g—"

Lady Hale dropped an empty teacup on the floor, breaking Bram's concentration. With a muffled *crack*, the delicate porcelain split into several pieces on the green brocade rug.

"Pick that up, Smithe," her ladyship drawled into the room's sudden silence.

Bram leapt forward, bending at his waist to gather the small, sharp pieces. A low groan came from the woman seated behind him, and he stilled momentarily. The hair on the back of his neck stood on end, and he realised all at once that she was staring at his arse.

He had to suppress his shiver of revulsion as he resumed cleaning the mess. The heat of her gaze burned through the hideous green material stretched across his rear, and Bram fought to keep the bile from rising in his throat.

With the small pieces contained in his gloved hands, Bram sketched a bow to the room and made his exit through the door leading to the kitchens.

He strode through the kitchens and disposed of the broken teacup, agitation evident in his stiff back and tightly clenched jaw.

"What has your dander up, Smithe?" Mrs. Patel asked from her position at the steaming pot over the monstrous open fireplace.

Bram shook his head. Even if he had been able to put to words the sickening roil in his stomach, he should not speak ill of his employers to the other staff.

"'Is lordship mistreatin' the poor Misses Wilkinson again?" the woman continued.

Bram looked up, startled at the cook's accurate presumption.

The small scullery maid, Harriet, nodded sagely, wiping a wet rag across the worktable's surface. "They's always treatin' 'em poorly. I heard tell from Lucy tha' she 'elped the misses bathe once." She leaned in and lowered her voice, as though the rest of the staff in the kitchens could not hear their discussion. "Says they was covered in bruises, if ye get my meanin'." She shook her head, the lace of her mobcap flapping with the movement. "Some in the shape o' men's 'ands and some wot could be from a fist…or a boot."

Bram's room companion, Stewart Davies, shook his head at the rough wooden table where he sat in the far-left corner of the kitchen. "I've seen it happen," he said across the space. "The misses say summat that 'is lordship doesn't like, and wham! They get a slap to the face. 'Tis a right shame. A man should have respect for kin, especially ladyfolk."

The knot of nauseating tension in Bram's stomach squeezed tighter.

"Poor gels." Mrs. Patel added dried tea leaves to the boiling pot and moved to prepare a tray for the servants' morning meal. "And them losin' their parents to that awful fever."

Two maids and a footman scurried past and through the doors of the morning room, presumably to clear the table after their masters had concluded their meal.

His heart slammed in his chest as more ghastly memories from his childhood appeared in his mind's eye. Swallowing past the bile in his throat, Bram pushed the old memories back and took a hard seat at the kitchen's table.

As a child, he'd vowed that as soon as he came of age, he would aid his mother with the issue of his father. But fate had intervened far sooner than expected and with a far grimmer outcome. It had left Bram and Yvie vulnerable. He'd had a second chance at living his life, however, but the Misses Wilkinson had not. And when this assignment was complete, Bram would aid the young sisters in ridding themselves of this unfortunate fate. This time, he would succeed where previously he'd failed.

At the present, however, Bram had to focus his efforts on ingratiating himself with Hale and unearthing irrefutable proof of the man's traitorous activities.

Chapter 3

Glass clinked as Algernon Chaisty, the Marquess of Hale, replaced the stopper on the decanter of port and replaced it in his study's tantalus.

Americus slouched in his seat and crossed his legs at the ankles, extending them out to the fire in the hearth. "Why not allow me to marry one of them, father? We would receive the dowry, and—"

"No," Hale grunted, cutting him off and taking his seat across from his son. "It is much more than that, boy. It's the bill, the support, the leverage."

"You would still have another sister—"

"I said no." He cut a hard glance at Americus. "We'll continue as we have. Our plans will succeed, and I'll then have the power."

Americus grumbled, and Hale scowled. "I'll not have your insolence, boy! Once our name has been elevated, you'll inherit the lot of it."

* * *

"I am fine, truly, Violet." Rose paced their shared bedchamber, belying her assertion, her fingers nervously toying with her delicate necklace.

Violet blocked Rose's path, forcing her to stop and look at the most recent bit of small writing on their shared sketchbook. "You do not appear fine."

Rose worried her bottom lip between her teeth, willing the telling prickle behind her eyelids to leave off.

"I suppose I should be used to it by now." Her now-free lip quivered.

Violet scribbled in the sketchbook once more, then placed a hand on one of Rose's cheeks. "We must remain strong, my dear. We will find a way out of this." She shook her head. "I am so sorry, Rose. I am so terribly sorry that I could not do more to help you."

Rose gripped Violet's hand in hers, pulling it gently from her face. "You should not take such a burden on yourself, Vi. Although I may seem weak of spirit of late, you must know that I will live through this."

Her sister's full lips quirked in a sad smile, and she scribbled again. "I know, dearest. You always survive."

Rose knew what Violet was referring to, but she preferred not to ruminate on the past. Their present was dreary enough without bringing past pains into the fray.

Violet startled, then glanced worriedly at Rose.

"What is it?" Rose asked.

Vi motioned for silence before tiptoeing to their bedchamber door, which she flung open.

And there he was. The Handsome Footman, his wig askew, his golden eyes wide and slightly crinkled in the corners as though he had a grand, secret joke. Rose wished she knew what that joke was; she could use some humour in her life.

Despite herself, her chest warmed as she greedily took him in. His jaw was strong but not overly pronounced, and his neck, mostly obscured by his shirt collar and neck cloth, was corded with tendons and sensuously curving muscles. His nose was straight—patrician— which led to devastatingly attractive lips. Rose suppressed the quivering sigh that threatened to escape every time she looked at his mouth. His lips were full, and, she was absolutely certain, made solely for the purpose of admiration…and pleasure.

Rose shook herself. She daren't think of such things but must instead ask herself why he'd come.

His golden gaze snapped upward to lock onto hers, concern and banked anger lurking there. Her stomach swirled uneasily, and the back of her neck prickled with embarrassment.

"I had through bring up a tray," he said, his beautiful lips moving, but the words not quite making sense. "I assumed…hungry."

She squinted as she considered his words, but quicky realized what he must mean.

A deep, longing quiver resonated through her as she noticed belatedly what he held in his hands. He had brought a tray of cold meats, fruits, rolls, and a steaming pot of tea with cream and sugar.

Finally, her eyes did mist, the salty tears perilously close to flowing over her lids. She discreetly took a deep breath, calming herself before offering a whispered, "Thank you."

The Handsome Footman's gaze darted around the bedchamber, presumably looking for a surface on which to place the tray. With an inward grimace, she followed his gaze. Two long, slender beds with moth-eaten counterpanes sat side by side against the right wall beneath two narrow windows overlooking the courtyard. Between them sat a short table with a well-worn copy of Jane Austen's *Pride and Prejudice* and Rose's reading spectacles.

The room was so miniscule that her calves sported constant bruises from being forced to walk sideways between the chest of drawers and her bed. A washstand stood against the wall at the foot of Violet's bed, closest to the door, while a privacy screen and a wardrobe monopolised the wall to the left of the entry. A worn, very nearly dangerous fireplace filled the wall beside the doorway; only heaven knew why their ancestors had placed it there, for it seemed greatly impractical.

Violet gestured toward Rose's bed, her lips moving too quickly for Rose to understand.

The man did as he was bid, keeping one hand carefully on the teapot, ensuring that it did not wobble or tip, before he backed away.

Rose stepped forward. "Thank you again…" *Oh dear. What is his name?*

"Smithe," he provided.

"Smith." She beamed.

With a small shake of his head and a charming smile, he corrected, "Smithe."

"Oh." Nerves fluttered in her abdomen. "My apologies. Your thoughtfulness is greatly appreciated."

He nodded. "If…have need of an ally," he said, facing her, "I am willing."

Sketching a rigid bow with a jaunty grin on his seductive lips, Smithe was gone.

Violet closed the door, her eyebrows high on her forehead as she faced Rose. She quickly wrote in the sketchbook, and turned it around. "What, pray tell, was that about?"

Rose could feel the blush rising in her cheeks, but she steadfastly ignored it.

"I don't rightly know."

"Balderdash!" Violet teased.

Rose's heart thumped. It had been so long since she had seen her strong, emotionally haunted sister smile, and she wanted more of that.

"What did he say his name was?" Rose asked.

Vi flipped the pencil over in her hand and wrote it out. "Smithe." Then described its pronunciation.

"Thank you." Rose sighed in relief.

"Come." Vi gripped her hands and led her to the bed and, on it, the tray of tempting food.

Rose's stomach grumbled, so she hastily took a bite, using that time to think of something to say. She inwardly sighed. Violet would know if she were telling an untruth, so she ought to save herself the trouble and be honest from the first.

She swallowed her bite of the buttery roll. "He opens the courtyard door for me every morning. I suppose he simply felt badly for me after what happened in the morning room."

Violet's grin grew, as she scribbled in the sketchbook. "You fancy him, don't you?"

Her heart fluttering, Rose resolutely shook her head. "You know that I cannot—"

"For heaven's sake, Rose!" Violet gestured her exasperation wildly with her hands, then resumed writing. "Your lack of virtue should not stop you from taking a lover."

"Violet!" Rose's cheeks flamed, despite herself. "Sometimes I wish I had never confided that fact to you."

"That you made love to your fiancé before he went to war? I do not see why not. I suppose if we were ladies of the *ton*, it would be a shocking thing, but surely not for our class." She raised her eyebrows defensively at Rose's expression, then bent back to the sketchbook. "Goodness, Rose, you behave as though it is so scandalous! Right now, we are below the notice of everyone. The neighbouring landowners are scarcely aware of our existence; I doubt they would give a fig if we took footmen as lovers."

"Violet! Do be serious…"

"I assure you, I am. That Smithe is devilishly fine. I daresay he leaves a string of broken hearts in his wake."

"Goodness, Violet." Rose shook her head. "I shan't take Smithe as a lover."

"So you say," Vi wrote, then winked and popped a berry into her mouth, smiling around the juicy red fruit. "Though I wager you will have him between your thighs within the month."

* * *

Sir Bramwell Stevens was acting the fool. He was nearly late for the mail coach's departure, but he couldn't leave Willow Hall without first speaking to Miss Rose Wilkinson. *Utter fool.*

He'd ventured to the sisters' bedchamber, but no one was within, and now he roamed the guest wing. Approaching a parlour, he slowed his steps and glanced inside.

Rose. There were the sisters, each reading a book, and—*Christ!*—an enchanting pair of wire-rimmed spectacles were perched on Miss Rose Wilkinson's nose.

He cleared his throat and tapped on the door's frame. Miss Violet's gaze swung upward just a moment before Miss Rose's. Bram inclined his head.

"Misses Wilkinson," he said in greeting. "Might I have a word?"

"Of course," Miss Rose said, rather louder than he'd have expected. "Do come in, Smithe."

His pseudonym on her lips rankled. Hell, most people he knew called him either Stevens or, more intimately, Bram.

Six months ago, Bram had been on an assignment to aid Hydra—Sir Charles Bradley—in the protection of his now lady wife. The man had perpetrated a scheme in which Bram was to hire Lady Bridget as a governess for his fictitious son in a castle in High Wycombe. It had gone mostly as planned, though none of them had expected the identity of the traitor. The outcome of the assignment had landed Hydra, his valet Jones, and Bram with knighthoods.

Bram had insisted that his comrades and acquaintances not address him as Sir Stevens, most particularly when others were about. He would not wish to become well-known and, subsequently, no longer be able to complete infiltration assignments.

He affected his customary charming smile and strode into the parlour. "Today begins my time of leave. I will return in two days' time."

A small crease formed between Miss Rose Wilkinson's brows. "Oh. Of course."

"I wanted to tell you that…" *That you'll be without an ally in Willow Hall and utterly at the mercy of the Chaisty family. That something is clearly wrong with me because I can't seem to stop thinking about you.* He cleared his throat. "…that I'll not be there to open the door for you in the mornings."

A slight blush coloured Miss Rose Wilkinson's cheeks, and Bram, despite himself, was utterly transfixed.

"Thank you for letting us know," Miss Violet Wilkinson said, her gaze sharply intrigued.

He'd not embarrass himself further. With a quirk of his lips and a swift bow, he turned and fled.

Sodding hell, what was that?

* * *

Rose's fingers hovered over the piano's keys, waiting for her aunt's signal for her to begin. Today was Lady Uriana's dancing lesson, and

Rose had been commandeered to play for them while Violet had been volunteered to turn the pages for her.

Playing the piano was one of the small joys that Rose; the high notes tinkled faintly in her ears, and the low keys vibrated through her chest.

Lady Uriana stood with her tall, slender dance instructor in the ready position, the top of her dark blonde head only reaching the middle of her partner's narrow chest.

Lady Hale flicked her wrist at Rose, who began to play the waltz. Violet flipped the page for her as the need arose. Suddenly, the air in the room changed. Violet nudged her side, and Rose looked up.

Lady Uriana flailed her arms. "How am I to turn the watch before…come-out next year if stupid Rose won't…music correctly?"

Squinting in confusion, Rose attempted to piece together what had happened.

Violet gripped Rose's hand in hers and gave it a comforting squeeze. Her lips moved, but Rose missed what was said.

Her heart in her throat, she darted a quick glance at Lady Hale's furiously pinched expression.

"Ten lashes, Violet."

Rose's pulse thumped unmercifully in her chest. *No!* Her horrified gaze snapped upward toward her twin sister. Violet's skin was starkly pale next to her nearly black hair, her lips a grim line. It was true, then.

Despite Violet's warning squeeze to her hand, Rose said, incredulous, "Surely you do not mean it!"

Their aunt's irate blue gaze turned on Rose. "Ten lashes, Rose."

Rose's jaw dropped open. *Squeeze.*

"But I haven't done anything!"

"Twenty. And cease your shouting, for pity's sake, I can scarcely hear myself *think!*"

Rose snapped her mouth shut.

"Continue to play, girl," Lady Hale said, affecting a deceptively pleasant demeanour. "And this time, no mistakes."

Chapter 4

Bram rubbed an agitated finger over his eyebrow as he sauntered around the side of Willow Hall, the soles of his boots crunching on the scattered stones. His trip to London had gone as well as could be expected under the circumstances. He had yet to find proof of Hale's guilt and therefore had nothing of import to report to Hydra.

With an inward curse, he gripped his satchel tighter and flung the kitchen door wide with his free hand. Within, there was chaos.

"More hot water, Maurice! Put another kettle on, Lucy!" Mrs. Patel barked orders to footmen and maids.

One tall maid scurried by with an armful of blood-soaked linens, and Bram's heart stalled in his chest.

"What the devil has happened?" he called over the din.

Stewart Davies, Bram's roommate, halted before him, his arms laden with clean linens. "The masters ordered twenty-five lashes each for the Misses Wilkinson. They—"

"*What?*" Bram roared. "*Lashes?* You mean they—"

"Took a whip to 'em." Mrs. Patel strode toward him. "They're right nasty ones, the Chaistys."

"But—"

"I know." She nodded. "It ain't right." She flicked her gaze to Davies. "Back to work. The Misses Wilkinson need fresh bandages. Off with you."

Davies jumped into action, his feet carrying him swiftly from the kitchens.

"But—" Bram whispered, his insides turning to ice and his pulse racing. *What in the actual sodding hell?* What kind of barbarous bastard would flog his own nieces? And what could they have possibly done for the "masters" to believe they deserved the flogging from the start?

"What they need is to get out of here." Mrs. Patel's voice broke into Bram's thoughts. "This house sucks the souls out of people. Those two young gels are far too bright to live out their days in this hellish place."

"Why would anyone do this?" he asked, though he thought it was mostly to himself.

"Because they can, I imagine." She clucked her tongue. "Only despicable people do such things."

Bram's jaw began to ache, and he made the attempt to unclench.

Mrs. Patel took a wary step back before she dusted her hands nervously on her apron. "Best get that hot water and poultice sent up to the Misses Wilkinson." She bustled away, barking more orders.

Bram remained where he stood, his blood crashing in his ears.

He couldn't. As much as he might wish to, he simply *couldn't* kill Lord Hale.

The man was a traitor, and once Bram found the proof, he would bring it to Hydra. Hydra would take it to the Home Office. Hale would go to trial. He would be found irrefutably guilty. Hale would hang.

Bram filled his lungs with a trembling breath and released it, encouraging his muscles to ease with it.

He'd been prepared for circumstances such as this; he merely needed to rely on his training to achieve his goals. If he could ingratiate himself with Lord Hale, if he were to earn the curst man's trust as a servant and be sent on increasingly personal tasks, he would find the evidence he required. For surely the man hid his documents *somewhere*. Bram must simply uncover their whereabouts.

His looming assignment—and the responsibilities therein—notwithstanding, there was no denying his desire to protect the Misses Wilkinson. They were vulnerable women at the mercy of a despicable man. If he could but find a way to release them from beneath their uncle's proverbial thumb.

A thought teased the back of his mind. What if there were a way for him to both gain entrée into Lord Hale's trusted staff and secure the sisters' freedom?

Mind working, he stepped forward to approach Mrs. Patel. "Is there something that I might do to help? Shall I bring refreshments to the Misses Wilkinson?"

Mrs. Patel swiped at a fallen hair with the back of her hand, her cheeks ruddy with exertion. "Aye. They missed their supper." She turned toward the massive stone fireplace. "Maurice, take that pot above stairs fer cleaning their wounds."

The lanky footman did as he was told, hurrying past the other servants crowding the kitchens.

"But"—Mrs. Patel turned back to Bram, her expression stern—"I'll not allow ye to bring this up, as you're not appropriately attired."

Bram turned his gaze to his clothing. *Damnation.* He'd completely forgotten that he'd just arrived from London. In fact, he still clutched his satchel tightly in one fist.

As much as he wished to see the Misses Wilkinson for himself, he could hardly argue with the woman.

Bram sketched a bow.

"Lucy, put some tea in that pot!" Mrs. Patel's orders followed him as he quit the room.

* * *

The repetitive *snick*, *rustle*, and *thump* of books being removed from their shelves, shaken, and replaced were the only sounds in Hale's study as Bramwell searched. The bastard of a man had taken the carriage and gone for drinks at another estate with his son, leaving his study pleasantly empty.

Bram had already searched Hale's study, but the blackguard didn't have any incriminating evidence at that time. Or, possibly, Bram simply hadn't found it. Something new could be added at any time, however, and he didn't want to miss his opportunity.

The blackguard was despicable, and the sooner Bram found his evidence, the sooner he could find a way to help the Misses Wilkinson.

Turning away from the bookshelves with a frustrated huff, he moved on to the desk. He carefully opened each drawer and examined them thoroughly, searching once more for a hidden panel or a lever that he might have somehow missed. *Nothing.*

Shite. He switched his attention to the tantalus, then the pedestals and tables, before examining the fireplace.

At least an hour had passed since he'd entered the study, and he still hadn't found a thing.

Damnation. How could he prove that Hale was guilty of treason when the man hadn't any of his paperwork at home?

* * *

Rose bit at her bottom lip, her eyes squeezed shut, as burning pain lanced through her. Her pillow pressed into her breasts while she lay on her stomach atop her narrow bed, Violet hovering over her.

A cool, comforting hand pressed gently into her shoulder; Rose was grateful for her sister's presence. Despite the state of constant fear in which they lived, they always had each other. Only moments ago, Rose had redressed Violet's wounds. They took turns in the silence to aid each other.

With a light warning squeeze, Violet continued.

Careful fingers dabbed at the oozing cuts on her back as Violet applied the poultice, bringing up memories of the previous afternoon. Vile images passed before Rose's mind's eye of her aunt and cousins exulting in every strike that her uncle delivered and every cry the strikes elicited.

Rose's fists tightened as a shiver of dread and hopelessness ran through her. No, not hopelessness. They would find a way to escape. They had to.

The moment her bandages had been set, she would go for a run; it helped clear her thoughts, and it was early enough in the morning that the Chaistys would still be abed. It would likely be a sight more sedate due to the pain in her back, but she would go regardless. Running was necessary.

It was only a few minutes more before Violet had concluded fastening the new bandage around Rose's rib cage. They then aided each other in dressing for the day. It took longer than it ordinarily would have, but such a delay was unavoidable in their current condition.

The moment she was clothed in her running frock, Rose retrieved her bonnet and gloves and hurried toward the large, ostentatious foyer.

Her heart stuttered in her chest as she spotted him. The Handsome Footman—Smithe—had returned from visiting family in London. He was in as fine a form as ever. *Is he a pugilist?* she wondered. And what of fencing? Perhaps he came from a family of crofters, tilling and working the land, to have earned his physique.

His gaze was aimed directly ahead of him, his back stiff against the far wall of the foyer, but she knew he was aware of her presence.

Slowing her steps, she employed the extra time to simply be in the footman's company. He was tall and broad. A thought struck her: Would he appear the same in the nude as Peter Jones had? Peter had a soft area of flesh around his middle that had been a pleasure to touch; would Smithe have the same soft spot? Or would he be harder there? And his *manhood…* Would it be as slender and long as Peter's had been?

A fresh blush heated her cheeks just as Smithe stepped forward to open the courtyard door for her. Her face flamed brighter.

Goodness, but he smelled of sandalwood and coffee—an utterly intoxicating combination. The sudden, visceral—and, most assuredly, absurd—urge to press her nose to his shirt collar and inhale deeply caught her entirely unaware.

Her gaze flicked up to meet his golden one, a grin hovering on his lips as he leaned toward her. Her pulse jumped, and her abdomen buzzed with anticipation. Was he going to kiss her?

His hot breath brushed her cheek as he whispered in her ear. Rose was hard pressed not to sigh aloud as his scent engulfed her senses.

He pulled back, and Rose blinked. What had he said?

She simply must get this attraction for the man under control. How had it happened so abruptly? One moment she was living her life in this hellish place, not expecting or even hoping for a better future. Then the absurdly lovely Smithe entered her life, and she was fantasising about his naked body.

Oh dear.

At sixes and sevens, she curtseyed. "Thank you," she mumbled before scurrying out the door and away from further humiliation.

Chapter 5

Bram watched in utter confusion as Miss Wilkinson darted out the door, her fresh, pretty face aflame. The woman was an enigma. One he dearly wished to decipher.

Curiosity and an entirely undeniable, burning desire to know more about her compelled him to follow her outside, his feet moving after her before the conscious thought truly entered his mind. Where did she go in the mornings?

He had learned from his years in service to the Crown never to make assumptions before one had evidence or had witnessed something with one's own eyes. It was for that reason that the sudden, disturbing image of Miss Wilkinson with a lover was pushed immediately from his thoughts. *Never jump to conclusions, especially ones that will adversely affect one's mood and cloud one's judgement.*

Slipping through the doorway behind her, he allowed some space between them as he observed. She was in the middle of the cloud-covered garden, slowly walking away from Willow Hall while putting her black bonnet atop her blonde chignon and pulling her gloves over her long, delicate fingers.

How did she fare after yesterday's flogging? She didn't appear to move differently than before, but surely she was in pain.

Bram stole along the edges of the path, keeping to the shadows behind the larger plants and shrubbery. Though it was a cloudy day, the grey skies did little to disguise him, particularly because he was dressed in such a hideous shade of green.

A fly buzzed past his face, and he swatted it away. Rose—no, it was dangerous to think of her on such personal terms—Miss Wilkinson kept her pace sedate, but Bram could tell that she wished to hurry. Clearly, she was eager to speed toward whatever it was that she was doing…or *whomever* it was that she was meeting.

The thought was lowering, but he again forced it aside as he crept through the back gardens of Willow Hall.

Finally, Miss Wilkinson reached an iron gate. She swung it open on creaking, rattling hinges, and slipped through. He followed behind her, taking care not to make a sound and to keep out of her sight.

He lost view of her for only a moment while he pressed his back to the garden wall. He waited for the span of a heartbeat before he snuck a glance through the gate's opening. But she was gone. She'd picked up her skirts and ran, hell bent, through the tall grass and toward the hills.

Bram's heart lurched in his chest. What was she thinking, running so recklessly? There could be snakes, burrows in the ground, holes, rocks, any number of unseen dangers lurking in the fields!

A low flash of movement caught his eye, and his stomach sank in an ominous swoop. A dog was chasing her.

Ballocks!

Bram picked up his own speed and sprinted after her.

"Miss Wilkinson!" he called.

His wig fell off, landing somewhere on the field behind him, but cared not; he could find it later. Right now, Miss Wilkinson was in danger, and he must help her!

He took a deep breath and bellowed, "*Miss Wilkinson!*"

She gave no indication of hearing him, but, he realised, she mightn't be able to when a dog was fast on her heels.

"Miss Wilkinson, I'm coming to help!" Heart racing, he gained on them, scarcely ten paces behind and still running. "Have no fear, miss!"

The dog's mouth opened, his teeth white and sharp in his large mouth, and the prickle of dread darted down his spine. *Dear God, no!* The dog was going to bite her! Bram was too far away; he couldn't stop it! The dog leaned forward, catching Miss Wilkinson's skirts in its teeth, and pulled. She stopped short, forcing Bram to nearly run into her back.

She spun toward him, her face a mask of alarm before recognition hit.

Without wasting a single second, Bram pushed past the dog and grabbed Miss Wilkinson in his arms, taking her to the ground with him and using his body as a shield from the inevitable attack.

"*What the devil are you doing?*" she shouted between panting breaths, her voice strained.

Bram waited, but no onslaught of vicious bites was forthcoming. He drew back from the young miss, his eyebrows drawn together in confusion.

"I said," she enunciated as though he were a dunce, though her expression held a grimace, "what are you doing?"

"That dog was going to attack you!"

"No, he wasn't!"

His frown deepened, very nearly becoming a scowl. "I saw him chasing you."

She huffed a breath, amusement quirking one corner of her mouth and adding a mischief to her warm brown eyes. It was entirely arousing.

"I run with Dog every day," she said.

His gaze slid toward the animal as it slumped in the grass beside them, his tongue lolling to one side as he panted out his breath. Bram faced Miss Wilkinson once more, incredulous. "You've named him Dog?"

She hesitated. "Yes."

"Bloody terrible, and, I'm afraid to say, an utterly predictable name for a dog."

She frowned, huffing a terse breath, the movement pushing against his ribs.

Christ, he was still lying atop her! He scrambled to his knees, then offered his hand to her. Her lips twisted in another grimace as she came to stand before him.

"If running with *Dog* is an everyday occurrence," he began curiously, rising to his feet as well, "then why did you not respond to me when I called out to you?"

Her gaze darted away as she chewed on her already swollen lip.

Suddenly, guilt assailed him. "My God! My most profound apologies, Miss Wilkinson! I had not thought… That is to say, I had not… I had forgotten that you'd been…" Hell, if he could but get a full sodding thought out, that would be lovely. "I did not mean to hurt you."

Her gaze dipped, but eventually lifted to meet his. "I am well enough, Smithe. I thank you for your apology, nonetheless." Her voice lilted with a breathiness that tugged at something in his chest.

She was a brave woman, this Rose. And strong. Despite the pain her injuries must have been causing her, she'd staunchly met with her dog for a run.

An incredulous laugh bubbled through his chest, but he refused to let it out. He was known for his quick grin, but Miss Rose Wilkinson brought out a side of him that he'd not known could resurface.

"Tell me, Miss Wilkinson, were you purposely trying to avoid me?" A breeze blew past them, chilling the spots on his green trousers that had been dampened by the ground.

She blanched. "Pardon?"

"Why ignore my warnings?" he asked again. "You…" his words trailed off as he caught her narrowed gaze watching his lips.

Acknowledgement and a sense of mystery about to be solved zipped through his chest, but he tamped it down, his gaze turning thoughtful. *Could she…* The thought half-formed in his mind, and he latched onto it.

"My apologies, Miss Wilkinson. It is not my place to question you."

"That is quite all right," she said gustily, the grey light of the cloud-filled day and her attire giving her an almost ghostly appearance. Her face was stark against a voluminous mass of black bombazine.

"I have not seen Dog in Willow Hall; does he have another home?" He was stymied. She continued to watch his lips as he spoke, and his heart tripped over in response. The pieces began to connect in his mind, the proverbial puzzle fitting into place, uncommon though his suspicion was.

With the exception of a few paltry facts about her life, Bram knew nothing about Miss Rose Wilkinson. Something indefinable was afire, burning deep inside him with the need to know all of her.

Her head tilted in an awkward shake. "My family detests dogs, and can never know of his presence." She spoke so softly that with the wind rushing past his ears, he could scarcely hear her. "With the help of my sister, I managed to create a structure in which he can sleep. I daresay he deserves far better; he is a wonderful companion." Her gaze rested fondly on the canine, and Bram felt an absurd clenching of his gut.

Damn it. Was he jealous of a dog? *Well,* he amended, *perhaps not jealous,* but he certainly wished she would look at him in such a way.

Bram nodded his understanding, then in a moment of daring—and obstinacy—turned his head to the side, looking out toward the horizon, and blurted, "I cannot stop thinking about you. I find you unavoidably in my thoughts at all hours." He paused, closing his eyes against the sun. "I dream of you. I lust after you. I know I cannot have you, but damn it, you're too tempting by half." He faced her once more, a grin on his lips, and waited.

The tempo of his breathing turned erratic, his pulse skipping as he waited for her response. If he was wrong, she would slap him for his impertinence, and he would have to beg her forgiveness—though God knew it was true. All of it.

He caught her frown before she smoothed her brow. She worried her bottom lip between her teeth and toyed with the necklace at her throat with one hand. *Hell.* She was thwarted, at a complete loss, wasn't she? He could see it in her troubled eyes: she had the look of a woman whose secret had just been uncovered.

His eyes widened in shock and his heart gave a hard thump as his chest tightened. *I'm right.*

He dipped his head, meeting her gaze, and voiced his suspicions aloud. "You cannot hear me, can you?"

* * *

Rose's heart halted terrifyingly in her chest before it began to pound, beating unmercifully against her ribs.

He knew. The Handsome Footman knew her deepest secret.

Despite herself—and to her utter mortification—her eyes misted over with unshed tears. She knew he was saying something to her, but she could not see his lips well enough to make out the words.

Shaking her head, she swiped at her eyes with the backs of her gloved hands. "I…" she hesitated. There was no sense in denying it any longer; he already knew, as much as she hated that fact. "I am deaf," she admitted.

She took a deep, steadying breath. *Good heavens, Rose,* she admonished herself. *Do not carry on so.*

No man would want a defective woman for a lover. She almost laughed as the thought rose to her mind. What had she hoped? That he would deign to take her to his bed? Preposterous! Though the hope must have hidden somewhere deep in her heart, for the ache in her chest felt very much like heartache. Another ridiculous notion, of course.

Resolutely blinking away the remainder of the moisture that had gathered in her eyes, she watched as his lips moved.

"I apologise…distress."

She gave him a damp, sad grin. "Do not concern yourself with my feelings, Smithe. I have become accustomed to my disability."

He dipped his head briefly before returning his gaze to hers, and she took the moment to admire his hair. What was a little more embarrassment on top of what she already felt? Why not be caught staring as well?

His wig had fallen off along the field somewhere, leaving the gloriously short-cropped brown hair open to the elements. It shone lustrous, even beneath the clouds. She had the distinct desire to run her fingers through it. Then her nose, to take in his scent.

"I do hope you pardon me for asking," he said, "but you speak quite clearly… Is your…your loss of hearing recent, then?"

Rose was absurdly glad that his expression held nary a hint of conceit or gloating but was simple, compassionate curiosity.

"Two years ago, a vicious fever tore through our estate, claiming the lives of many people. Several others, like me, lost their hearing, either entirely or partially, and some lost their eyesight. Violet was fine, but the lives of Mama, Papa, and our sister, Helen, were lost.

"The hearing loss was gradual, slowly degrading until naught was left. Well," she amended, "I am able to faintly hear very high notes, and deep tones, but I'm unable to discern words."

Memories flooded Rose's mind: awaking that long-ago morning to the painful realisation that the process had been completed, followed by unbridled panic that threatened to consume her soul...

Smithe's eyelids dipped over his beguiling golden eyes, a remorseful grimace on his beautiful lips. "I'm so sorry, Miss Wilkinson."

She nodded. "Thank you. I have practiced reading lips with Violet, but I fear most people speak too quickly or don't form the words fully, and I am unable to understand them. Vi and I have found that if she writes what she wishes to say, we converse with greater ease."

Smithe nodded. "Do Lord and Lady Hale know of—?"

"No." She shook her head, alarm spiking in her chest. "And please do not tell them. I fear that if they discovered the truth, they would send me to a convent. And while I mightn't be in daily danger there, it is not the life that I want."

He almost appeared offended by her request, but replied clearly. "I would not betray your confidence."

Her relieved breath came out in a *whoosh*. "Neither the Chaistys, nor our estranged aunt, have even the slightest inkling. My sister is the only one who knows."

He gave her a quick frown. "Aunt?"

"Yes." She shifted her stance in the tall grass. "She is my mother's sister, who lives in London."

"Again, pardon me for prying, Miss Wilkinson, but why in God's name would...Lord and Lady Hale rather than with your aunt in London? Surely...entreat upon her the conditions in which you live and beg her to take...on?"

Rose swallowed past the sorrow lodged in her throat. "We have tried," she said, shrugging one shoulder, and hoping that she understood his meaning correctly. "We believe that our family here monitors our mail. We have her address but have not yet found a way in which we might get word to her."

Smithe frowned fiercely. "And you believe that if she knew, she would rescue you both from this hellish place?"

The sadness in her heart deepened to sorrow. "I do not know. We have not seen Aunt Maureen since we were children, and, at the time, she was already estranged."

His golden gaze scanned her face, his cheeks hollowing as he considered his next words. Another breeze tugged at her damp frock. He stepped closer, closing the distance between them and enveloping her in his warm scent of sandalwood and coffee. Gooseflesh spread across her skin at his nearness.

"Would you permit me to kiss you, Miss Wilkinson?"

Blimey. Had she heard him correctly?

"I-I beg your pardon?"

His lips quirked, and he replied slowly. "Would you permit me to kiss you?"

Her pulse hummed, and her instincts took hold. Without a word, Rose surged upward on her toes and captured his lips with hers.

Chapter 6

For the briefest of moments, shock at her own boldness stiffened Rose's spine, but raw desire softened her lips. She was kissing the Handsome Footman!

Anticipation thrummed through her, her heart suddenly lighter in her chest, her stomach tight with excitement.

Would he deepen the kiss?

Oh yes. She opened her mouth willingly beneath his as he tentatively dipped his tongue inside. Tingling heat darted its way down her spine and pooled low in her belly.

Her skin felt alive, from the top of her head to the tips of her toes, her whole body aflame with desire. Pulse erratic and excitement tingling along her nerves, she realised this was precisely what she'd wanted—what she'd hoped for.

Giving in to her curiosity, she reached one hand up to tangle her fingers in his hair. The short, smooth locks tickled her palm, each strand seemingly darting in a different direction. It was an arousing mix of chaos and design, as though he had strategically arranged his hair to be disordered.

A rumbling vibration came from his throat, and a responding molten heat rushed to her womanly core. Rose marvelled that her body reacted so quickly to him.

Grasping at his lapels, she tugged him closer. She wanted to feel the hardness of him against her, to lose herself in his kisses, his touches…in him.

He broke the kiss to press his lips to the throbbing pulse at her throat, and her jaw dropped open on a sigh. The touch of his lips on her sensitive skin felt like a series of small fires igniting down her neck, each touch a fiery brand.

She could feel his lips move, and she recognised that he was speaking. "I cannot hear you," she gasped, her fingers tightening in his hair.

He pulled back, and, for a brief moment, she thought he would repeat himself so she could see, but instead, his lips caught hers in another passionate tangling of their lips and tongues. Her pulse skipped, and her stomach swooped in nervous anticipation.

Abruptly, the darkening grey sky rumbled and opened up, and fat, heavy droplets of rain splattered them, causing them to spring apart.

Rose blinked up into the abrupt downpour and laughed. Of all the things to interrupt such an ardent interlude, she was glad that it was rain.

With a pleased grin on his lips, Smithe trailed the back of one finger along her cheekbone.

Contentment stole over her, and she had the absurd urge to giggle, standing there in the rain on this grassy hill. Smithe's grin deepened, his cheek creasing near the corner of his lip. "You make me lose my head, Miss Wilkinson…"

Lose one's head, indeed. "I confess, you quite take me out of myself as well." A naughty urge provoked her to continue, "But you may address me as Rose, in private."

He ran both hands through his wet hair, his eyes sparking with renewed interest. "Then you shall call me Bramwell, or Bram, should you prefer."

"Bram…" she tried the word on her lips. It felt like him; beautiful, charming, yet with something unfathomable hidden within. She liked it.

"Come. We…return to Willow Hall. I…you will be missed by now."

The reminder of her expected reception dampened her mood, but not entirely. She was walking with a strikingly attractive footman—with whom she had just shared a tingling, swoon-worthy kiss—after all.

They walked in silence for several moments, the softening ground sucking at Rose's half boots and the rain pummelling them with almost warm, spring droplets. It would take them far longer to return to Willow Hall at this sedate pace; despite the punishment she suspected she would receive as a result, Rose was inclined to continue on as they were, slowly walking, side by side, Dog prancing about them.

Goodness, if it weren't for my black bombazine, Bram's livery, and the pouring rain, one might think us a courting couple out for a pleasant stroll. The notion made her smile, though sadness touched her heart. As happy as the thought was, she knew that a man like Bram could not be for her. Who would want a deaf, unchaste woman as a lover, let alone a wife? How could she hear their children calling for her or listen to their laughter? Her chest tightened. My, but that thought was depressing. *I might just cry.*

Out of the corner of her eye, she saw Bram's head swing toward her. Grateful for the respite from her lowering thoughts, Rose met his gaze.

"I an understand how why your response to be this morning was so odd."

She bit her lip, squinting as she pieced together what he must have said. "I—"

He smiled at her, his toothy charm adding a flutter to her stomach. "There is no need to explain, Rose. I understand."

"Thank you." She hesitated before asking, "What did you say? This morning at the door."

Making sure to keep his face directed at her, he replied, "I asked if you required any aid."

Rose responded with a quick laugh. "I can understand why my meagre 'thank you' was an insufficient answer."

Bram nodded. "I worried that you might require immediate help—and, I confess, I was curious—which is why I followed you."

His gloved hand brushed hers as their arms swung at their sides, and a jolt of heat tingled up her arm, despite the damp chill in the air.

The rain continued to pour on them as they walked, the cool spring water quenching the thirst of the vegetation growing from the earth. Rose had always adored the rain: the rejuvenation; the crisp, clean scent; the sound of it splattering against windows. Of course, she did not hear it any longer, but she remembered it, and she cherished the thought of it all the same.

Willow Hall came into view and anxiousness began to gnaw at her stomach. Would her aunt and uncle have questioned Violet on Rose's absence, or had they even noticed? Would they have taken their anger with Rose out on Violet once again? What of Violet's wounds of yesterday? Would they require redressing? Rose was certain that her own would.

A noise of distress rose up in her throat, and she swallowed it down.

Bramwell's hand touched hers again, and she nearly jumped from her skin. Instead, she turned her head to gaze at him.

"Are you well?" he asked.

She sent him a tight-lipped smile. "Of course. Why do you ask?"

"You…" His expression of concern smoothed, replaced by another one of his grins. "No particular reason, Rose."

* * *

Bramwell gazed surreptitiously at Rose from the corner of his eye. He knew she would notice if he turned his head fully in her direction, but a small glance could easily be missed.

She watched the ground as they navigated the muddy, grassy terrain, Dog prancing happily along beside her, his tongue bouncing out the side of his mouth as he panted and lapped at the rain.

Bram found it curious that she did not realise when she made noise; it came with being unable to hear, he supposed. But she did it. A noise of distress gurgled from her throat as they neared Willow Hall; it made him both curious about the source of the sound and furious that, if his assumptions were correct, the likely cause was her abusive uncle. Did she worry that Hale would be angry upon her return? Did she fear her cousins? It was too repulsive to consider the reasons.

He glanced at her again, the veil of rain between them doing nothing to diminish the brightness of her beauty. Her cheeks and the tip of her nose were flushed from the slight chill to the air, while water flowed over her defined features despite the wide-rimmed black bonnet she wore. Her full, alluring lips stood plump in her profile.

Blast. He wanted to grip her head in his hands and spend hours exploring those delectable lips. As impossible as it was, he thought her mouth tasted of chocolate, sunshine, and pure, insatiate lust. Damn, but he wanted another taste of her.

While desire continued to drive him and he battled to control the eager appendage in his trousers, he still felt a measure of shock at what he'd discovered. Rose was deaf. How could he not have seen it before? How could Lord and Lady Hale not have noticed such a thing? Either Rose Wilkinson was exceptionally skilled at keeping such a monumental secret and had merely slipped in Bramwell's presence, or she had chosen to reveal it to him—whether she was cognizant of the decision or not. He favoured the latter, for it made his chest absurdly fill with pride.

The reasoning behind it notwithstanding, she had given voice to her secret to him, of all people. He felt a connection to her. A deep, emotional connection that—God help him—he actually liked. Hell, if he were honest with himself, he would admit to feeling more than just fondness for this woman. But he was not ready to admit that just yet. His feelings made no sense. He'd shared scarcely a handful of words with her, and yet, he could not deny the truth of what he felt.

Those kisses, however… *Holy hell.* They were more than he could have hoped for.

He spotted a sodden white ball of hair just ahead and to his left, and he trotted forward to pick it up. If he were not a spy, he would lament the loss of the wig, for it would cost him a flogging and a pretty penny. But Bram was prepared for such eventualities. He would simply be obliged to use the spare wig that he had hidden away for just such an occasion.

"Oh, dear." Rose's soft voice came from beside him, barely audible over the pounding rain. "It's ruined."

He turned to her, watching her eyes to be sure she could see his lips. "Please do not fret over its loss. I have another."

Her expressive coffee-brown eyes crinkled in the corners. "You are very fortunate, indeed."

Bram hedged a glance at the estate garden's iron gate. They were but twenty paces from another, more dangerous, world. Within a few minutes, their encounter must be forgotten for the purposes of his assignment and for Rose's safety. The moment they crossed into the copse of willow trees, their mostly innocent tryst would have to come to its conclusion.

He was not ready for that to happen.

Bram cupped her jaw in one hand, his thumb running lightly over her sodden cheek. Her lips were still rouged from their kisses, and the sight fired his blood.

He wanted so badly to speak his mind. To tell her what he thought of her. *You are a brave woman, Miss Rose Wilkinson,* he would say. *You sustained terrible losses, both in heart and in body, and still continue to exhibit hope and dignity on the daily. I cannot possibly express how much I admire you for your courage.* Bram struggled in vain to put into words the combination of emotions quarrelling within him. To speak openly to this strong, yet frightened, woman.

He settled for satisfying his unearthly urge to kiss her again.

Her lips opened beneath his on a startled gasp. His dripping wig fell from his fist as he brought his hand up to frame her jaw with his palms.

His pego thickened as her small hands flitted over the shoulders of his livery to tangle her fingers in his hair.

He could not take it any longer. With the knowledge of her injuries at the back of his mind, he gripped her soft hips through the dark fabric of her dress, pulling her against him until her full breasts pressed against his chest, her hips aligning with his. A deep growl escaped him. Her responding moan only made him more desperate to rip their clothes away and have her naked and writhing on this very meadow, pouring rain and threat of discovery notwithstanding.

It was for that reason that he broke the kiss. He might have fancied himself out of sight and away from threat of discovery, but the truth of it was that he was always in danger of being found out. Hale was a man known to have done despicable things, and Bram must return his focus to finding proof, for both the sake of England…and the sisters Wilkinson.

Chapter 7

With the placement of one last pin in Rose's hair, Violet stepped back to admire her work. The shadows of rain splattering their small bedchamber window played across Violet's features as she nodded in satisfaction.

"Perfect," Violet wrote in the sketchbook.

"Thank you."

Violet's lips pursed, and her gaze narrowed in thought as she wrote again. "Where did your mind go just now, Rose? You're rather flushed."

To Bramwell, she thought. How droll to think of the Handsome Footman on such personal terms! It was rather uplifting to know that she had something pleasing to look forward to on the morrow.

Violet crooked her index finger under Rose's chin, gently turning her head so they faced one another.

"What is this?" her sister asked, her glinting blue eyes scanning her features.

Violet had always been too perceptive for Rose's liking. Since their tragic losses, Violet had taken on the role of protector for Rose, regardless of whether Rose felt that she required it. They were in dire enough circumstances, and while Rose appreciated her sister's enthusiasm for defending her, she found it significantly increased her internal turmoil, adding guilt and pain for them both.

Violet's perfectly shaped, plump lips dropped open on a gasp, before she wrote. "Something good has happened!"

Rose could not help the revealing blush that stole over her cheeks. *Drat.*

If it was the only happy thing in their lives, she should share the joy—however fleeting—with her sister. "Very well."

Violet animatedly clapped her hands, then wrote once more. "Oh, good! I long for a bit of excitement."

Rose laughed at her sister's enthusiasm. "The Handsome Footman," she whispered.

Vi's brow wrinkled in confusion, but her eyes were lit with anticipation. "Oh! Smithe? The one with the golden eyes?"

Rose nodded and regaled her sister with the events of that morning.

Violet clapped again, her features alight with pleasure. "Oh, Rose! I told you that you would have him between your thighs within the month. Just you wait; I'm absolutely certain that's coming." She winked, then leaned forward eagerly. "Tell me, how was it? Was he as skilled a kisser as Peter?"

Rose's skin tingled as she recalled the magical way Bram's lips had fit over hers, the slide of his tongue… "I daresay his aptitude for kissing surpasses innumerable gentlemen, Vi, Peter Jones included."

"Then it's settled."

Rose blinked. "What is settled?"

"You shall marry him!" She shrugged a shoulder. "At the very least you ought to take him as a lover."

"*Vi!*"

"Come, now, you cannot claim to still be in possession of your maidenhead, and the prospect of a life living here with this vile family is not to be borne." She leaned forward and gripped Rose's hands in hers. "For the sake of your sanity and, at the very least, for the sake of finding some enjoyment in this hellish place, do yourself the great favour of taking that man to your bed."

"I am confused," Rose confessed. "You *wish* for me to flout propriety? What of the dangers of such an arrangement?"

Vi bent to the sketchbook once again. "Your reputation can hardly suffer. Society in the country is far more lenient than in London, and the lords and ladies in the neighbouring estates haven't the faintest idea who we are. Word of your transgression—should it ever become known—will not travel far."

"And of conception?" Though heaven knew that whatever child Bramwell fathered would be breathtakingly adorable.

"Well, you simply take precautions." She listed them off on her fingers. "You could soak a sponge in vinegar and insert it within you, he could use a condom—either linen soaked in a chemist's liquid and dried, or specially treated lamb's or sheep's intestine or bladder, made to fit over a man's penis—or he could remove himself from you before he finds completion. There is always the possibility that—"

"Good gracious, Violet!" Rose gasped, her hands clapped to her flaming cheeks. "How do you know about such things?"

"For a woman with no virtue, you really are a prude." Despite her words, Vi's lips curved up in a Machiavellian grin. "I have waited for some time to give this to you, and I've not found an opportune moment before now."

Violet dropped to her hands and knees upon the threadbare rug of undistinguishable colour and searched about beneath the bed.

"Ready for what, precisely?" Rose asked warily.

Her sister reappeared, her features flushed from having been bent over, with barely suppressed excitement lighting her eyes. "A book!"

"A book," Rose repeated dully.

"I dare you not to blush when you see it, Rose." She thrust her hand from behind her back to reveal an ordinary leather-bound book scarcely the height and width of her hand. "I will not judge you if you do, however, for I, too, found myself embarrassed when I first saw it."

Rose accepted the book from her sister, curiosity forcing her fingers faster. The spine was soft, the supple leather smooth to the touch as she ran her hands over it.

She reached for her reading spectacles upon the bedside table and placed them carefully on the bridge of her nose. Flipping the book open to the title page, she read aloud, *"The Schoole of Venus, or the Ladies Delight, Reduced into Rules of Practice."*

She looked up and saw her sister was speaking. "It is written by a Frenchman by the name of Michel Millot, but it was translated to

English in the 1600s. I must admit to being shocked at first, but I came to admire his penchant for humour."

Rose flipped through the pages and paused to read a passage. *A Prick hath a fine soft loose skin, which though the Wench take it in her Hand, When it is loose and lank, will soon grow stiff...* She choked on her own gasp as she snapped the book shut.

She sent an incredulous look at her smirking sister. "You've *read* this?"

Vi nodded once, and scribbled in the sketchbook. "Indeed. Several times, in fact."

"But how could you... That is to say... When did...? Where did you...?"

Violet laughed. "I found it several years ago at a bookshop in a section labelled 'Gentlemen Only.' I enjoyed it so much that I bought a second copy for you when you had become engaged to Peter. I'd thought to gift it to you on your wedding day, alas. I am pleased to finally have an excuse."

Without another word, Vi snatched the book from Rose's limp fingers and stuffed it beneath her pillow. "Read it later. You've a previous engagement with Mr. Darcy."

Chapter 8

Rose adjusted the reading spectacles on her nose before she put a small piece of biscuit in her mouth. She'd entirely forgotten to remove the spectacles when she'd been called for lunch, after having donned them to read Jane Austen's *Pride and Prejudice*. She'd read the well-worn copy twelve times in the two years since her mother had gifted it to her, and she loved it ever more with each reading.

That morning, however, she'd struggled to focus on the witty dialogue between the strong-willed Miss Elizabeth Bennet and the shy yet dashing Mr. Darcy, her thoughts continuously drawn back to her conversation with Violet.

As appealing as an *affaire* with her captivating footman—Bramwell Smithe—would be, Rose knew it to be impossible. She had been in love with Peter when she had given him her maidenhead, and they had been betrothed, for pity's sake! Making love to Bram when all she felt for him was friendship—and a healthy amount of desire—would be… Well, it would be *sordid*. Would it not?

She broke another chunk of biscuit with her fingers and flicked her gaze up toward the man himself. His back rigid and mien impassive, Bram stood in the corner of the dining room, waiting to be called upon.

I kissed those lips, she recalled, her stomach giving a wobble.

Uriana waved a hand in the air, drawing Rose's attention.

"This tea is frigid. Get me another one," she said.

Bram hurried forward to take the teacup, and left the room.

Rain continued to fall outside, splashing against the window across from Rose. She recalled the sound it used to make and imagined it doing so now, its peaceful tapping offering comfort in a stormy life.

Across the table, Violet nudged her sliver of pigeon pie with her fork. They were always given such small portions of food and then punished for eating it too quickly after they'd inevitably gone hungry.

Ignoring her family, Rose turned her gaze out the window once more, chewing on her own piece of cooling pigeon pie. The garden was obscured by a veil of rain, the pearly droplets spilling from the sky to quench the earth's thirst. The leaves of the trees and the petals of every flower flickered and waved with the tap of each droplet. It was like a symphony—if one could hear the music—perfectly orchestrated from the heavens to play on the beauty below.

No butterflies flew today; they remained ensconced in their hidden, leafy homes, protected from the showering rain. Rose rather enjoyed the rain in spring; it smelled of earth and flowers. It was refreshing while she ran, and warm enough that she would not catch a chill on the walk home.

Home. How odd the notion was that she considered Willow Hall her home. It was hardly welcoming, as a home ought to be. Nor was it warm or comforting, where one could find a benevolent greeting or a familial embrace. No, indeed. Would that she and Violet could purchase a hidden cottage to live out the remainder of their lives in peace and contentment.

Of course, that was not for them.

* * *

Bramwell Stevens stood at his post against the wall in the sizeable dining room at Willow Hall, vigilant in his position but also very aware of Rose's presence. She ate apathetically, much like her sister, her head bowed and several blonde locks falling over her brow.

"I was trying to speak, Papa," Lady Uriana groused, waving her fork indignantly in the air.

"Oh, Lord Hale." Lady Hale waved a limp, bejewelled hand through the air. "You say such droll things."

"*Does no one hear me?*" Lady Uriana shrieked, forcing Bram to suppress a grimace. The high sound echoed so shrilly through the room that Bram could swear he heard the china rattle in its cupboards.

"Of course we do, my dear." Lady Hale patted her daughter's hand before dabbing at her lips with a napkin.

Lord Americus Chaisty, the Baron of Bristol, picked at his teeth with one prong of his fork. The awful scraping was nearly as distasteful as Lady Uriana's jarring voice. "I'm certain that even the neighbours hear you, Uriana. Christ, but your voice is awful."

"Well, *you* are the worst brother in all of—"

"Pray go on, Uriana." Lord Hale cut her off, frowning into his glass of wine.

Lady Uriana huffed an irritated breath as she put her long nose higher in the air. "Dorothea and Fanny's families are taking the waters in Bath next month, and I want to go with them!" She stomped one foot beneath the table, a delicate frown on her perfectly sculpted dark-blonde eyebrows. "I daresay that I will be the only one among my friends not going, and I—"

"But of course you may go, my dear," Lord Hale drawled, startling his daughter into silence.

Rose's gaze swung between them, visibly struggling to understand the conversation.

"I… what?" Lady Uriana gazed wide-eyed at Hale.

"You may go with your mother and Americus to Bath with a handful of servants. I will have other business to attend to."

The young lady's squeal of glee and overly chipper clapping filled the room as Lady Hale waved her hand at Bram and the other footmen stationed around the perimeter of the dining room, signalling the end of that course.

He swiftly stepped forward, coolly gathering a dish in each hand and leaving through the far door.

The air in the kitchens was dense with steam as the maids boiled water for washing the dishes.

"Lucy!" Mrs. Patel barked at the young maid, sweat beading on her brow as she sliced a lemon cake. "Put that teapot on the tray and get the platter for the desserts."

The tall maid did as she was asked.

Mrs. Patel wiped her hands on her apron. "Maurice and Davies, bring port and more wine to the table. You know how 'is lordship likes his drink after a good meal."

"Yes, mum." Both footmen disappeared.

Bram waited until the tiered decorative silver platter was adorned with an assortment of cakes and pastries before he followed with a stack of small plates into the dining room. Having already delivered the port and wine to the table, Davies strode behind him, carrying the tray laden with a selection of berries and other fresh fruits.

The desserts, fruit, and tea were placed in the centre of the table as the family exclaimed with delight over the appearance of their favourite sweets. The hair on the back of Bram's neck stood on end, and his gaze lifted to catch Rose's.

Her brown eyes, wide and unblemished by cynicism, glittered in the bright, candlelit room. The stubborn set to her chin proved that she was brave, despite how her uncle's treatment cowed her.

His gaze settled on her lush lips, and their addictive flavour sprang to mind. A blush rapidly stained her cheeks. She must have been thinking of their kisses as well. Lord knew he had not stopped thinking of them.

He smiled imperceptibly and resumed his post against the wall, the slightest twitch of his lips and crinkle to his eye the only indications of his thoughts. It would not do to attract attention to them both.

"Mmm," Lord Bristol hummed, his black eyes glinting ominously across the table at Rose and Violet and his mouth full of raspberry tart. He swallowed. "I've always had a fondness for tarts." He said it so caustically that one could not mistake his meaning.

Bram clenched his jaw, grateful that Rose had turned her gaze to her plate of selected fruit. She peeled her orange with quieted zeal. He could sense her anticipation for the fruit from where he stood. The first section of the peel came off and she brought it to her nose, her eyes closed.

In that instant, Bram absurdly wished he were that orange: desired, admired, and coveted by such a beautiful woman.

Rose bent the orange's skin, discreetly squeezing the peel and squirting its fragrant juices upon her slender neck. He had to suppress a groan. He felt like a hound salivating at the scent of its next meal.

Damn and blazes, think of something else, Bram, old boy. It would not do to get a cockstand in the middle of the dining room. You're a spy, damn it! Control yourself!

His self-admonishment notwithstanding, he was forced to bite the inside of his cheek as fevered images of himself licking those tart-sweet juices off her neck filled his vision. He wanted her, and that was a bloody dangerous thing. He had an assignment to complete, and she had her reputation to uphold.

The chatter of the Chaisty family speaking animatedly on one topic or another settled down to absolute, threatening silence as the clinking of a spoon against a teacup filled the air. *Oh no.* Bram's stomach plummeted.

Four sets of eyes stared incredulously at Rose, who sat, oblivious to the gauche noise she made while stirring her tea, her gaze fixed happily on the swirling liquid in her teacup.

Rose, stop stirring, he willed her with his thoughts. *Please, Rose, look up!*

Bram caught Violet attempting to nudge Rose with her feet beneath the table, but it was too late. Lady Hale's arm had already drawn back, then extended over the corner of the table to deliver a punishing slap to her niece's cheek. The motion surprised Rose into knocking over her teacup, its contents spilling across the table's cloth, before she lost her balance entirely and toppled from her chair onto the floor with a resounding *thud.* Rose's jaw dropped open on a silent cry of shock and pain as her aunt proceeded to shout at her.

Eyes watering, Rose gamely retrieved her spectacles—which had been knocked from her face—and put them back on. She attempted to hide her fear, her anger…her humiliation. But Bram was trained to see the truth of people, and he saw her feelings clearly. Her throat bobbed, her chest rose and fell rapidly as she held back tears, her jaw clenched with anger and determination… She was a spitfire, fully capable, he was certain, of finding a way to free herself. And he still wanted to save her.

Bram's body grew taut—his hands fisted, his jaw tight, his toes gripping the floor through his shoes. His entire being wished to intervene. But how could he? What could he possibly do to make things better for her?

Chapter 9

"We need to leave," Violet wrote after helping Rose into her night rail, her poultice and bandages newly reapplied.

Rose grunted her agreement, pulling her knees to her chest and resting her chin atop them, facing Vi in her bed. "How in heaven's name would you suppose we do that?"

"We could escape," Vi offered, finding her brush and settling in to brush her dark hair.

"Yes, I surmised that, and I've certainly thought of doing so before, but we are two young women of little means and connections. How would we travel with no money and no hope to acquire any? Where would we go? To Aunt Maureen? We don't even know if she is still alive! Nor our grandparents in Glasgow. We have not heard from them in years."

Vi lifted her hands in a gesture of helplessness, the brush flopping in her slackened grip, before she took the pencil up once more. "What else are we to do, Rose? We cannot very well remain here."

Fear mingled with strength and bravery in her eyes. Rose felt it, too. The fear. They were both very aware of what their uncle was capable, and it was entirely terrifying.

"Of course, you are correct, Vi. We must go." A strange sense of relief washed over her as she said the words, before logic crept in once more. "I believe that a plan is in order."

Vi's blue eyes lit with anticipation. "We could borrow horses and ride into town, claiming to be widows that have run down on our luck—our bombazine is the ideal disguise."

"And we ought to merely hope that someone will heroically offer their help?" Rose shook her head. "I daresay most of the people we might happen across will be as impoverished as we."

Violet chewed on her bottom lip. "Quite."

"Do you suppose that our uncle gets a stipend from Papa's estate, in order to keep us?

"I imagine so," Violet confirmed, "but we'll not see a shilling of it. Even after we escape, I'm afraid that those funds would still go to our uncle."

"Until we marry."

Violet scoffed. "I'm not getting married."

The words hung in the air and, for a moment, Rose wanted to protest. Violet was her own woman, however, and Rose did not want to tell her how to live her life; they'd experienced controlling relatives, and that was the very last thing Rose wished to resemble.

"Very well," she said resolutely. Their plan would not involve finding men with whom to elope. "I daresay that money is ours, isn't it?" She nodded as the idea formed in her mind. "I suggest we retrieve our funds from our family, arm ourselves, and prepare to fight our way free of this place."

Her twin's eyebrows lifted nigh to her hairline, a wry smile quirking the corner of her lips. "My, my. Bloodthirsty, are we? You're beginning to sound like me, Rose." She winked. "I love it."

"Then let us plan."

Rose felt a swell of hope as they talked and plaited their hair, slowly preparing for bed as a renewed vigour for their future surged.

One thought played at the back of her mind while they spoke: Bramwell Smithe. She would, regrettably, be forced to leave him behind. Perhaps she ought to speak with him, ask him to meet with her in London. At the very least, she would seek out another of his kisses before she left—though she imagined he might have been put off after that display in the dining room.

Violet's hands stilled where they'd been toying with the end of her plait before she gestured toward the door. Someone was here.

The bed shifted as Violet stood. Rose lifted her chin from her knees to see her sister answer the door, using her body to block the other's view of Rose sitting on the bed.

Hot coffee and sandalwood. She closed her eyes and inhaled as the fragrance reached her. Such a masculine and… arousing combination. But why was Bram here?

Her eyes snapped open again. Violet turned from the door, allowing Bramwell through the narrow space. Heavens, she had nearly forgotten how remarkable he was. His tall, broad body dwarfed everything in the room, and his hideously green livery clashed with the space at large.

His concerned gaze rose to hers as she stood from the bed, crossing her arms anxiously beneath her thinly clad breasts.

"How are you, Rose?" he asked.

She bobbed her head. "Well enough," she lied.

What is he doing here? An irritating nervous flutter had begun in her stomach, buzzing and whirling without a care for her distaste for it.

He pulled his wig indecently from his absurdly beautiful head of dark brown hair and worried it in his hands, his gaze never leaving hers.

"I came…speak…about a matter of…importance. I…should inform…sennight…Lord Hale is to attend a house party at Kerr House…outskirts of Eastbourne. Not…Willow Hall, but far enough away to give you some peace. A few…servants and I are to attend him there."

The hope that had been blossoming in her chest took hold and bloomed. "Truly? We shall have a sennight without our uncle?"

"As long…house party…cut short, yes." Bram nodded.

Rose beamed, turning her gaze to Violet. "Our aunt and cousins will still be in residence, but this is our opportunity to begin our search."

Bram waited before Rose had turned back to face him before he asked, "Search?"

"We intend to escape," Rose explained. "We are searching for items that might help us."

His lips twitched. "Admirable, indeed. Please…me know if you require…assistance. Oh!" He reached into his pocket and retrieved a folded napkin. "I noticed that…unable to hide food away for Dog, so I pilfered…Mrs. Patel."

Rose accepted the small parcel and opened it to reveal two cooked cuts of meat, a halved tomato, and a short, curved carrot.

She was aware of Violet turning her back to them, giving them a moment of privacy, which Rose appreciated.

"Thank you, Bram," she said, letting the strength and warmth in his golden gaze reach her heart. "I'm truly touched that you would think of him."

Beaming at her, he nodded. "I know some dogs that enjoy the vegetables…more than…meat, but if he doesn't take to it—"

"He adores them," she interjected.

Their gazes locked for a long moment, and her chest tightened with nerves.

His gaze lowered to her lips, his eyelids dipping, and a responding flutter erupted in her abdomen. He was thinking about kissing her again, she was almost entirely certain.

Her smile slipped ever so slightly. The thrumming of desire pumping through her veins was enough to terrify any maiden. Gratefully, she was no longer a maiden, but an experienced woman— albeit with only one such experience.

* * *

Christ, but Rose's citrus scent filled Bram's senses and had him wanting far more than an innocent conversation. Her sister's cinnamon scent faded into the background when compared to Rose.

Her gorgeous brown eyes darkened with desire, drawing Bram closer still. Until a throat cleared.

"Might I have a word, Mr. Smithe?" Miss Violet Wilkinson asked, one brow arched at him.

Blast. "Of course."

Rose's gaze swung around, no doubt attempting to catch up on the conversation.

"I wish to have a word with Mr. Smithe in the corridor," Violet explained to Rose, before marching past him and out the door.

Bram followed, closing the door quietly behind himself.

"Can we trust you?" Violet turned to face him, her eyes narrowed in thought.

He blinked, taken aback. "I would like to believe that you can."

"What I mean to say is, where do your loyalties lie? Are you a trusted servant to our uncle?"

Ah. Understanding dawned. "I've been in service to Lord Hale for only a short while, and I cannot abide the way in which you and Rose are treated. I'll not entrap you, you have my word."

Her stance relaxed, and she sighed. "Excellent. Rose could certainly use another ally. Be good to her."

Chapter 10

A chill ran down Rose's spine as she neared the guest parlour's French doors, rainwater dripping from her frock and bonnet. Nearly a sennight had passed since she'd last seen her Handsome Footman, and while she missed him terribly, his return would also bring Hale. The time of Hale's absence hadn't been entirely peaceful, as her aunt and cousins had remained in residence, continuously belittling and abusing the Wilkinson sisters, but there was something to be said for the relief it gave her to know that Hale would not surprise her with a slap or a flogging.

She pulled open the French doors and stepped inside.

They'd had little luck in searching for weaponry, as there'd been someone around nearly every turn. This afternoon could change things, however.

"I am returned from my run, Vi," Rose announced as she spotted her twin reading upon the well-worn *chaise longue*. The faded periwinkle-blue upholstery brought out the sapphire of her eyes.

Vi put her book down to smile at Rose. "You're sopping wet, dear. Perhaps you had best bathe," she said, carefully enunciating each word.

"I believe I shall." Rose grinned. "Our aunt and cousins have an afternoon tea scheduled at the estate of one of Lady Hale's acquaintances; it shall provide us the perfect opportunity for our search."

"Superb!" Violet brightened.

Rose strode toward her sister, rubbing her chilled, wet hands together as she walked.

"Are you reading that naughty book again, Vi?"

Violet raised her eyebrows at Rose. "But of course! One must keep abreast of such knowledge."

"Fear you that the mechanics will change? Or do you wish to please a stable hand?" Rose teased. "Perhaps you mean to become a courtesan?"

Her sister shrugged one shoulder nonchalantly, though Rose could see the tension in the gesture. "Such would suit me fine, dear. Anything would be better than a life with Lord and Lady Hale and their vile offspring."

Rose could not argue with that statement. "Quite so. Though I certainly hope that becoming a courtesan will not be necessary."

* * *

"Have you seen Americus with a pistol before, Vi?" Rose asked as Violet slowly opened their cousin's bedchamber door.

"No," her sister replied over her shoulder. "But the man's surely prepared to be called out."

It was their best course of action. If they pilfered one of Hale's pistols, he would surely notice within days of his return home, but Americus… He wasn't as attached to his weaponry—though he was decidedly just as violent as Hale—and would likely not notice one missing until someone actually wished to duel him.

They entered, though Rose could not be certain how silent they were, and began their search, each starting at different ends of the room and working her way inward.

Rose inspected the chest of drawers, which smelled sickeningly of cigarillos and lavender, carefully opening each drawer and lifting the items within, ensuring that she put them back just how she'd found them. She opened the last drawer and lifted some folded cravats, then bent to peer beneath. Nothing.

With a furtive glance toward the bedchamber door, she moved on to the bed while Violet examined first the writing desk, then the wardrobe. She lowered herself to her hands and knees, bending low to peer beneath the bed.

There were several boxes, and she withdrew the first one, lifting its lid. Cigarillos. She moved on to the next. Old wellingtons.

She'd searched through three more boxes of much the same nonsense before she felt a tap on her shoulder. Despite herself, she jumped.

"I found something," Violet said, crouching beside her to show the box in her hands.

She lifted the lid to reveal a modest stack of bank notes. Rose's eyes grew wide.

"Good heavens, what could he be saving this for, do you suppose?" Rose asked, bemused.

"I cannot say. But…" Violet's nose wrinkled. "Should we take it?"

An admonishment sprang instantly to Rose's lips, but she bit it back. Should they take it? "When we had formulated our plan, we spoke of relieving Lord Hale of funds, not Lord Bristol."

Violet shrugged one shoulder. "From the purse of the father so onto the son? Would that not make this our money as well?"

If their cousin was benefiting from whatever stipend went to their uncle, then Vi's logic was sound. At the very least, it was what Rose chose to believe. She nodded. "Let's take it."

"Thank you, Americus," Violet said, palming the stack of notes and slipping them into the bodice of her old frock. "Keep looking, Rose."

With a nod, Rose returned to examining the boxes beneath her cousin's bed. There was another pair of shoes, a stash of French letters that sent a shiver of revulsion down Rose's spine, and another box of cigarillos.

She sighed, reaching for a small wooden chest nearest to the head of the bed, then opened it.

"Here," she gasped out. Inside the box was a pair of pistols, a sachet of shot, and other accoutrement.

Violet appeared at her side and clapped her hands together. "Perfect, Rose!" She removed one of the pistols from the box and lifted a brow. "Now to prepare for the remainder of our plan."

Chapter 11

Rose closed her eyes, shutting herself away from the brightly lit music room as her hands danced over the ivory keys of the piano, her heart connected to the instrument and the music it allowed her to create. Every note vibrated through her body, the highs only faintly reaching her, and lows humming in her ears.

She recalled the notes of music she'd learned, but now she didn't follow any rules, didn't have someone there to rap her on the hands or tug at her hair when she played a note incorrectly; she played for herself. She played by how it made her feel.

They'd been successful in their search that afternoon, and while her aunt and cousins were still at tea, and her uncle at the house party, she'd taken to the music room in the familial wing while Violet practised her watercolours in their bedchamber. It was very likely the last time she would ever get to play on a piano as beautiful as this, and she would not waste the opportunity.

Striking a low chord, the heavy notes quaked through her, and she relished them.

* * *

Bram felt strangely good-humoured as he strode into the Willow Hall foyer, his arms laden with the master's trunks. The traitors' rendezvous had gone ill, indeed, and his lordship was in a wicked temper. Bram had not spoken to his fellow spy, Gabe; close friend and fellow agent, Mary; or his superior, Hydra, since the Sheffield ball and, therefore, hadn't the faintest idea how their assignment had concluded. But if Hale's paroxysm was any indication, Bram would say it was a success—at least in part.

Lord Hale and the cohorts that had not been under Bram's and his fellows' watchful eyes had decided to journey together to Willow Hall to continue their unquestionably treasonous revelry. If luck was with him while the men were here, Bram should be able to find *something* that would be of use to conclude his assignment and to see Hale swinging from a noose.

Though despite how pleased that should make him, it was not that which had him so inordinately cheerful. Indeed, that honour fell to one person in particular.

The moment he had stepped through the front doors, the fragrance of tallow wax, silver polish, floor cleaners, cinnamon, and countless other things surrounded him, but beneath it all was oranges. *Rose.* He inhaled deeply, filling his lungs. He, selfish man that he was, would get to see her again, to talk to her. He longed to learn more about her: what her favourite foods were, what books she enjoyed, whether she had ever applied her running to sport. Largely, however, he wanted to see if she would be receptive to another kiss, for Lord knew he'd regretted not kissing her farewell before he'd left nearly a sennight ago.

"Good morning, Garrott," he greeted the butler.

The thin man wrung his hands, flicking his gaze toward the rear of the foyer and back. "His lordship did not send word of his arrival."

Odd. Bram's brow furrowed. "He and his guests are in the carriage behind ours. He sent the trunks ahead."

"Yes, yes. Good." He sent another nervous glance toward the rear of the foyer where the halls to both wings stood.

"Hurry it up." Lord Hale's valet pushed past him toward the family's wing. "Must have 'is lordship's things put to rights afore he arrives."

"And how soon will that be?" Garrott called after him.

Bram stood gazing at the butler, suspicion roiling in his stomach. Something was not right.

"Is there anything the matter, sir?" Bram asked.

"No, no," he rushed. "Of course not." Garrott showed his teeth in a false smile before standing back to allow another two footmen in, each carrying trunks.

"His lordship has three guests," Bram volunteered.

"Very good, very good." He pointed toward the family wing. "Bring those to the master's suite, if you will, Smithe."

The man's hands shook like leaves in a windstorm. Something was very wrong. Had something happened to Rose? To Violet? *Damn.* There was no time to find out without being conspicuous. He would have to speak with the butler when he returned for more trunks.

He spun on his heel and strode toward the family wing. He chanced a glance over his shoulder at the shaky butler, but the man was already scurrying toward the hidden doorway to the servants' passages.

As he reached the hall to the family wing, lilting music reached his ears. Sweet heaven, the tune was…*moving.* He had never heard such a song. Who had composed it?

His chest was caught like a fish on a hook. It pulled him forward, the trunks forgotten as they fell to the floor.

The keys were hit hard, each note precise and deliberately done, but with a flourish that was akin to the melody of emotion. Up, down, high, low, ambiguous yet certain. Love, laughter, sadness… It all rolled from the piano in a symphony of feeling.

Blazes, but it had him well and truly caught.

His feet carried him faster down the hall. He turned a corner and strode directly into someone, the petite form bouncing off his side and nearly falling to the floor. *Violet.* Bram reached out and grabbed her arm, gently holding her until she regained her balance.

"My apologies, Miss Wilkinson." His lips curled up in one corner.

She gazed at him with wide, frightened eyes, her breath suddenly coming rapidly.

He frowned. "I will not harm you. Surely you know that by now."

"No! No, no, *no!*" Her hands drew up to cup her cheeks as she turned her terrified gaze to the hall behind her. "*Ballocks!*"

Bram nearly choked on his tongue, the sound coming out in a garbled cough.

A string of dark curses flowed from the small woman's delicate lips.

Bram's coughing continued, his eyes watering. "My pardon, Miss Wilkinson, but you have the mouth of a seaman."

She ignored his comment and gripped his upper arms, her thin fingers digging into his flesh like talons. "How far behind is he?" she asked urgently. Her words rushed out. "Did he come with you? Is he here now? *Tell me!*"

"Lord Hale?"

Her fierce expression deepened into a scowl. "Don't play thick, Smithe. Of course, Lord Hale."

"He's in the carriage just behind—"

"Damnation!" She turned and sprinted down the hall, her black skirts hiked up to her knees.

"Wait!" he called, rushing after her.

She hesitated, glancing over her shoulder at him. "There is no time! Rose is in—"

"*Shh!*" Bram held out his hand as deep voices came from around the corner, far too close for his comfort. "That's Hale. They're coming!"

He gripped her arm and pulled her toward a vacant room.

"No!" She pulled against his grasp. "I must warn Rose!"

"If we do not hide in here now, all three of us will be caught in the familial wing."

Her expression told him she hated that he was right. He hated it, too, damn it.

"I must go to her. She does not deserve Hale's wrath."

"Neither do you," he replied. "It is Rose playing the piano, yes?"

She twitched her head in a jerky nod.

He ought to have known. Such soulful music could not come from a purer heart or more stunning woman. No matter how much he hated to leave Rose vulnerable, he couldn't allow her sister to put herself in peril as well.

Painfully aware of the fast-approaching traitors, he forced himself to think quickly. "*Hide.*"

He took Miss Wilkinson's fearful murmur as her assent and tugged her arm toward the vacant parlour.

"We will hide until they pass." His sternly hushed words brooked no argument. "I promise you I will find a way to help her. But we must hide if my plan is to work."

As quietly as possible, he closed the door behind them. He pressed his index finger to his lips in a signal for silence. Miss Wilkinson nodded in understanding.

The room reeked of wilting flowers. With the curtains closed, the parlour was dim, but still light enough for him to see his surroundings. Pieces of furniture scattered the room; however, he and Miss Wilkinson remained with their ears pressed to the door.

Beyond his heart hammering in his ears, Bram could hear distinct, heavy treads along the runner in the hall. The men had stopped talking, the echoing music likely causing a distraction. *Blazes.*

The footsteps faded down the corridor, and Miss Wilkinson reached for the door's latch.

"No," he whispered.

She frowned fiercely at him. "You said we could help Rose!" she hissed.

He shook his head once. "*I* shall help her."

In the distance the music stopped. Bram's heart followed suit.

He turned to Rose's sister, gripping her shoulders. "Go to your bedchamber and close the door. I will find a way to get her out of there. Wait for her."

A piercing scream echoed down the hall and Bram's stomach plummeted. He hated himself for letting her face Hale alone.

"*Bloody hell,*" Miss Wilkinson breathed.

She graced him with a gimlet eye. "Save her."

He could not answer for he was already pulling open the door. His feet propelled him toward Rose's agonised cries. His heart clutched in his chest as he wished, guiltily, that he had allowed Miss Violet Wilkinson to warn Rose. What had possessed him to halt her? *Foolish, unthinking…*

He skidded to a halt before the music room door, not allowing himself any time to gather his wits or catch his breath before he stepped inside.

He couldn't look at her. Out of the corner of his eye he could see her curled into a ball on the floor, her arms defensively wrapped over her head while Lord Hale stood over her and his cronies looked on in morbid excitement. But the confounding magnetic pull she had on him notwithstanding, Bram couldn't look at her. His gaze remained fixed on Lord Hale's cravat as a good footman should do. Diminutive and subservient.

"What is it, Smithe?" the bastard barked, his hand still poised to deliver another blow to Rose.

Damn. He had not thought that far.

"I have come to inquire after your comfort," he said on a whim. "Would you care for tea or refreshments? I would be pleased to serve."

Was that too forward? Too impertinent? He didn't care as long as they allowed Rose to leave!

Hale turned to the other three male occupants of the music room. "What say you, gentlemen? Shall we adjourn to the drawing room for a whisky while we discuss matters?"

"I am amenable to a whisky while we converse," Sir Wycliff drawled, his beady eyes narrowed menacingly on Rose.

The other two men, Lord Reddington and Mr. Piper, nodded their agreement.

Hale smiled at his traitorous friends, the lines on his face deepening, showing his advancing age.

"Off you go, poppet." He bent to pat Rose on the bottom, then laughed as she squeaked at the contact.

Bram tucked the inside of his cheek between his back teeth and bit down. He was desperate to intervene, to tell Rose that she could escape. But then these villainous cads would know her secret.

Rose, now is your chance! Run!

Chapter 12

Rose's body throbbed with each pounding beat of her heart. The site of each punishing blow Hale had delivered burned and swelled: her back, her ribs, her arms, and face. He had pounced on her like a wildcat, teeth barred and claws out.

The hurt. The humiliation. She could not—she *would* not—stand for it any longer. They would find another life somewhere beyond this purgatory; she didn't rightly care how.

A swift slap to her bottom startled her after a moment of respite. She tensed. Would he begin his assault anew?

For a terrified moment, Rose remained as she was. The low rumble of someone shouting reached her ears, but she could not discern the words. Despite her instinctive desire to protect her head, she slowly uncurled herself, to find out what was being shouted.

There he was. Her gaze immediately found Bramwell's, his glorious eyes full of pity and anger, and her embarrassment increased tenfold. How mortifying to have him see her thusly, as her uncle shouted, his arms flapping about.

Bram's head twitched to the side, ever so slightly. He was signalling her to leave. If this was her chance to flee these monstrous men, she would not squander another second.

Forcing the pain of her injuries from her mind, Rose scrambled to rise, and fled the room on swift feet. She picked up her skirts and ran. The halls were bustling with servants preparing the house after the master's arrival, but Rose spared them not a moment's concern. Their curious stares followed her as she raced past.

She swiftly opened the door to the courtyard, bursting into the warmth of the midday sun. The ground was still soggy from rain, the muddiness sucking gently at her slippers.

Her eyes stung and watered as she ran through the gardens and out the back gate; she did not know if it was from the wind in her eyes or if she wept, but she let the tears come. Her mama had always said that shedding tears was a cathartic release. And she could use a soulful cleanse right now.

She forced her arms and legs to move faster. Tears streamed backward into the hairline at her temples, and her chignon was woefully windblown. Her arms pumped at her sides, and her skirts whipped at her legs. And she continued to run.

Time faded away. Her lungs and muscles burned mercilessly, her bones ached, and her cheeks had gone numb long ago, but she pushed through the pain. This land was entirely new to her having passed Willow Hall's estate boundaries countless minutes ago. She didn't care. She simply had to get away.

She would return for Violet before nightfall, and they would take their newly acquired funds and pilfered pistol and leave. They would—

With a sudden gasp, Rose skidded to a halt as the end of the world drew up before her.

Her knees wobbled, her muscles trembling with exhaustion, but she stared in wonder.

She stood only steps from the edge of a cliff that curved outward into a peninsular point over a dense, rolling fog. The effect was startling in its beauty. It gave one the feeling of being poised high above the clouds, looking out over the bright sky.

The muscles in her legs finally gave way, and she slumped to the ground, her rumpled black skirts folding beneath her. A bead of sweat trickled down her throbbing temple to her bruised neck, sliding its way between her breasts as her lungs still laboured for breath.

The early afternoon sun warmed her exertion-heated skin through her black dress and glinted off the moisture in the fog, giving it the appearance of dancing sparkles. A bird flew over the cliff, swooping down to touch its wings to the fog, causing a swirling billow in its wake. Her lungs heaved as she took in the scenic splendour. How could such a place exist? It appeared to be something out of a painting, a place that someone might imagine.

Rose swivelled onto her bottom, situating herself more comfortably on the hard, grassy ground.

A wet nose prodded her hand, and she nearly jumped out of her skin.

"Dog!" she gasped. "I did not know you followed me, boy."

She gave his head a scratch and ran her hand over his warm fur, his own breath coming quickly.

Turning her gaze back out to the view, Rose wrapped an arm around her companion. "Is it not a breathtaking view, Dog?"

She tilted her face toward the sun and closed her eyes.

She scratched him absently under the chin as she spoke. "Will you come with me when Violet and I leave, Dog?"

* * *

Bramwell poured another dram of whisky into a crystal goblet, then returned it to Lord Reddington's waiting hand.

"Tell us the rest of your proposition, Hale," Sir Wycliff drawled, his own glass of whisky nearly empty. "Now that we've seen one of the chits—of whom I heartily approve—let us begin the negotiations."

Bram pressed his back against the wall of Hale's drawing room, and attempted to become invisible.

The room was adorned in midnight blue and deep green, with touches of mahogany wood furnishings. The low-burning fire lent warmth to the space while the opened windows brought in light. It was anything but ostentatious. Curse the bastard for that. The room, in fact, resembled the man: strong, fit, sleek-lined, and tainted with a heavy scent of liquor and sin.

"What are your terms, Hale?" Reddington grimaced as he gulped down a deep swill of whisky.

Hale's expression was too self-assured by half. Bram wanted to knock the cocksure smile from the villain's face.

Hale crossed one stocking-clad ankle over the other and reclined in his armchair, presumably at his ease. "Ten thousand quid and your vote on my next bill."

Reddington choked on his drink, coughing and sputtering, while the others looked on.

His eyes watering, Reddington clapped his chest. "For *that* chit?"

Bram fought the frown that threatened. What the devil were these negotiations for?

Hale gazed thoughtfully at the liquid in his glass. "Yes."

The younger man chewed on his bottom lip. "Would you advance the funds to me until such time that my grandmother releases my stipend?"

Hale inclined his head. "Indeed, I would."

Reddington clapped his hands together. "Capital!"

"Now, just a moment here," Wycliff interjected. "Which of us gets first choice of the chits? And how can we be assured that they will breed? The blonde one took abuse well, but will she easily show unsightly bruises?"

Chits? Breed? What the hell? Bram's pulse sped. Surely they weren't discussing the *purchase* of the Wilkinson sisters?

"One is never assured that a female will produce an heir. And that one does bruise, I'm afraid." Hale examined his fingernails before taking another swill of his whisky. "The weddings will take place in a sennight by special licence. No exceptions."

Wycliff rubbed his index finger and thumb together greedily, his lips curled back in…arousal? Disgust roiled through Bram. *Bloody hell!*

"I find myself rather fond of the young Miss Rose Wilkinson, Hale," Wycliff said, his voice deepening ominously. "I will pay you twelve thousand pounds if I can have her right away. I board a frigate on the morrow and will not lose her to damned Reddington because of a bloody stipulation."

Reddington had an odd expression of combined outrage and smugness. "What of the wedding? Hale said no exceptions."

"Reddington, you fool, the captain can marry us. But if I don't collect those documents from curst Anthony Spencer and throw him overboard, we'll all be hung."

Anthony Spencer was the alternate identity of Bramwell's fellow spy, Gabe Ashley. Gabe had attended the house party at Kerr House and acquired important documents from these villains, then obtained passage on an America-bound frigate—which he did not intend to board. The trap was well and truly set for Wycliff, but Bram couldn't let either of the Wilkinson sisters be caught in the middle of it.

Hale's avaricious smile grew, his eyes narrowing with greed. "Of course you may have her."

Reddington uncrossed his legs and sat up in indignation. "Oi! But what if the other one is ugly? Why does he get to choose?"

With all his might, Bram fought to remain calm. He very carefully evened his breathing, forcing his heart rate to slow to normal. He would help them. He would find a way to aid their escape before Wycliff boarded that frigate. He must.

The other men glared at the young, treasonous collaborator.

"Reddington, you blasted ass."

The fool frowned in confusion at his elder cohorts.

The fourth bastard in the room, Mr. Piper, sat forward eagerly, finally breaking his silence. "This is enjoyable business, eh wot? The Misses Wilkinson seem enjoyable for sport. The blonde one takes abuse well, which is pleasing, wot, wot?"

The others nodded in agreement and Bram clenched his jaw. *You mustn't break, Bramwell.*

"Well!" Hale wiggled his glass, signalling Bram to refill it.

Bram hurried to do as he was bid, accepting the glass from the devil's hand and bringing it to the liquor tantalus.

"As we seem to have concluded this aspect of our meeting, barring the signing of the contracts, which I shall have my solicitor draw up, I believe we must move on to *this*." Hale removed a short piece of parchment from the inner breast pocket of his cobalt coat and waved it briefly in the air.

Bram's interest flared.

Hale accepted the refilled refreshment in his free hand while Bram retrieved the others' empty crystal tumblers and began to refill them at the tantalus.

"After the disaster of our last meeting, this is—" Hale stopped as Bram delivered the men's refilled whiskies. "That will be all, Smithe."

Damn. Bramwell needed to know what was on that piece of parchment. From what he had learned, their rendezvous had gone horribly awry, ending in the death of two other traitors after the discovery of some forged documents, but proof of Hale's guilt still eluded him. If he could make a rubbing of that parchment, he might very well be able to conclude his assignment!

He meekly bowed to the room before he exited, slowly closing the door behind him.

"This letter," Hale continued as the door shut, "contains orders from our superiors, directing us on which of our bloody English-supporting counterparts are secreting away information that would benefit Bonaparte…"

Bram pressed his ear eagerly to the closed door, his heart flipping over in his chest. *Good God! Which of my fellow spies' identities have been compromised?*

"…the first of which is my own damned neighbour…"

Bram's gut tightened. Christian Samuels, the Viscount Leeds, resided in the neighbouring estate. He was also the lead cryptologist in their band of spies. He must be warned.

* * *

The early evening sun lowered slowly into the hazy pink sky as Rose absently scratched Dog behind the ears. The cliff was breathtaking, the fog below reflecting the pinks and reds of the sky above. The world stretched out endlessly before her.

She wished she could remain in this spot. But she had to return to Violet and to their plan.

With a sigh, she rolled to her knees and stood, her temporarily forgotten injuries making themselves known once more. The moisture from the ground had dampened her bombazine frock, and the air was heavy with humidity after the rain. As the sun lowered in the early June sky, the air began to chill, the cool, damp breeze sending gooseflesh skittering along her skin.

It was time to leave Willow Hall.

Chapter 13

"It is against my sworn duties as a footman," Bram whispered, "to reveal such intimate details of my master's discussion, but I feel honour-bound to warn you of your uncle's intentions."

Miss Violet Wilkinson's blue gaze was stormy in the dim light of the corridor outside her bedchamber.

"Thank you, Smithe."

Bram nodded, his white wig going askew, and lowered his voice even further. "I would suggest an escape, as soon as may be. What can I do to help?"

Her eyebrows rose. "You have done so much already, Smithe. I would hate for you to bear Hale's wrath."

He shook his head, his sagging wig tilting further. Frustrated, he lifted the thing from his head and tossed it to the ground at his feet. "I wish to aid you in your escape, Miss Wilkinson. Tell me what I can do."

She gazed thoughtfully at him, then blurted, "Do you have amorous feelings for my sister, Smithe?"

Hell. What had Rose told her sister about them? He could not very well tell her of his physical attraction to Rose, but perhaps part of the truth would suffice.

"I am fond of Rose, but that is not why I wish to help."

"Of course." She grinned. "Have you expressed your feelings to her?"

"No, I—" he halted, his eyes narrowed. "I see what you've done, wily woman. But you aren't going to trick me that easily."

She winked. "I shall find a way." Her grin slipped slightly as she continued. "Rose and I have begun planning an escape, but there are missing parts to the scheme that pose a problem."

"What are they?"

She grimaced. "Now that I am aware of our uncle's plans to sell us, Rose and I will need to separate. If we journey in different directions, our uncle will have increased difficulty in finding either one of us, should he decide to follow. I intend to travel north to Glasgow, where our grandmama and grandpapa reside. The how is not important right now. Rose, however, requires help." Her gaze turned hopeful. "Rose needs to travel to London, but she will need someone with her. I'd thought that could be you."

Bram's eyes snapped wide with shock even as his mind worked. "With *me*? But what of—"

"She would not reside with you in London, of course. Our aunt, Maureen, resides in town. I am certain she would be of help to her."

Christ, but he wanted to be that man; he wanted to ensure Rose's safety while she travelled to London, but his assignment had not yet been completed. Could he secret her away somehow, before concluding his business, and *then* reunite her with her aunt? It was entirely possible.

Once he had her on the road, however, how would they travel? As brother and sister? He knew what to do from the position of an agent, but what did innocent women expect? And how could he be expected to spend so much time alone with her and keep her reputation intact?

"What of propriety?" he asked. "What of Rose's reputation?" He distractedly ran a hand through his hair before squeezing the muscles at the back of his neck. "She is—"

"She is not a maiden," Violet burst out before biting her lips together.

Despite himself, his pulse sped, and his cock twitched. *Hell.*

Miss Wilkinson's eyes widened slightly, and she cleared her throat. "I-I mean," she stammered, "that is to say, Rose's reputation is of little importance when compared to our dire circumstance at Willow Hall."

"Of course," he replied half-heartedly.

Passing over her foible, she reached for one of his hands, grasping it tightly in her own. "Will you do it?"

"Pardon?"

"Will you take Rose to safety? To our aunt in London? But you must leave before dawn if you are to escape our uncle and his horrid guests."

There was no choice to be made. He couldn't leave Rose to be purchased like sodding cattle. He would find a way to do all of it at once. "I will, though I daresay that Rose is more than capable of making this choice on her own."

Relief slackened Miss Wilkinson's spine. "Oh, thank heavens!" She clasped her hands together at her chest.

"Might I speak with Rose before I prepare for departure?" he asked, flicking a glance toward the closed bedchamber door. "You both ought to begin packing if we are to depart before dawn."

Her features froze. "But she was with you!"

Bram's heart slammed once in his chest. "She is not."

She scowled at him. "You told me you would rescue her from the music room! You said you would—"

"I did, damn it! I sent her to you." He rubbed a hand over his face, his other resting on his hip as panic threatened. "She ran from the music room, and I thought she would return here to you. I would have followed her had I not been required to remain.

"The sun will set soon," he continued. "Would she have gone running with Dog?"

She wrung her hands. "Yes. Yes, I believe she might."

"Blast. You remain here. If she returns, she will need you to examine her wounds."

With that, he dashed down the corridor.

* * *

Rose's legs shook with each step. The rooftop points of Willow Hall were visible just over the last hill, each window reflecting the bright oranges pinks of the sun behind her. Her lungs burned with each breath, her left eye was nearly swollen shut, and a stabbing pain radiated through her back with every slight movement.

Dog nudged the hand hanging at her side, and she weakly patted his head. "I…" She heaved a breath through the pain. "I can't…."

Her legs gave out beneath her and she dropped, scarcely aware of her contact with the damp, grassy ground. She merely required a short rest to regain her strength.

"Do not worry…Dog," she gasped. "I will rest for but a moment…then I shall…I shall"—she wheezed another breath—"continue on."

* * *

The halls were quiet as Bram crept downstairs in search of Rose. Would she enter through the foyer or would she use an alternate door? He didn't know, curse it, so he checked each potential entrance for any sign of her. When that was unsuccessful, he ventured out of doors.

The early evening sky was clear and bright with hues of pink, orange, and yellow.

Keeping off the garden path so as not to call attention to his location with that telltale *crunch* of the gravel, and grateful for the uniform that matched the landscape, Bram slunk through the gardens.

"Bram." A whispered female voice came from a nearby stone bench.

Tamping down the pang of alarm in his chest, Bram sauntered to the shadowed figure, a grin on his lips. "Amelia West. Bloody hell, what are you doing here?" He raised an eyebrow. "Is there a poor soul you're here to murder? I'm sorry…*assassinate*?"

Even as he spoke, he kept his ears trained for any sound that could be Rose.

Amelia was the best assassin in their band of spies. She was quick on her feet and deadly accurate with a bow and arrow.

The *snick* of her blade against a tree's branch sounded loud in the dark garden. "You know very well Hydra hasn't sent me on that sort of assignment in some time." There were more sounds of her whittling. "I'm tailing Porter."

Bram nodded, his gaze slipping to roam around them for any sign of Rose. "Ah, yes. Porter. Any particular reason?"

Amelia stood, abandoning her seat on the bench, the blade and branch still in her hands. The bright light of the sky silhouetted her figure, delineating the angle of her bow as it rested over her shoulder, and the crossed arrows she often kept in her hair.

"After the house party, Hydra assigned the lot of us to the other known traitors," she said. "Callum's resumed training Harris, and they tailed Wycliff until they boarded a frigate yesterday morn."

"Have you seen Mary?" Bram asked. Mary Wright was their fellow spy and his close friend—had been so since they had both begun their training. She was a valued part of his life and nearly as close to him as a sister would be. She'd been attacked the last time he'd seen her.

Amelia nodded once. "She's well. Happy, as far as I can tell."

Relief filled him. He turned his attention back to her previous comment. "Is Harris well enough to make such a journey? I thought he was still in recovery at Hydra's town house." The young man had been injured while tailing a spy for Bonaparte.

Amelia shrugged.

Bram shook his head. It made no sense. "If Callum and Harris boarded yesterday, then what frigate is Wycliff boarding on the morrow?" Again, his gaze roamed the gardens.

He could hear Amelia's lips pull back in a grin. "Callum is taking on the position that as of yet he's only been able to conjure in his dreams."

Bram released a barked laugh. "Tell me he isn't to be a pirate…"

"Oh, yes."

"By damn."

"Off you go then, Bramwell Stevens. Find your lady."

Bram frowned. "How the devil are you always so perceptive?"

She clucked her tongue. "Your gaze has been searching the gardens since before we began speaking. Is she well? Would you like some help?"

"No, thank you. I will find her on my own. If you hear her in the garden without me by her side, do ensure she enters the house safely. And damn it, Amelia, don't frighten her."

"Come now," she protested. "I do not frighten innocent people."

"I'm a grown man, and you frighten the devil out of me most of the time."

She cuffed him on the shoulder, and Bram grimaced, rubbing at it to soothe away the pain. "Curst woman," he grumbled.

"Bastard charmer." She smiled. "Good luck."

As quietly and as quickly as he could, Bram made his way to the garden's gate. Clearly, Rose was not within its confines, so she must still be running with Dog. She would be exhausted by now.

He closed the gate behind him and ventured out over the grass, scanning his gaze over the hills in each direction. He would call her name, but that would be fruitless. But perhaps if he—

A thought occurred to him, and he would have grinned if he had not been so concerned for Rose's wellbeing. Pursing his lips, Bram blew, a light, high-pitched whistle resounding through the air around him.

He paused, listening. A responding bark came almost immediately from just over the closest knoll, and Bram broke into a run before Dog crested the hill.

"Dog!" Bram called, jogging to the animal.

He patted the beast's flank. "Where is she, boy?" Bram lifted his head to look out over the hill as he spoke. "Take me to her."

Dog broke into a sprint and Bram followed close after him. The run was short, for within moments he spotted a lone form slumped in the grass.

His heart twisted in his chest. "Rose!"

He skidded to a halt before her, entirely at sixes and sevens. What should he do? He dropped to his knees at her side.

Having sensed his presence, she lifted her head; one of her startled brown eyes was wide in her pale face while the other was nearly swollen shut and a horrid shade of purple.

"Bram?"

"I'm here." He cupped her face in his hands, his swarthy skin making her appear ever paler. "Where are you hurt?"

She gripped his hands in hers, pulling them gently from her cheeks. "I am well enough. Merely too tired to walk any longer."

He searched her uninjured eye for validity in her words. She may well believe she was in earnest, but Bram could see pain lurking in

He froze, his expression stilling and his lips forming a grim line. "Bram?"

She could not hear it, but the self-depreciating grimace and the rumble beneath her palm told her that he groaned. "I must speak with you on a very important matter, Rose."

Clearing her own throat, she allowed Bram to assist her to a seated position, the movement sending shooting pain through her back and side.

Bramwell gripped her hands, concern lighting his golden eyes. His lips moved, but she must have blinked, for she couldn't understand a word of it.

"Pardon?" she asked.

"Are you well?" he repeated.

She took a steadying breath and nodded. "Do go on. What is it you wish to say to me?"

His shoulders rose and fell with a sigh and then he spoke. Rose watched as he carefully described her uncle's atrocious plan to sell her and her twin sister to other monstrous men as broodmares and sparring dummies. Her heart sank lower and lower with each word until he concluded with a detailed recitation of his discussion with Violet. Some of his words had been lost, but she understood the crux of it.

He gazed at her with uncertain hopefulness as he awaited her response. It was rather a lot to take in all at once.

"Will you make the journey with me to London? To your aunt?" He appeared so discomfited that she wished she could put him at ease.

She blurted, "What of the funds required for travel?" It was a tactless inquiry, but the concern needed to be voiced. "I have a small amount, but not nearly enough," she admitted. She and Violet were meant to use the pilfered money together; splitting it up meant fewer bank notes each.

His lips curved in a grin. "Rest assured, Rose, I have more than enough to make the journey three times over."

Rose could not help but feel impressed with his judicious saving.

But one glaringly obvious matter was holding her back.

She looked at him regretfully. "I cannot go until I am assured that Violet will be safe. Our uncle is a vile man, and I will not have her alone in Willow Hall with him."

Bramwell nodded his understanding. "Do discuss this with your sister. I will await…decision. Meet me before dawn?"

Relief flooded her. She could not possibly take such a large proverbial step in her life without first ensuring that Violet would be secure, despite how fervently she wished to throw caution to the wind and abscond to London with Bram.

"Of course," she confirmed. "At the stables?"

He grinned at her, and she had the sudden urge to kiss it from his lips, to feel his body pressed against hers, his stiffness against her *mons… What a wanton I have become!*

"Are you able to walk?" He watched her with concern.

Rose pulled her bottom lip between her teeth in one of her habitual gestures but winced as her teeth scraped the split and swelling there. She had briefly forgotten about that inconvenience. "I'm afraid not. Perhaps if I remove my slippers…"

She reached down to her woefully inadequate footwear, but he brushed her hands aside.

"Allow me."

Rose extended her leg to him as he slowly and intimately removed her severely worn black satin slippers. She hissed a breath between her teeth at the abrupt stinging.

His wide eyes rose to search her face. "Your stockings are crusted with blood, Rose!" Suddenly his shock turned to anger, his dark, shaggy eyebrows angling downward in a fierce frown. "Why did you not tell me you were in such pain?"

Rising to his feet, he crumpled her slippers in his fist and shoved them into the inner breast pocket of his coat.

"I-I'm sorry. I did not real—"

He waved in a dismissive gesture, halting her flow of words before he bent down and lifted her carefully in his arms. She ignored the stabbing pain shooting through her back and side and wrapped her arms around his strong neck. She would have time to recover soon enough, but for now she pushed through the hurt.

Every movement jostled her, causing her to cringe, but it was a far sight better than having to walk. And for that she was grateful.

Bramwell took his steps slowly, each one deliberate and careful, while Dog trotted alongside him. The air had cooled greatly in the past hour, causing Bram's every breath to puff in a white, misty cloud, drawing her gaze. Such energy he exerted…and it was for her. He was not obliged to carry her, but he'd seen her in pain, so he'd acted.

Had she ever met a man as gallant as he? Rose did not think so.

She closed her eyes, giving in to temptation and pressing her nose to his neck, inhaling his heady scent. An insistent jolt of pain went through her with each of Bramwell's steps, and she clung to him, immersing herself in his coffee-and-sandalwood fragrance. He was the perfect distraction.

His throat vibrated with his voice and the deep notes rumbled through her chest. But she daren't pull back to watch his lips, for she knew if she left this world of coffee and sandalwood, pain would engulf her.

* * *

"You found her." Amelia's soft voice called to Bram through the dim light of Willow Hall's gardens. "How is she?"

Bram bit back the curse that threatened to escape. "In a great deal of pain," he grunted.

"Hale's a right bastard," she muttered from somewhere over his right shoulder as he strode purposefully down the garden path.

"I can think of several stronger choice words for the blackguard." He took long strides, carrying them quickly toward the courtyard. "I have business to attend to tonight," he said softly to Amelia, whom he assumed was following him. "I plan to depart for London by dawn."

The sky grew darker by the moment, but Bram knew his way. He pressed himself faster, not waiting to listen for a reply from Amelia.

Rose's sweet breath brushed the underside of his jaw, the feeling sending an odd sizzling sensation over his skin. He could feel her jagged gasps with each of his movements, and his heart stuttered.

He hastened his steps while also being cautious not to jar her, striding across the courtyard. He struggled for a mere moment with the door's latch before he steadfastly turned into the guest wing of the house. He made quick work of each set of stairs, finally reaching the sisters' bedchamber door unseen.

"We're here, Rose," he murmured. He knew that she could not hear him, but he spoke nonetheless, hoping that the vibration of his voice was comforting to her.

With one outstretched knuckle, Bram tapped lightly on the door.

It swiftly opened, a *whoosh* of wind rushing past him into the room as Miss Violet Wilkinson pulled the door from the other side.

"Rose!" Miss Wilkinson stood aside to allow Bram to pass before she fluttered around them. "Her bed is this one." She pointed to the one farthest from the door.

As carefully as he could, Bram placed Rose upon the bed. Her grasp around his neck was tight, but once she realised where they were, she slackened her grip.

"What happened?" Violet gazed down into Rose's one opened eye, then retrieved a bound sketchbook and wrote swiftly with a pencil. "Oh dear, look at your face. Are you hurting very badly?"

Rose licked her dried lips. "I feel fine but for my back and my feet." Her voice was strong, though Bram could sense her struggle with her pain.

He placed his hands upon his hips as he watched Violet remove Rose's crusted stockings.

Violet hissed a breath as she gazed at her sister's sorely damaged soles. She wrote in the book once more. "Oh, my poor sweet Rose. You should not have pushed yourself so."

"I know a skilled doctor in London," Bramwell blurted.

Doctor Simon Claridge, the Earl of Merrington, was a superb doctor and one who had become the only medical aid to Hydra's band of crown spies. Claridge knew of their association with the Home Office and patched them up when they'd been shot, stabbed, or otherwise injured while on assignment. He would most certainly help Rose should Bram request it.

Miss Violet gazed at him, her cobalt eyes wide with worry. "Her breathing is shallow. Would she make it to London well enough, do you imagine?"

"I am fine!" Rose asserted, her eyes wide and slightly alarmed. "I do not require a doctor."

Bram nodded jerkily in response to Miss Violet. "I believe that it is her only hope for a full recovery. If you both are to remain, there is a greater chance for further injury."

After a quick, scratching of the pencil in the sketchbook, Miss Violet turned it around for Rose to read. "Your injuries are more than I can tend to, dearest. You require help."

Bram glanced at Rose's bruised face and away again, hiding his sympathetic cringe. "I have much to do before we depart in the morn, and I believe that Rose wished to speak with you. I will leave you two to gather your things in privacy."

Bram stepped closer to Rose's bedside, ensuring that she could see his lips as he spoke. "We daren't meet at the stables as agreed, Rose. I will return here before dawn to fetch you."

She nodded with a wince. "Thank you, Bramwell."

His lips curved upward in a sad grin before he spun on his heel and left the room. He was on an assignment, damn it, and he would complete it successfully, save the Misses Wilkinson, and if he were fortunate, perhaps examine this feral lust for Rose that consumed him. Once his assignment had concluded.

Chapter 15

"He fancies you, Rose," Violet wrote, clearly attempting to lighten the atmosphere of their bedchamber while she packed their meagre belongings into two large, aged hatboxes.

They had once possessed great trunks filled with gowns and fripperies, but their many frocks had long since been ruined beyond repair and their trunks sold by Hale to, as he'd sneered, "cover the very great expense of feeding their ungrateful mouths." The only means for carrying their belongings were the hatboxes they'd found stuffed haphazardly in a cupboard.

Rose kept a cold, damp strip of folded linen to her swollen eye as she sat upon her bed, her aching back propped against the blissfully cool wall. She toyed with the material of her coverlet where it rested on her lap. Her stomach was a nervous jumble. "It is kind of you to say, Vi, but I know that—"

"Here now!" Violet interrupted. "Do not diminish your value, dear heart. You would be the toast of the season if we were out in society." She winked. "Besides, he has already kissed you, has he not? Surely you know that means that he desires you."

Rose pressed her swollen, cracked lips together to suppress the tumultuous grin that threatened. Despite their circumstances, Rose anticipated her journey to London. It was potentially perilous, and undoubtedly painful in her current state, but not only would she at last be free from her uncle's clutches, she had a rather dashing travelling companion.

They would be alone for the duration of the journey. The possibilities of what might happen in such close confines were endless!

Violet paused in her packing to take Rose's free hand in hers, foregoing their customary use of the sketchbook. "Promise me something, Rose…"

She blinked. "Of course."

"Promise me that if he is amenable—and I'm certain that he is—and if an opportunity presents itself, you will make love to Smithe on the journey to London."

Rose's jaw dropped briefly before she caught it. "*Violet!*" Her heart beat a tattoo in her chest. Much to her consternation, her reaction was one of not scandalous outrage but unmitigated hope…and excitement.

"Do not…scandalised, dear." Violet rolled her eyes. "I know you've peeked at that book I gave you. Besides…done the deed before…shan't be anything new."

Rose's hand fluttered to her onyx pendant. "But goodness, Vi, of all the things for you to wish for me to promise…"

"It is the very best of things to promise!" Violet insisted. "I shall know…sister is happy and satisfied. And with a man who would risk life and limb to protect her! Shouldn't I wish joy upon my sister?"

"Well, yes…"

"Precisely! So promise me, Rose, if the opportunity should arise…not squander it!"

Rose chewed on her bottom lip. Her mind screamed for her to say yes. She wanted Bramwell in her bed and in her body. Indeed, she thought of him frequently in such circumstances. But something in the back of her mind begged her not to flout propriety again, to follow the rules of society and be a good— *Oh, who am I attempting to fool?* she asked herself. Her days of expecting a good match were so far from the realm of possibility that she might as well enjoy a few stolen kisses and caresses before she became an elderly spinster obsessed with cats and employed as a companion to some wealthy widow.

"Very well," Rose agreed, odd though it was.

Vi's expression brightened, and she flounced from the bed.

Rose's insides were knotted with anticipation; she could scarcely endure it for another moment. If she permitted herself to think on the subject of Bramwell Smithe much longer, she would positively burst.

She flipped over the cold compress on her eye, placing the air-cooled side against her skin.

"What of you, Vi?" she asked. "Will you give your maidenhead to some fellow in your travels?"

Her sister lifted one shoulder before letting it fall. "If I find a decent man. I'll not wish to bed a blackguard."

"I should say not."

Violet returned her attention to packing their boxes.

Rose licked at her dry lips. "How do you plan to journey to Grandmama and Grandpapa's? I refuse to leave unless I am assured of your safety."

Violet spun to face her with a roll of her eyes. "Why, it is simple, dear." She dug her hand into the side of her overlarge hatbox and pulled free the dulled metal duelling pistol—its handle glimmering with an inlaid design—that they had purloined from their cousin. "I shall use *this*."

* * *

On silent feet, Bram slunk from the dimly lit corridor into the dark sitting room adjoining Hale's study and closed the door quietly behind himself.

He crept to the study's door and pressed his ear to the cool wood, listening intently. There was nary a sound, so he slowly pressed the latch and pulled the door open.

Empty. Perfect.

He strode quickly inside and opened the curtains wide, allowing the evening's moonlight to lend its soft, milky glow to the room. He had searched each of Hale's strongboxes once before, so he knew where they were concealed. He made quick work of checking those first.

He *must* find those orders.

* * *

"Please tell me that you do not intend to shoot someone." Rose leaned forward, dropping the damp compress to her lap and ignoring the jolting pain in her back. She gazed into her sister's glimmering eyes. "Do you plan to kill Lord Hale?"

Violet laughed, then took up the sketchbook. "Heavens, no, Rose! I fear I am incapable of murder, no matter how vilely our uncle behaves."

"If you are not joining Bramwell and me while we travel to London, and you are not committing murder here at Willow Hall, what do you intend to do?"

Vi's blue eyes sparkled, and her grin deepened. "It is an ingenious plot, really. I will simply walk to the neighbouring estate and gently persuade the landowner—a Christian Samuels, Viscount Leeds—to take me to the nearest inn and pay for my passage aboard a mail coach."

Rose frowned. "You are going to threaten him?"

Violet shrugged one shoulder as she folded her night rail and stuffed it into her hatbox, then wrote. "At first, I shall play upon his pride and gentlemanly urge to aid a lady in distress. If that fails to garner his assistance, then yes, I shall threaten him. It is purely as a precaution, Rose, as I am certain that he will leap to lend his aid. I've seen him from afar; he's an elderly man with silver hair and a pronounced limp who surely will not leave me in peril."

Pushing past the curiosity at how her sister knew so much about the neighbouring landowner, Rose forged onward. "You will then take the mail coach all the way to Scotland?"

"Naturally."

Rose nodded. She could not claim to be terribly fond of the idea of her sister travelling alone, but with so many others in the mail coach, she knew that help would not be far away if Violet should require it. With the added protection of the duelling pistol, Vi could certainly defend herself if the need arose.

"Tell them that you're a widow," she said. "Your fellow travellers will ask fewer questions of you."

Vi swept close to buss Rose's cheek, then pulled back to smile at her. "You're a genius, dear one."

Rose pointed at the small pile of black bombazine that Violet had placed at the foot of Rose's bed. "Would you care for some help?"

"Absolutely not, Rose. You must rest, at least until Smithe's doctor can examine you. Lord knows what damage has occurred beneath that horribly bruised skin." She shook her head angrily as she wrote, her motions agitated. "Not only do you suffer from the same healing lashes as I, but that rotten bastard had the nerve to kick you after he'd punched your eye and knocked you to the ground. Why, if I had—"

Rose waved a hand through the air. "That's enough, Violet. While I appreciate your defence, I am far too exhausted to become enraged over it. Even listening to his offences again is tiresome."

Vi clenched her jaw, visibly struggling with her outrage. "Very well." She dipped her head, and scribbled. "But that doesn't stop me from wishing I could cut off his ballocks in his sleep."

* * *

Bram slid another heavy tome from the bookshelf and flipped through the pages. Surely if there was a book with a secret compartment, he would have found it by now. *Damn.* He was beginning to run out of places to search.

He turned to face the room, frustration riding him. There were no false bottoms to Hale's drawers, nor were there any hidden panels in the walls…

Just a moment. Perhaps he was looking at this in the wrong way.

Hale was a devious sort; he would not place such important documents in the obvious places. Perhaps Bram was looking for the wrong type of hiding spot.

He dropped to his knees and knocked on the leg of a short table.

* * *

"But what if I don't like the chit?" Reddington's grating voice crawled up Hale's spine.

"Damn it, Reddington, I've told you before what she looks like." Hale increased his pace down the corridor, their footsteps muffled on the hall's carpet runner.

"But if I could just sample her—"

Hale spun to face him, halting in his tracks. "If I let you have a sample then Wycliff will want one, too."

"Bloody right I would." Sir Wycliff stopped to stand beside Hale in the poorly lit hall.

"Well of course *he* would—he gets the blonde!"

Hale clenched his jaw in barely suppressed irritation. What he wouldn't give to punch the man in the nose. But if Reddington managed to come up with the funds to pay for Miss Violet Wilkinson, then he was worth keeping around. Besides, Reddington was useful in other ways as well.

"I propose we suspend this discussion for the moment," Hale said as calmly as he could manage. "There are other matters to discuss. Come. My study awaits."

* * *

Bram cursed under his breath as he crawled across Hale's study floor to the next piece of furniture. The desk and decorative pedestals made the most sense as possible hiding places for a secret compartment. The pedestals had already been checked, so he moved on to the desk.

Knock, knock, he rapped on the thick, elaborately carved wooden sides. He moved over an inch. *Knock, knock*. He moved over yet more. *Knock, thunk*.

His heart rate elevated with the buzz of triumph that shot through him.

He tapped again. *Thunk, thunk*. He'd found it!

* * *

"Just a moment, Garrott," Hale called to his fool butler from the top of the foyer's stairs.

The man halted in his retreat. He had clearly begun to ready himself for bed but had come out to lock the door. Hale didn't give a damn. The man was a servant and would serve him regardless of the hour.

Garrott turned and bowed at the three men descending the stairs. "Good evening, my lords, Sir Wycliff."

Hale reached the bottom of the steps and stared down his nose at Garrott. "Have refreshments brought to my study at once."

The man's eyes shifted nervously between Hale and his guests. *Good. The man should be afraid of me.*

"B-but the maids are all t-to bed, your lordship."

Hale could feel his face reddening with the force of his ire. *"Then make it your bloody self."*

With a trembling bow and a mumbled, "Yes, my lord," the butler scurried toward the kitchens.

Reddington snickered openly.

"Damnably difficult to find good help these days," Wycliff murmured.

Hale turned to face him, his blood still running high. "Isn't it just?"

* * *

Bram's fingers ran over the intricate carvings on the side of Hale's desk. He knew where the compartment was hidden; he simply needed to find the latch to open it. He pressed along seams, pushed knots in the wood. Nothing. *Damn.*

He was tracing his index finger along a circular pattern when an idea hit him. He pressed the circle and turned it. *Aha!*

A *buzz* and a *whirr* echoed through the grand room, followed by a small *pop* as a door in the side of the desk sprang open. He peered inside, and his heart leapt. The document was within!

Without hesitation, Bram retrieved the parchment and laid it out on the desk. Good God, it wasn't even coded well. The fools had made this far too easy to decipher.

Jubilation raced through his veins. He'd done it. This was his evidence against Hale! It was clearly addressed to the man, and the orders to carry out treason in the form of murder against agents for the Home Office was the proof Bram needed to see Hale swing. Once Bram took the letter to Hydra, it would be the beginning of the end for the marquess.

Gently running his fingers over the writing, he felt for any ridges. *Excellent.* A thrill bubbled up his spine. The writer of the note had pressed firmly enough to emboss the parchment.

Bram found another piece of parchment and gently placed it overtop, then hurried to the cold hearth and picked up a small fragment of charcoal. He hastened to create the rubbing. It was not the best, but one could not mistake the message.

With the rubbing rolled, he set about returning Hale's study to rights.

* * *

"I am eager to learn of your news, Reddington," Wycliff said as Hale led them down the hall to his study.

Hale was inclined to agree. As much as he found Reddington a dandified fool, the man was skilled at scheming and violence.

They reached the door to his study and Hale pressed the latch, swinging the door wide.

"Have a seat, gentlemen." Hale swept his arm into the room and waited for Reddington and Wycliff to enter.

With both men inside, he turned to retrieve a candle from a nearby sconce before he followed, closing the door behind them.

Hale strode about the room, lighting the candles until the space was brightened with an ambient glow.

"Now"—he settled himself in his dark-brown leather armchair—"do share with us your news, Reddington."

The man looked entirely too smug for Hale's liking. His news had better be good if it required Hale to delay his ablutions before bed.

"I have kept it secret for just over a month now…"

"Out with it, damn you," Wycliff rumbled.

Reddington's conceited grin grew. "I have myself a little captive."

Hale frowned, intrigue firing his gut. "Captive, you say?"

"Indeed. One of the Home Office's little minions… I caught him sneaking around, and I captured him."

* * *

Bram's heart beat a staccato rhythm. *Captive? My God!* They must be speaking about Hugh! He'd been missing since the beginning of May.

He pressed his ear harder against the door, eager to glean any information he could.

"Have you learned anything of interest?" Hale asked.

"Not a blasted thing. Yet. I still intend to continue the interrogation."

"Where are you keeping him?" Wycliff questioned. "What if he escapes? Have you guards?"

Reddington laughed, and Bram's stomach clenched. "He is hidden in a hut no larger than a wardrobe on my estate in Leicester, chained within and covered in his own piss and vomit," the villainous cur guffawed. "My men at the estate are keeping him just alive enough to answer questions."

The others laughed along with him, and Bram's last meal threatened to resurface. He needed to inform Hydra. Poor Hugh… What he must be going through, Bram couldn't imagine.

He backed away from the door and the raucous laughter beyond and moved to put the rolled rubbing into his breast pocket. But he encountered something that blocked his way. He reached in and withdrew Rose's slippers. His lips cracked in a grim smile as he placed the parchment and the slippers in opposite pockets. He would have to return her items to her later, ruined though they were.

Right now, however, he had to warn Hale's neighbour of the forthcoming attack.

Chapter 16

Rose hissed a breath between her teeth as she reclined on her bed and ever so carefully rolled to her side. Her ribs and back pained her greatly, but she would not miss this last night with her sister for anything.

Violet climbed beneath the bedclothes of Rose's bed, facing her.

"I am going to miss you," Rose murmured. "I cannot help but wonder how long it will be before we see each other again."

Vi covered a yawn with the back of her hand. They had to depart in just a few short hours.

"I…miss you as well. It…for our safety that we separate, dearest."

Rose nodded, the motion mussing her plaited hair. "I know. I merely worry for your safety."

Violet clasped Rose's hand in hers. "Fear not. I…be well." She gave her hand a comforting squeeze.

"Will you send my well wishes to Grandmama and Grandpapa?"

Vi smiled at her. "Of course I shall. And will…the same with Aunt Maureen?"

"Mmm," Rose hummed in confirmation.

"We had best sleep." Violet smoothed a wayward strand of hair over Rose's ear. "We must awaken soon, and I desire an hour or more…before…make the journey."

Pushing past the pain of the movement, Rose leaned forward to buss her sister's cheek.

"Good night, Violet."

"Sleep sweetly, Rose."

* * *

The window was easy enough to enter…if one broke the lock.

Bram hated to do it, but he knew that the locks on Samuels' doors would be nigh impossible to pick.

Viscount Leeds' parlour was nearly black as pitch but for the faint moonlight shining through the window. Bram quickly and quietly wove around the strategically placed pieces of furniture until he reached the door to the hall.

The hair on his nape abruptly stood at full attention. He hesitated in the doorway; this was not right.

Something whizzed past his cheek and hit the door's frame with a *thud*. He spun his head around to see a dagger dug deeply into the wood.

"Bloody hell, Samuels," Bram cursed.

"Your entrance lacked subtlety," a deep, cultured voice intoned from the darkness of the corridor. "I thought you ought to know."

Bram crossed his arms over his chest and leaned his shoulder against the doorframe below the dagger. "Yes, well, I could have managed far better if I had not been in this state of urgency."

There was silence in the darkness for a moment before the man spoke. "Come along, then." His uneven footsteps receded down the corridor, and Bram followed.

Christian Samuels, the Viscount Leeds, was Bram's superior in all but his station within their group of spies. Both of them reported to Hydra; therefore, Bram considered them equals on that score.

Samuels had grown up in the spy world because his father before him—rest his soul—had been one of the first men among the Home Office's agents. He knew every detail, every facet of their world of intelligence. He trained other spies in the skill of cryptology; indeed, Bram rather felt the man had turned it into an art.

Ever since his injury, however, Samuels had become reclusive. He was still their lead cryptologist, but he rarely ventured further than his estate grounds, particularly in inclement weather.

They entered his study; the room was brightly lit with a fire in the hearth and candles set about the room. It was evident that he had been working late on decoding some document or another.

Samuels strode to his grand desk, and Bram grinned at the sight of him. He wore only a cerulean banyan that crossed low on his chest, revealing his prematurely greying hairs; at one-and-thirty, the man was a year Bram's senior.

"Have a seat, Stevens, and tell me what this urgency is about." Samuels crossed his fingers over his middle.

Bram did as he was bade, sitting in the hard leather-upholstered chair. "You are in danger, friend," he blurted.

Samuels inclined his head. "I have been informed as much by Hydra. He says my identity has been compromised, thus my need for increased protection."

Bram shook his head and retrieved the rubbing from his pocket, extending the document across the desk to Samuels. "They know where you live, and they aim to pursue the lead directly."

Samuels accepted the rolled parchment and scanned it. He laughed, the sound a gruff, gravelly noise. "It was a fool who wrote this." He tossed it upon his desk. "The code is so simple a babe could figure it out."

"Yes, but the message is clear."

His fellow spy ran his fingers through his silver hair. "Indeed. I imagine I shall make myself scarce for a short time. I will report to Hydra on the matter. Thank you, Stevens; you have done me a kindness."

Bram brushed off his thanks with a shrug. "I begin the return journey to London before dawn. The Misses Wilkinson are in daily danger in that hellish place."

Samuels' thick silver eyebrows rose. "You plan to journey with both young ladies?"

"No." Bram shook his head. "Just Miss Rose Wilkinson—under pseudonyms, naturally. Miss Violet Wilkinson has another mysterious plan to escape Hale and his vile machinations."

Samuels notched his chin toward Bram and crossed his fingers over his belly once more. "Tell me."

* * *

Bram was awoken from a dead sleep by a noise in his room. He was not scheduled to rise for another hour. After speaking with Samuels the previous evening and then returning to prepare their equipage for a quick escape, Bram had slid between his bedclothes in utter exhaustion.

But something woke him unnaturally.

His frown deepened as he took in a vile odour. *Blimey. It's the aroma of…*

Bloody hell! His eyes sprang open just as his bed dipped with the weight of Lady Hale crawling nude toward him, a predatory gleam in her eye.

Unbidden, a shout of alarm escaped him as he scrambled to leave the bed. "What the devil?" Panic gripped him. He had certainly not accounted for this in his plans to escape.

He was eternally grateful that he had chosen to wear trousers to bed in the interest of making an expedient exit. But damn. *This* he hadn't expected. He'd not even known that Lady Hale and her dreadful children had returned from Bath!

She crooked her finger at him. "Return to bed, Smithe, and I promise you shan't be disappointed."

"Whazzit?" Davies mumbled from his bed as he rubbed sleep from his eyes. "*My lady!*" His sleep suddenly gone, the young footman leapt from his bed, holding his thin bedclothes to his chest.

Lady Hale lowered herself to her back, her head resting upon Bram's pillow as she splayed her legs distressingly wide. Bram swallowed the bile that jumped to his throat.

Davies' terrified gaze darted between Lady Hale's nakedness and Bram's own wide eyes, trying to make sense of the situation.

"Mmm." Lady Hale's voice lowered in what Bram assumed was meant to be a seductive thrum. "Do say you'll join us, Davies."

The poor lad's eyes widened ever further, a squeak rising from his throat as his fingers clutched desperately at his coverlet. Evidently realising the dangers of remaining, Davies fled the room, his quick footsteps echoing down the hall.

"He doesn't have the cods anyway." Lady Hale turned her low-lidded gaze on Bram. "It shall just be you and I, lovely man."

A bead of sweat trailed down his spine, adding to the shiver of disgust that wracked him. "I believe there has been some mistake, my lady."

Booming, heavy steps echoed through the corridor, and Bram's gut knotted.

Hale. Sodding hell. He may not be a soldier, but he was a damned good spy. And he knew when to retreat.

Bram retrieved his packed satchel from beneath his bed and pulled a shirt on over his head as Hale's footsteps drew closer.

"Come, love, do not make me wait." Lady Hale touched his shirtsleeve with the tips of her toes, and Bram quickly withdrew his arm.

"I would not partake, madam, if you were the last bloody woman in existence."

She huffed in outrage, her jaw dropping to her wrinkled chest just as Hale burst through the small servants' bedchamber door.

He let out a mighty roar as he gazed at the room's occupants.

Bram braced himself. Hale was across the room in three large strides, and his fists connected with Bram's jaw and stomach simultaneously. He doubled over in pain, but maintained his footing.

"Oh!" A breathy sigh escaped Lady Hale as she rushed to her husband's side. "I love it when you're violent. Hit him again."

Hale turned to Bram, his brows drawn together in a fierce scowl. "You're to pack your things and be gone from this house forthwith." He punctuated the demand with another jab to Bram's gut.

Lady Hale let out another aroused exclamation. "*Oh!*"

She rose and clung to Lord Hale's arm, and he turned to meet her sultry gaze. "You enjoyed that, did you, my lady?" His voice had deepened.

Good God, to what am I a witness? Bram's upper lip curled back in abhorrence.

His lordship and her ladyship slowly moved toward Bram's bed, and without hesitation, Bram made a hasty exit. His large satchel, coat, and boots gathered in his arms, he sped down the corridor and down the stairs toward the Misses Wilkinsons' bedchamber.

* * *

Rose frowned, trying to dispel the pull of consciousness threatening to take her from her sinfully delicious dreams. Bram had been there before her, in naked glory, though his true image eluded her. He motioned her toward him.

Slowly, the dream faded away and Rose was aware of Violet stirring beside her. Was it time to awaken already? She felt as though she had only just fallen asleep.

The room was still dark; the only light was that of the low-hanging moon.

Vi sat upright in the bed, a comforting hand on Rose's shoulder. Had someone knocked? Violet left the bed and cautiously went to the door.

Determinedly ignoring the searing pain wracking her body, Rose sat up, her heart in her throat, as she clutched the bedclothes to her chin and watched Vi's movements. Had someone discovered their plans to escape? Or, heaven forefend, was it one of their uncle's abominable friends come to—

The door swung open, and Rose's fears fled. There stood Bram…in his shirtsleeves? Oh, dear. His expression was harried, his arms laden with his things, and blood trickled from a split in his bottom lip.

Violet was saying something to him, but Rose—disregarding the pain lancing through her—stood from the bed and rushed to the doorway.

"What has happened?" she breathed, reaching out to touch her fingers to his jaw. "Someone struck you!"

He turned his worried gaze on her and inclined his head in a terse nod. His lips moved, but Rose could not make the words out in the darkness of the room.

Vi dashed away and returned with their sketchbook and pencil and gave them to Bram.

Without missing a beat, he wrote. "Lord and Lady Hale are awake but are…briefly occupied." Rose's heart plummeted as Bramwell spoke. "If we are to make our escape, now is the moment."

Chapter 17

Violet was the first to move. She spun on her heel and flurried about the small, dark bedchamber.

For the briefest of moments, Rose's heart sank and doubt consumed her. *Our plan is doomed to fail. I shall be forced to wed a vile man and—*

Her stomach knotted nauseatingly, but she shook the negativity from her mind. All was not doomed if she would but *move*! With a blink, Rose whirled around, following Vi's example, and quickly retrieved her overlarge hatbox containing her meagre belongings. It was light, as she only owned three frocks, one of which she would don that morning. Hale had personally examined their belongings when they had taken residence at Willow Hall, and removed everything that he deemed "unnecessary." There had been but a few small items that they had managed to withhold from his greedy grasp. She quickly placed the hatbox by the opened doorway, where Bram stood, his gaze averted.

It was then that she realised what she wore, and a fierce blush blossomed on her cheeks. Her night rail was so thin as to be transparent! *Drat.* With faltering breath and eyes squeezed tightly shut against the agony searing her back and face, she put on her midnight black bombazine walking dress. The style was two years out of fashion and the edges were frayed, but she cared not. Her very life was in peril, for pity's sake!

With her gown fastened and her half boots tied by Vi, Rose knotted her hair haphazardly at her crown and put her favourite book and her reading spectacles in her over-filled, tattered reticule.

"I am ready," she announced in a whisper as she faced the doorway.

Bram and Violet stood in urgent conversation as Bram tied his cravat about his neck. He'd donned his coat as well; he wore all black but for his shirt and cravat, and nary a stitch of lace or frill. The overall effect was stunning. A dandy this man was not. Neither was he in want of funds, clearly, for his attire was of very fine quality.

Despite their dire circumstance, his swollen lip curved upward in a heart-pounding grin.

Rose's throat swallowed of its own accord. *Heavens.* The sober, simple suit of clothes was screaming for a woman's hands to tear them off. And she dearly wanted to be that woman.

He bent to retrieve her hatbox, putting a halt to her inappropriate thoughts.

With a nod in her direction and an odd tilt to his head, he led them down the cool, dark hall.

Rose's pulse sped, her heart beating wildly against her ribs. Were they making noise? Could someone hear them? Oh dear. Was she stepping too noisily with her damaged feet? Surely Violet would let her know if she were in danger of attracting attention. Her rationale didn't calm her nerves, however.

Pay attention, Rose.

Bramwell led them to the rear of the house, his head tilting every which way presumably to listen for any other footfalls. They descended several sets of stairs and traversed many a corridor before they reached the rear door of the kitchen.

He halted, forcing Violet and Rose to do so as well. He caught her gaze, ensuring that she could see him through the dark. Bless him for that. Withdrawing the sketchbook from beneath his arm, he wrote.

His expression turned regretful. "We haven't the time to retrieve your bonnets and gloves, I'm afraid."

Rose shook her head and kept her voice as soft as she thought possible—she hadn't the ability to accurately judge the volume of her voice, after all. "They are naught to me anyway."

Violet linked her arm affectionately through Rose's, giving her a gentle squeeze.

"I will lead the way to the stables," he continued to write, "where I have prepared our equipage. From there, Miss Wilkinson will perpetrate her own plan for escape, and Rose and I shall journey on to London." His face turned stony. "I remain uncertain about your plans, Miss Wilkinson. Are you positive that you do not wish to join Rose and me?"

Vi shook her head, then took the book, and wrote beneath his scrawled script. "I am quite determined on my path, Mr. Smithe. Though I thank you for your concern."

"Then we haven't a moment to lose." Bramwell pressed the latch on the door and swung it wide, pulling with it a whirling gust of cool night air.

With a glance about, Bram led them through the darkness toward the stables. Gloomy shadows surrounded them, each one spiking apprehension in her chest.

Be brave, Rose, she told herself.

Her thin frock was nigh useless protection against the chill out of doors. The gnarled claws of the night air found their way through the scant material, skittering gooseflesh across her skin.

Each cautious step sent needles of pain through the raw skin on her feet, and the muscles in her back ached with each movement, but she pushed on. She would have time to rest while they travelled. She would focus her energy on looking forward to taking a long, soothing soak in a bathing tub and recovering in a comfortable, warm bed. Whenever that might be.

Keeping to the darkest shadows, they slunk through the night until they reached the outer walls of the stables. Bram turned to them, his index finger upon his lips in the signal for silence. Of course, the stable hands would be sleeping above the stables. Were one of them to be alerted to their presence, all would be lost.

Violet put her hatbox on the ground and gripped Rose's hands tightly in hers, her eyes swimming with unshed tears and her expression grim. "Be careful, Rose."

Heart lurching painfully in her chest, Rose blinked away the sudden prickle at the back of her eyes and breathed through the tightness in her chest. "You as well, Vi. I shall miss you dreadfully."

Violet pulled her lips between her teeth in a familiar attempt to keep from weeping. The sight made Rose's gaze blur, and she pulled Violet into an embrace. She soaked it in: warmth, the familiar scent of cinnamon, and *Violet*. The moment they parted, Vi retrieved her large hatbox and gazed solemnly at Rose.

"We are twins, Rose. We shall always remain connected, no matter how far apart we might be."

Rose inclined her head, thick emotion clogging her throat.

Vi raised one thin, dark eyebrow. "Do you recall the promise you made me?"

Cursing the blush that suddenly flamed her cheeks, Rose nodded. She refused to give in to the urge to glance at Bram.

"Good." Violet turned to gaze sternly at Bram, and returned the sketchbook to him. "Take care of her."

Then she was off, running in the direction of the neighbouring estate.

Bram placed his hand solicitously at the curve of Rose's back, igniting a fire beneath her skin. Suddenly, the air did not seem so chilled. Her stomach fluttered, and her fingers shook. My, and with only one touch!

"Come. Our transportation awaits."

His golden eyes somehow brightened in the darkness of night; their depths held a wealth of meaning that she was desperate to know.

"I am sorry," she whispered.

His shaggy brows dipped in a frown. "For what?"

With a regretful grimace, Rose whistled. She knew not how loud it was, but from Bram's stunned expression she could deduce that it was not in keeping with their intent for stealth.

A dark mass came bounding around the far side of the stables, and Bram swung around, pressing his back to her front in a chivalrous gesture of protection. Rose smiled broadly as Dog leapt up, pressing his front paws to Bramwell's coat.

Clearly understanding they were in no real danger from the beastie, Bram set Dog aside and put a hand to Rose's elbow, gently leading her inside the grand stables. The scent of manure, hay, horseflesh, and leather assailed her senses. She could imagine the horses' soft snorts and their hooves pawing at the stable floors, but it had been two years since she had heard any such sounds.

A dimmed lamp lit the far corner of the stables: their beacon toward freedom. With one hand clutching Rose's hatbox and the other her elbow, Bram sped them forward between the rows of stalls.

* * *

There was something decidedly wrong with Bramwell Stevens. He had been on countless assignments before, fought many a foe, even rescued several persons in danger, but never had he felt so damned… No, he couldn't be *fearful*. Could he?

Blazes! His heart was in his stomach, his stomach was in his throat; he was a mass of anxious energy. It was entirely unsettling.

Rose's whistle for Dog had doubtless alerted someone to their presence. It was now a matter of escaping before that person—or, God forbid, *persons*—entered to see them fleeing.

His gut clenched tighter. He could not—he *would* not—fail Rose.

Bram released a sigh of relief as they reached the gig, and he fastened Rose's hatbox beside his satchel at the rear. The realisation of how few belongings she had brought sprang to his mind. Was this all she possessed? Damn, but he hoped her aunt would provide well for her in London.

While he finished fastening the last strap, Rose helped Dog onto the gig, where he promptly sat, his tongue lolling to one side.

Bram turned to assist Rose onto the seat, but at the sight of her in the lamplight, he hesitated. Her left eye was not nearly as swollen as it had been last evening, but it was blackened and still slightly puffy. Bruises outlined her jaw and cheekbone as well. He could only imagine the state of her ribs and back…and, damn it, her feet. He had entirely forgotten about the bloody state of her stockings last night. Christ, he was a cad.

Upon returning to his shared bedchamber in the wee hours of the morning, he had examined the state of her slippers, and he had tossed them into the fire.

"Are you well, Rose?" he could not help but mouth the question. "Are you in a great deal of pain?"

A pretty blush stained her already pinkened cheeks. His breath quickened, and for one startling moment, he wondered if what her sister said was true…that Rose was unchaste. Not that it should matter to him, for she was a gentlewoman and not to be touched by the likes of him. Again.

Her tongue darted out to lick her lips, and he nearly groaned.

"I am well enough," she said, her voice barely above a whisper. "It will do me well to rest once I reach my aunt in London."

He shook himself. "Of course," he mumbled. *Of course? What's wrong with me? We're in peril of being caught, for Christ's sake.*

Meaning to lift her onto the gig's narrow seat, Bram gripped her around the waist. Then his good intentions fled his mind. The feel of her lithe body beneath the thin material of her dress gripped his cods in a vice.

Her breath hitched, her wide, coffee-coloured gaze met his, and he was lost. The air between them abruptly crackled with tension and desire. His breath quickened as his gaze lowered to her full lips. He recalled the taste of them, the texture.

You're in the middle of an escape, Bram, old boy! his mind screamed at him. But one kiss couldn't hurt, could it?

His cock was straining at the falls of his breeches, begging to be released into her hands. But no. She was of quality and he was a lowly spy. They were not to be… No matter how much he might desire it.

Rose pulled her bottom lip between her teeth, a low moan rising from her throat, and this time he groaned. He stepped closer, until there was nary a breath between them. The scent of oranges swirled around him, pulling him closer…and closer.

His heart stuttered at her sultry and heavy-lidded—though bruised—gaze. Her hands slid up his arms and over his shoulders as his mouth crashed down upon hers. For the briefest of moments, he feared that he may have hurt her, but her lips opened willingly beneath his own.

His heart exulted. His mouth and hands daringly explored. *God,* how he wanted to touch her! To feel her body beneath his hands, to mould her softness, to—

Bram froze at the *click* that sounded from his back. Dog barked, the sound sharp and deep.

Ballocks.

Breaking their kiss, Bram pulled back to give Rose a reassuring glance. She was understandably perplexed until she glanced over his shoulder and squeaked in alarm.

"B-back away from the g-gig now, an' I won't have t-te shoot ye," a stable hand said in a faltering voice.

They ought never to have tarried. Bram should have kept his damned hands and lips to himself. Should have thought with his mind, and not with his prick.

He had hoped that they would make a clean escape, that Lord Hale would not learn of their departure until he awoke in the morn… But he supposed there was no hope for it. This would undoubtedly alert all and sundry to their flight.

"I-I said te back away from the gig." Trepidation seeped through the stable hand's voice. "I'll sh-shoot ye, I will."

Bram hated to have to frighten the lad…

He discreetly reached into his coat pocket and retrieved his own pistol. Judging from the direction of the stable hand's voice, he was nearly twenty paces behind Bram's left shoulder. The click had very clearly come from a blunderbuss, and an ill-crafted one, at that.

Taking the facts into account, Bram spun, aiming and cocking his pistol in one smooth motion.

Bang! He pulled the trigger.

Chapter 18

Rose flinched, the blast of the pistol reverberating through her chest and the sound muffled to her ears. Smoke filled the air, but she could see the stunned stable hand gaping at them, his weapon gone from his hand.

Bramwell had expertly shot the blunderbuss from the boy's hand! But how had he done it?

Without giving her a moment more to think, Bram gripped her around the waist and lifted her effortlessly onto the gig's seat next to Dog, following directly behind her. He picked up the reins for the grey gelding and flicked, sending the gig jolting forward and out into the stable yard.

Rose brought an arm around Dog, holding him tightly to her as they sped along. The gig's lanterns swayed with their movement, taking the light from the stables and out into the darkness of predawn.

The cold of the wind hit her as they increased their pace, but with her blood heated from their ill-timed embrace and the alarm of their discovery and flight, Rose scarcely took notice. Her back ached with every jounce and jolt of the equipage as they trundled down the gravelled front drive.

The sound of the gunshot had likely awoken the other stable hands and grooms, along with many within Willow Hall. They had little time before others were in pursuit.

The vibrations of the gig's two wheels changed as they reached the end of the gravel drive. The lamps gave little light to navigate, but Rose felt oddly confident that Bramwell could keep them safe.

Their direction was off, however. They had turned to the right from the drive, rather than the left, toward the roads to London. Alarm spiked in her chest, and she turned in question.

"We are going the wrong way," she stated, hoping that he could hear her above the horse's hooves and gig's wheels.

He tilted his face toward her enough for her to see his lips move as he spoke while keeping his gaze on the dirt road ahead of them. "We are going to be followed." His sensuous lips told her. "If we journey toward London, they will know our ultimate destination." He shook his head. "We mustn't allow that. We will make several stops in different routes in order to confuse them."

Rose silently agreed with his astute and startlingly well-calculated assessment. A man, woman, and dog were easy enough to follow in an equipage such as this. Perhaps if they rode north for a short while, her uncle would assume that they had journeyed to Gretna and he would halt his pursuit.

Her heart raced in her chest, and she gripped Dog tighter as they navigated a sharp turn.

Heaven forbid her uncle travel to London to question Aunt Maureen. Lord knew what the vile man would do to her poor aunt if he guessed the truth.

* * *

"*They what?*" Hale roared at his head groom.

Hale had just finished dressing after a satisfyingly aggressive tup with his wife when this putrid *shit* announced that his plans to garner funds while gaining alliances had gone the way of the chamber pot.

The coward pushed the small stable boy forward. "'E says they shot at 'im, yer lordship." He nudged the boy. "Tell 'im, Pete."

Hale turned his irate gaze on the pale child before returning it to the head groom. "You let *this* protect the stables, *alone?*"

"Well, no, milord…" The groom squeezed the life out of the brim of his hat as he spoke.

He was out of patience. "Were both the females with the damned footman?"

The boy shook his head. "I-I don't rightly know, m-milord. It 'appened right quick. B-but they 'ad a-a dog."

Hale pulled his loaded and cocked pistol from his desk, aimed at the snivelling head groom, and pulled the trigger.

The boy shrieked, and the footman at the door jumped, a low curse falling from his lips.

The former head groom made a solid, and unfortunately dissatisfying, *thunk* as he hit the floor of Hale's study.

Hale glared at the footman. "Get the corpse out of here."

The footman bowed deeply before bending to his task.

Hale turned his gaze on the stable boy. "Tell one of the other grooms that he's been promoted to head groom. I don't give a damn who it is."

The boy nodded his head fearfully. Good. It would serve him well to know that Hale would brook no failures among his staff.

"Then you may also tell him to send out more men than the two already sent." When the boy continued to stand there staring at him, Hale growled, "*Go!*" and the child bowed and scurried from the room.

This was a damned nuisance. The next time he saw Smithe, he was going to kill the bastard.

* * *

The journey to the nearest inn on the road to Brighton was short but jarring. Rose's complexion had become increasingly pallid with each rut in the road, much to Bram's dismay.

Morning light seeped through grey clouds low in the sky as the day dawned. It would be a difficult one, undoubtedly, but he would see to it that Rose was cared for. Just as he'd promised her sister.

He steered the gelding into the yard of the Cackle Inn and whistled for the groom. Dog hopped to the ground while Bram carefully lifted Rose from her seat. She was clearly in pain. He just didn't know what to do about it. Had Hale broken one of her ribs? Did she bleed internally?

Blazes, even the thought of it turned his stomach into knots.

He steadied her on the ground and clasped her hand, curving it around his elbow, before he slowly led her into the main taproom of the inn.

There were only four inhabitants of the large room: two men at separate tables reading papers and sipping on mysterious brews, a sickly-looking taproom maid with gaunt features, and the innkeeper behind a counter. Bram could not risk leaving Rose alone for a single moment, so they cautiously made their way toward the innkeeper.

"Mornin', sir, miss," the man greeted them.

Bram grinned at the friendly fellow, the motion pulling at the healing split in his lip. "Good morning to you as well, sir."

The thin man beamed at them. "What can I help you with?" His smile slipped as he took in Rose's bruised state then noted Bram's injuries.

Bram leaned toward the man as if to impart a confidence. "We had a carriage accident some miles back, and my sister is in a great deal of pain, I'm afraid. A fellow down the road was kind enough to loan us his gig, but we need to rent another for our journey on to Brighton to visit a physician. Do you happen to have one available?"

The innkeeper's disposition cheered once more, eased by Bram's speech.

With only a moment's more discussion, Bram had Rose seated at one of the rough wooden tables while they awaited their ale and sustenance. It would only be a few minutes for the grooms to transfer their luggage.

Rose gave him a wan smile from her seat across from him, her absurdly large reticule clutched to her stomach. "Thank you," she uttered softly.

Bram nodded, oddly unsettled by the admiration gleaming in her eyes.

"What did you say?" she asked, her narrow brows drawn together in confusion.

Bram drew out the sketchbook that was covered in half of countless conversations, and wrote. "I told him that you were my sister, and that we'd had a carriage accident and required an equipage.

We've arranged to rent one, and the grooms are transferring our effects now."

She gave a half smile and a nod. "Thank you."

"We have but moments to continue our journey," he wrote. "Undoubtedly, Hale has men following us." He eyed her carefully. "The ale will dull your pain, which should make the next leg of our journey more tolerable for you."

Rose kept her expression hidden behind a clenched jaw, but Bram could see the poorly banked fear in her pretty brown eyes. Her hair was charmingly windswept, and her cheeks and nose were rouged from the chill air, her bruises in stark relief against her skin.

Anger gripped him anew, but he forced it down. The rubbing he kept in his pocket was enough to have Lord Hale hung for treason. And, by God, he would hang.

* * *

"We had an agreement, Hale. The funds for the girl," Sir Wycliff snarled.

Hale's study was brightening with the light of dawn, but Hale's disposition was darkening by the moment.

"You can have her when you return," Hale grunted.

Wycliff's lip pulled back in a feral growl. "That is months away, damn it! You agreed that I should take her on the ship with me to be wed by the captain." His hands clenched into fists at his side.

"You cannot have her if she is not here, Wycliff." Hale sent a glare out the window of his study. His men had better damned well find them soon.

Wycliff shouted inarticulately then shifted his footing, pointing warningly at Hale. "Know this, Hale: the moment I return to England's shores, I expect a swift wedding to that chit. I like a good tup after I've been away at sea." His eyes held a wealth of meaning. "If she is still unavailable, I shall have the pleasure of ridding your daughter of her maidenhead."

Hale would be damned if Wycliff sullied his daughter. He was saving her for another advantageous union. "You have my word, Wycliff. If I have to ride out to find them myself, I shall."

* * *

As much as Rose had not believed Bram's assertions that consuming ale would alleviate some pain, she must grudgingly admit that for several hours after their stop at the inn, she had felt little discomfort. Now, however, as they passed midday, she felt the ache in her muscles all the more.

They had stopped at two additional inns merely to exchange gigs and cater to their necessary needs. It wouldn't do to deprive Dog of his occasional jaunts among the shrubbery, either.

The midday sun was high in the cloudless sky, the warmth of the day heating their backs with every mile they passed. The terror of being caught gradually lifted from her shoulders the farther they travelled from Willow Hall. Her uncle's men were doubtless in pursuit, but being with Bramwell so far from her troubles was a liberating feeling—one she wasn't desirous to lose.

He sat next to her, sturdy and comforting, the sketchbook wedged between his back, and the seat. Rose was heartened that Bram had taken to writing, rather than forcing her to always attempt to decipher his words. She was adequate at reading lips, but it was a challenging endeavour, to be sure, and his acceptance and willingness to make it easier on her was a comfort.

His body was warm, the heat of him filling the space between them. Over the course of the past hours, they had slowly migrated closer together on the perch, until his arm and thigh brushed hers with every bounce and turn of the gig.

Despite the hurt of her injuries and the constant concern for her sister, Rose could not help but feel the tingle of awareness that a large, virile man sat so near to her. Her heart beat wildly as she thought of her promise to Violet. Could she bring herself to fulfill such a weighty bargain?

She glanced at him out of the corner of her eye. His shaggy brown head of hair blew in the wind, his golden eyes watching the road ahead of them, his noble jaw set in determination… Such a man was he that he did not hesitate to save her from a living purgatory, even at the risk of his own safety.

Oh yes. She could certainly—and gladly—fulfill her oath to Violet. And it would not be merely for the sake of fulfilling the oath, but to satisfy her own burning need for him. She had only borne one dissatisfying experience of making love, but then, she had heard that the first time was never very pleasing; somehow, she instinctively knew that her first time with Bramwell would be so much more than her night with Peter.

Rose touched the pendant at her throat as she thought.

She had but to find an opportune moment for a seduction.

Chapter 19

If they pressed on, they would reach London by the supper hour, for their frequent change of gigs ensured each horse was fresh and rested, thus allowing them to make excellent time for the journey. Bram knew that Rose grew weary, however, and Lord knew they were both famished.

Having her so close beside him as he drove the gig was eternally distracting. He was hard all over: his muscles tense with desire and the optimistic appendage in his breeches springing to full attention with each of her movements and wholly arousing noises. Despite the wind at his front, the horse leading them, and the dust of travel, he would swear that he could still smell her fresh orange scent. And it drove him nigh into madness with lust.

Bram kept hearing Miss Violet Wilkinson's words in his ears. *She is not a maiden.* Miss Wilkinson had recovered from her slip well enough, but Bram suspected that she spoke the truth about her sister. There was only one true method to learn the veracity of the statement, but despite Bram's burning desire to have Rose in his bed, he knew that he mustn't.

She was under his protection.

He was on assignment.

And he was a sodding spy.

He must bring her, unsullied, to her aunt in London.

The sound of running water caught his attention over the din of the horse's hooves, and he steered the animal off the road toward it. They could use a moment of respite, and a source of fresh water would do quite nicely. They bounced along through the tall grass at the side of the narrow road and into the thick of the trees. He would hate for the gig to become stuck, but it would be unwise for them to leave it on the road for Hale's men to find. They hadn't a choice.

Beside him, Rose clutched Dog tighter while the hand nearest him gripped his thigh for balance. The heat of her small hand upon his leg brought his erection roaring back, and he stifled a groan. It was sweet torture, indeed.

The copse of trees became increasingly dense, scarcely able to admit their gig, until it opened into a bright clearing before a small pond. Water trickled down a short rock face and into the rippled pool. Birds chirped and whistled among the trees surrounding them as other creatures scurried about along the forest floor. A dragonfly flew before the horse's ears, causing them to twitch. *This is an ideal spot to rest*, he mused. Indeed, he could not imagine a more tranquil setting.

Bram pulled the gelding up short, and Rose's hand slipped slowly from his thigh. With a hard blink, he turned to her. His heart jumped to his throat. She gazed in awe at their surroundings, a hint of a smile upon her lips and the colour high in her cheeks. The sudden urge to turn her sigh of contentment into a moan of desire quickened his breath. Damn, but this woman turned him into a solid mass of need.

Clearing his throat, he lightly touched the sleeve of her black day dress, garnering her attention, and showed her the writing on the sketchbook. "I brought the implements for fishing. I had thought you might enjoy a meal of fish, should we catch one."

Her smile made his heart falter. Her eyes were warm like hot coffee. "I would very much enjoy that." The point was punctuated by the growl of her stomach.

He grinned at her. "Excellent. Are you able to search for twigs for a fire?"

She nodded eagerly, and his grin deepened.

He dropped to the ground from the gig's perch and aided Rose down, Dog jumping to the ground after her.

But Bram didn't let go. His hands fisted in the material of her dress at her waist, the memory of their last kiss fresh in his mind. His gaze found her sensuously curved lips, and his heartbeat reverberated in his ears. He could kiss her right now. He could *touch* her. He was certain that if he dared, she would allow him any liberty he wished to take...

But no. He was not so much of a cad that he would use a woman for her charms when she was under his protection.

He closed his eyes against the tempting sight of her. "There is much to do," he mumbled before he forced himself to release her.

* * *

Rose's heart clamoured beneath her breast, imploring Bramwell to return to her with each harried beat. He had looked as though he were about to kiss her. Well, she amended, she had *hoped* he would kiss her. She supposed that was a vastly different thing.

She took a steadying breath and set about the task he had requested of her. If he did not wish to bed her, she would not press the matter.

He had kissed her readily enough on the other occasions, though. What made this moment any different? Could it be the bruises upon her face and neck? Could it be a misguided sense of honour? Or, perhaps, did he merely wish to secure a meal and a place in which to bed down before night fell? She was unsure.

If he would but take her upon the clearing floor...

That thought oddly excited her. To have him make love to her with such a wild, abandoned passion that he could not wait until they reached the soft comfort of a bed sent her heart to fluttering and her stomach to buzzing. Would he—*could he*—desire her in such a reckless, ardent manner?

She bent at her waist, the ache in her body crying for rest as she gathered twig after twig in a bundle in her arms. She pondered the possibilities. What would a woman have to do to inspire such lust in a man? Peter had never been one to exude such passions. Indeed, he was rather staid and stoic in his habits. It was Rose who had insisted upon his taking her maidenhead. He had been careful and apologetic during their encounter, which was hardly the lustful experience that Violet assumed and certainly nothing like what the book she gifted Rose had described.

Her gaze drifted over to where Bramwell hunched at the lakeside— *Oh!* He had removed his coat and rolled up his sleeves as he reached one arm beneath the water's surface. His expression scrunched before he withdrew a smooth stone and placed it upon the ground with several others.

Rose's insides flipped over as her gaze caught on the corded muscles and tendons of his forearms. Had he truly held her with those arms?

Dog bounded in circles before hopping along the lakeside. His nose dipped eagerly toward the slowly moving water, watching what swam below its surface.

Rose caught her lower lip between her teeth in thought. If she was so affected by the sight of something as simple as Bramwell's bared forearms, could the sight of her without an article of clothing just as easily affect him? She was willing to wager it was—if she had ever been one to wager.

With an alluring thought forming in her mind, Rose strode toward the centre of the clearing, her arms laden with sticks.

* * *

Dog let out several happy barks at the fish beneath the lake's surface. Bram suspected the pup had never before seen a fish in its natural habitat. Well, if Bram succeeded in catching any, the three of them would enjoy the trout cooked over the fire.

He brought the stones into the centre of the clearing and placed several of them in a circle. The fire was easy enough to build with the sticks Rose had collected and the flint he carried in his satchel. The trick had been to find the correct stone for the cooking. Many a man preferred to roast his trout upon a stick, but Bram fancied his way of preparing fish as vastly superior.

After arranging the rocks and twigs to his liking, Bram strode toward the gig to retrieve the other required items.

He had unhitched the gelding from the gig to allow him freedom to graze, drink, and rest. After a well-deserved respite, the horse should be ready for the remainder of their journey to London.

Bram retrieved the items from his bags. The fishing twine was strong enough to strangle a man, should the need arise, yet thin enough to slice through skin like a blade. But in this instance, it was perfect for fishing.

Returning to the newly made fire pit, Bramwell set to work lighting a fire. Dog scampered to him and settled himself on the grass at Bram's side. It took several minutes of working the flint, but soon the blaze was bright and hot, heating the stone he meant to use to cook the fish.

Dog settled himself comfortably on the grass near the fire and closed his eyes with a sniff.

Bram dusted his hands on his breeches as he stood, then settled himself at the lakeside and deftly attached a hook to the end of the twine before bobbing it in the water.

A splash sounded to his left and he turned, alert and, he was ashamed to admit, startled. His gaze darted around, and his heart stopped. *Rose! Dear God, has she fallen in? Does she know how to swim?*

Before he could rise to his feet, her head breached the surface of the water, a Machiavellian grin on her lips. He sat, stunned, and entirely unable to move as she swam toward him.

Beneath the water she was decidedly pale… *My God! Has she discarded her gown?* His throat bobbed as he swallowed convulsively. *Or…is she nude?* His cock swelled even before the thought occurred to him. The curst eager thing was straining the falls of his breeches.

He could not hear anything over the pulse of his heart pounding unmercifully in his ears. Nor, for the life of him, could his gaze be torn from that decidedly lascivious expression upon her beautiful face.

"Will you not join me?" he thought he heard her say.

She reached the edge of the lake, where the deep water met rock, which met the grass upon which he sat.

"No," he forced himself to ground out. "I cannot swim." He didn't know what made him admit it, but he could not bring himself to care.

Rose is nude…and wet. His mind had officially gone blank.

For a moment she appeared uncertain, but that was quickly replaced with determination, which only served to arouse him further.

"Then I shall have to come to you," she purred.

Good God! She removed the fishing twine from Bram's numb hands and placed it beside him on the grass before she braced herself upon the lake's edge and lifted. She grimaced in pain, but attempted to disguise it with another sultry grin.

By God, she was magnificent. And remarkably talented at seduction for a novice. Hell, she was as talented at seduction as a woman of some experience. *Damn.* He could be in some serious trouble.

His eyes widened, his gaze riveted on her as she rose from the water.

Nude. Yes, indeed, she was entirely bared but for the small onyx pendant at her neck. Her breasts swayed jauntily in front of his face as she lifted herself from the water, each breast perfectly and pertly rounded with small, saucy buff nipples—just a shade darker than his favourite pair of tan breeches—puckered from the chill of the water.

Her body narrowed around her waist, curving ever so slightly. Her skin was akin to porcelain, her belly soft and covered in gooseflesh as the air blew around her. He had the urge to spread his hands over her wet skin and dip his tongue to the smoothness around her navel. It was such a pretty navel.

Finally, she was out of the water, and he had an arousingly full view of her sweet thatch of curls. The blonde, springy ringlets drove him mad with want. He burned at the thought of touching them…of tasting them…of her allowing him to penetrate her over and over until they both shouted their bliss into the echoing woods around them.

His breath came fast and hard, his hands clenched into tight fists. Water sluiced in rivulets down her body. She was so near that she dripped on him. His mind was utterly lost. Could she truly want what he thought—nay, what he *wished*—she did?

His gaze darted upward to meet hers.

Oh yes. She wanted him. But he could not take her without adding a shadow of shame to the moral standards he set for himself.

However…he could certainly give in to his desire to give her pleasure. She clearly wished it. But he must be absolutely certain.

"Will you permit me to give you pleasure?" he mouthed.

Her lips parted on a gasp. "Yes."

Unwilling to waste another moment on thought, Bram reached for her hand and slowly ushered her to the ground, allowing her the time to settle herself without causing further pain. With her lying on the ground, he nudged her legs apart. Bracing himself on his knees, and without preamble, he spread her folds and pressed his mouth to her *mons*.

Oh, sweet blazes! She tasted better than he'd ever imagined. Damp with fresh, cool pond water, while also hot, sweet, musky *woman*. His cods tightened. He could feast on her forever.

* * *

Rose gripped grass in her fists as she was swept away by Bramwell's ministrations. Her breath came in gasps as his tongue flipped and swirled between her folds.

She was surprised that a man could do such an intimate thing to a woman, but she was even more amazed that it felt so…*carnal*. Her heart thundered as his tongue flicked over her sensitive nub, her passions in wonderful upheaval.

His smooth lips played over her sensitive flesh, the texture of his tongue gently abrading her cleft almost too much to bear. His day's growth of beard grazed the skin of her thighs, adding to the sensual delight.

Somewhere deep inside her, a coil wound tighter and tighter, until she was certain it would snap. Surely it would stop her heart! But she daren't ask Bram to stop.

Her hips rocked of their own accord, seeking friction and pleasure. His breath puffed against her, hot and erotic, and a quiver ran through her. The coil tightened ever further as he continued to delve between her folds with his hot tongue, her breath coming in staccato gasps.

Suddenly she snapped, stars exploding behind her eyelids, her body shaking, her pulse pounding through her veins, and her entire being throbbing with the delight of it.

Bramwell pressed slow, light kisses along her inner thighs as she caught her breath. Heavens, what was that wondrous feeling? What had happened to her? She had never felt such a thing before. *Could this be what Vi had called "the little death"?*

She smiled at the treetops as she came down from the clouds.

Despite the bliss rushing through her, a sudden ill feeling swept in. Why had Bramwell not penetrated her? She knew he had not found his own release, so why had he pulled away?

She rose to her elbows to look at him, her aches notwithstanding. His hungry gaze swept her body, and his chest heaved. Her gaze lowered to the bulge straining his breeches. *My!* If that was any indication, he was indeed larger than Peter had been.

Bram *was* affected by her, but his expression remained shuttered. Something held him back from taking her.

She reached an arm to him, silently imploring him to enter her. As pleasurable as that had been, it was not what she craved. She wanted *him*. She wanted him to be inside her. To move with her. She wanted him to find as much delight in their joining as she.

"Come to me, Bramwell Smithe."

* * *

A siren. That was what she was. A bloody siren. For who else could tempt him to violate his principles? And enjoying such a perfect specimen of femininity out of wedlock would indeed be a violation.

But hearing his pseudonym on her lips rankled. He was not a Smithe, nor would he ever be. He was a Stevens and damned proud of it. Not that he could tell her.

Her hand hovered in the air, reaching out to him. She tempted him. Oh yes, she tempted him.

But… He did not have to enter her in order to gain his own fulfillment.

Ignoring her hand, he crawled overtop of her and took her lips with his, laying her carefully back against the grass once more. Her mouth was hot and welcoming. He poured his passion into that kiss, every feeling of unspent lust seeping through his lips to hers.

With one hand, he led hers to his breeches, encouraging her to rub him through the material.

Then she was opening his falls with her small, feminine fingers and, blackguard though he was, he didn't stop her. He wanted her hands on him too damned much.

Her cry of delight from when she'd come apart for him still echoed in his ears, causing his cock to throb once more in anticipation.

Undeterred by the randy appendage, Rose explored, her hand gripping his hard shaft then cupping his ballocks.

She broke their kiss. "I-I don't know what to do," she whispered uncertainly.

He made sure she could see his lips as he spoke. "What you're doing feels heavenly. But…" He reached his hand down to guide her. "This will make me come faster. If that's what you desire." He groaned as she worked her hand up and down his length.

His jaw clenched and his eyes rolled back as she squeezed experimentally.

"Come?"

He gasped as her hand worked its magic. "What?" he asked, confused.

"You said 'come.' What do you mean?"

"Oh." Somehow his foggy brain understood. "There are many names for it, but it is an orgasm, sweetheart. The little explosion."

The puzzlement cleared from her features, and she began to stroke him in earnest.

"*God*, I can't—" On an oath, he captured her mouth with his.

He bucked helplessly in her hand, his rising pleasure and her hands driving him mad.

It was on him before he could make sense of it. His body jerked, and a savage growl escaped him, his head thrown back, as he spilled his seed onto her belly.

Chapter 20

Contentment stole over Rose as Bram touched his forehead to hers. The rapid thud of his pulse beat a tattoo against her chest, even through his layers of clothing, and she revelled in the closeness. His ribs expanded and contracted swiftly with each breath, the heat of it creating dampness against her neck and his jaw.

A smile stole over her lips as she trailed a fingertip over his back.

Rose hadn't any notion of how sinfully magical relations between men and women could be. To be sure, she had felt a wealth of amorous feelings for Peter, but nothing such as what she felt with Bramwell. He had not entered her, yet she felt far closer to him than she had Peter.

She must admit to finding herself curious, however. How would making love to Bramwell in the *full* sense compare to what she had just experienced? Would it have the same result? Suddenly, she burned to know what secrets were contained in that naughty book Vi had gifted her. Perhaps if she read it, she would know more about the art of seduction. She was admittedly curious about what more could transpire between the sexes.

In that moment, she vowed to read that book from cover to cover, furious blushes aside.

Heavens, had she truly just behaved so wantonly? It was positively delicious!

Bram slowly pulled himself back to gaze at her from beneath heavy eyelids. "You are—" He stilled, his muscles suddenly tense as his gaze flicked upward.

"What is it?" she whispered prudently, frowning.

He sent her a look of warning with a finger to his lips. But his eyes spoke for him. He looked at her for just a fraction of a moment, but she could see the dread within their depths.

Whatever it was that concerned Bramwell, it should concern her as well.

Then there was a flurry of movement. Bram swiftly stood and aided Rose to her feet, despite the persistent ache in her back. "Get dressed," he said as he buttoned his breeches. "*Quickly!*"

Oh no. Without wasting a moment, even in a nod, Rose dashed to do as she was bid. She had draped her garments over a large boulder by the lake. She swiftly scooped a handful of water and splashed it over her abdomen, cleaning Bram's seed from her.

A blush rose to her cheeks. *Goodness gracious, Rose, now is hardly an appropriate moment!*

Grimacing at the strain on her injuries, she hurriedly dressed, slipped her hand through the ties of her reticule, then slid her feet into her half boots. She hadn't the time to tie them before Bramwell swept her up into his arms.

As she had all day, Rose gritted her teeth against the throbbing aches, focusing instead on their present circumstance.

Bram's arms held her tightly as he broke into a run, carrying her across the clearing to their waiting horse. Her large hatbox lay open with the lacy items tossed out. It seemed that Bram had transferred several of Rose's meagre belongings and the sketchbook into his own satchel and fastened it to his back. Fear forced her heart rate faster. They were abandoning their gig.

He tossed her up onto the carriage horse's bare back, her skirts hitched up between her legs as she sat astride. The beastie sidestepped and shook its head, and Rose very much feared that it would throw her off. Within the span of a breath, Bram was mounted behind her, his body warm against her back and his thighs tight against hers.

Bram pulled a small, deadly sharp blade from his boot and sliced the horse's long reins to a manageable length. For the briefest of moments, Rose feared for their safety upon the horse. Even if Bram knew how to ride, how could he possibly manage a carriage horse?

They were notoriously difficult to ride, not having been trained to run with weight on their backs.

With an arm wrapped around her waist and one hand expertly handling the horse's reins, Bram quickly nudged the beast into a gallop.

Rose turned her head to call for Dog to follow, but what she saw stopped her heart. Four of Hale's largest grooms burst into the clearing on black bays.

* * *

"*Dog!*" Rose's hoarse shout echoed through the forest around them and in Bram's heart. He could hear the ache in her voice, the fear.

He pulled her closer against his chest, forcing her to return her gaze forward. Her long, wet hair soaked his front, but it hardly signified. The only thing that mattered was getting Rose safely away from her uncle's men.

Dog would follow, he was certain. The dog could sense the danger well before it had arrived. He had danced nervously about as Bram had snuffed the fire and prepared the satchel and horse, anxious for them to be well enough away from any threat.

Bram grimaced as he guided the horse around a particularly large tree, jostling them on its back.

Riding bareback was comfortable for neither them nor the beast, but he would be damned if he entered into a chase in a gig.

A shot echoed in the forest behind them, the ball splintering the bark of a nearby tree and frightening the horse. The beast whinnied, shying to one side, despite Bram's attempt to guide it.

Damn.

He kneed the gelding faster. The poor thing was having a time of it carrying the both of them. The beastie wasn't pleased. Bram suspected that he hadn't been broken for riding, but he was handling the uncommon labour damned well.

The horse's hooves thudded dully against the soft forest floor, his breath coming heavily in short snuffs. Shouts of the men rose up behind them, their mounts' whinnies growing louder as they drew closer. Birds and other forest animals flew and scurried away, chattering angrily at the interruption to their peaceful day.

Bram knew that Rose was frightened. And in pain. Of course she was. She hadn't the faintest idea what was happening. She only knew that he'd told her to hurry. He should have explained, but there'd been no time. She sat tensely in front of him, discomfort, pain, and distress apparent in every stiff line of her body.

Lord knew he could have spent all afternoon and into the evening lying on the grass with Rose. She had the body of a siren-goddess, if ever there were such a thing. He'd wanted her. *Hell's teeth*, how he'd wanted her! To sheath himself in her warm heat and have her come again… But he couldn't.

In retrospect, he supposed it was a good thing that he hadn't, for then Hale's men would have caught them and either murdered them or imprisoned them for torture…or both. Hell, for all he knew, Hale could have ordered his men to murder Bram and return Rose to Willow Hall in order to be sold as originally intended. And Bram would be damned if he let that happen.

Indeed, as much as his body might protest, he knew that what he had done was right.

They took a sharp turn around a tree and Rose squeaked, gripping the arm that held her. There was no time for reassurances. They must escape with their lives.

Bram's brow lowered in concentration. Dog would not last long following them at this pace. Nor would the gelding last much longer. Each of the grooms were likely to have two pistols on their person, which left them with a greater chance of a bullet meeting their targets.

Bram's own pistol had been spent and now sat useless in his coat's pocket. His knife would do them little good if he threw it at their pursuers. While it might hit one of them, he would have no way of retrieving it before the others overtook them.

Damn, damn, damn! Think, Bram…

The grooms' shouts and their horses' hoofbeats trampling the forest floor were coming closer. There was no hope for it. They would never outrun them.

Rose trembled in his arms as Bram directed their gelding between the trees.

Then there it was. Hope at last.

Through a narrow opening in the dense forest, Bram saw water flowing. It was gentler than a river but stronger than a stream. The size scarcely mattered. It was the boulder at the water's edge that had caught his attention.

He pushed the gelding harder toward it, and the beast grudgingly obliged, his coat shiny with sweat and his sides heaving. Their pursuers were not far behind, though with the dense trees obscuring their view and hindering their speed, Bram hoped they would not see as well as he feared.

As the horse entered the water, Bram suddenly pulled the animal to a halt. With nary a moment to lose, Bram leapt down and lifted Rose off after him.

"Behind the boulder," he mouthed to Rose as he slapped the gelding's rump, sending the beast off through to the opposite bank and into the forest beyond.

With a nod, Rose spun, her skirts lifted in her hands as she hurried to the stone. Bram followed directly behind her, keeping his ears alert and his eyes trained on the back to the way they'd come. He could not control the hitch in Rose's breathing, but he prayed that the sound of the slowly running water disguised any noise they made.

Rose sat upon the hard ground, her back to the stone and her knees pulled up against her heaving chest, her sodden skirts wrapped around her ankles. Bram sat beside her, putting a comforting arm about her shoulders as they waited.

Something vaulted from the forest's edge, and Bram reached for his blade, his heart in his throat.

* * *

Rose smiled at the familiar nudge to her hand as Dog begged for affection and praise. The band that constricted her heart eased slightly, and Bram's tense arm loosened.

Her back ached as it pressed against the large boulder, and her feet and ankles were soaked through to her skin. If it meant that her life could be spared, however, she would endure any such pains or inconveniences.

The earth began to quake and tremble, and the birds in the trees around them took flight into the late afternoon sky. The low rumble faint to her ears.

Bram held her tighter, his arms wrapped protectively around her and Dog, keeping them close and, hopefully, hidden behind the large rock. Rose squeezed her eyes shut and turned her mind away from the approaching riders.

Fear had dug its ugly talons into her chest, yet despite the danger in which they found themselves, Rose was warmed by Bram's gallantry. Such an amazing man was he that he would defend her, protect her, save her…and all at great risk to his own safety. How could one footman possess such generosity of spirit? And such a skill at shooting and talent with horses?

To be sure, the events of the day had given her many questions, but those were best saved for a more opportune moment.

Then the thought struck her. Would she see Bramwell again after she had reached Aunt Maureen in London? Her heart hiccoughed, and she realised, alarmingly, how sad that thought made her.

Slowly, Bram loosened his grip on her, turning to gaze across the water. Rose could only assume that her uncle's grooms had passed. Soon they would come across the riderless gelding and realise that they had been fooled.

Would they come back this way to search? *Oh no.* Would they be searching for Violet as well? Rose could only hope that, having seen her and Bramwell's trail, her uncle's men had focused on her journey and not Vi's.

"How do we go on from here?" she asked.

His jaw tightened as he turned his gaze on her, his lips working as he thought.

Goodness, had those lips truly touched her so intimately?

"We might walk to the nearest inn," he proposed. "But I would wager that to be rather difficult with your injuries. I would suggest our better option of reaching the main road and placing our fate in the hands of a passerby."

He reached his hand out to smooth a wayward wisp of hair that had fallen across her brow, his warm fingers brushing over the side of her cheek and around her ear. The contact sent a shiver of awareness through her, followed closely by a tingle of delight down her spine.

Her head twitched in a halting nod. "Very well."

* * *

Rose felt certain that hours had passed as they walked through the forest to the main road—the pain in her back and feet were absolutely positive of that fact. But as the sun had not moved in the sky, she knew it could have been only minutes.

As providence would have it, the rumble of hooves vibrated through the ground beneath her feet.

Bram turned to her. "Remain here."

Bram strode into the middle of the road, his hands held high, as an enclosed carriage approached. The equipage slowed then rolled to a halt, the coachman leaning closer to Bram.

She could not discern the words in their exchange, but was intrigued by their body language. Bram appeared distressed and the coachman looked on in concern. Bram gestured toward Rose, and she straightened—as much as her injuries would allow—as the coachman searched her with his gaze.

The men spoke again, their exchange brief.

With a shallow bow of gratitude, Bramwell turned and made his way back to Rose, a grin on his lips. He retrieved the sketchbook from his satchel and wrote.

"This kind man travels with two maids and their masters' trunks to Canterbury. He has generously offered to bring us to the next inn. It will take us in the wrong direction for a mile or so, but I believe this to be an excellent opportunity."

Relief coursed through her, and she smiled at him with a nod.

* * *

The inn bedchamber's air was heavy with humidity and the scent of citrus. As grateful as Rose had been to the innkeeper's wife for providing her signature scent, Bram cursed the kindness. It would undoubtedly drive him mad by the time they reached London.

Their carriage ride to the inn had been uneventful but for the curious stares of the maids. Bram had given the excuse that their own conveyance had overturned and they had attempted to make the journey on foot, but it did not stop the young women from staring openly at the bruising and dishevelment that had overcome their appearances.

A slosh of water echoed in the room behind him, and Bram gazed sightlessly at the low-burning fire in the hearth. He had promised Rose that they would eat and bathe at the inn before they hired a coachman to resume their drive to London. He hadn't accounted for the fact that he would suffer with a determined arousal for the entirety of their respite.

He had bathed in the adjoining room while Rose ate her repast, but as the innkeeper required the bedchamber for a new arrival, Bram was forced to join Rose before she had concluded her own bath. And now he had to endure the erotic torture of listening to her.

An image of her rising from the lake flashed in his mind's eye, and he groaned. Damn this curst insatiable lust for her!

He squeezed his eyes tightly shut as he heard her stand from the tub and step out. She hissed a pained breath between her teeth, and Bram's gut clenched.

He could not stop himself. He spun, prepared to aid her should she need it. Then his heart stopped beating and his throat closed.

Several dark curses flowed through his mind as he stared, utterly unable to speak. Her back was marred with purple and blue overtop many healed scars from floggings. The blotches covered her pale skin nearly in its entirety. He hated the thought of her suffering from each of those wounds, but he admired her strength. He also very much wanted to see Hale brought to justice for what he'd done against his country and to the Wilkinson sisters.

Rose finished towelling herself and pulled a clean chemise over her head, a groan rumbling from behind her clenched jaw. Then the spell was broken. Bram's heart resumed its hard beating, and the breath he'd been holding rushed out in a *whoosh*.

He needed to get her to London quickly. He knew that Dr. Claridge would be in town, for he had been scheduled to examine several of Bram's fellows over the following days. They needed to arrive in time for him to aid Rose before he returned to his family seat in the country. She was in dire need of a doctor's exam.

She eschewed the use of stays or a corset and reached into his satchel for her petticoat and a wrinkled black frock.

He shook his head as she struggled to put them on, then went to her aid.

She jumped as he rounded in front of her, and he grinned, attempting to calm her.

"Will you allow me to help you?" he asked, showing her the words written upon the page of the sketchbook.

Her gaze searched his face, and his heart gave a responding *thump*. What was the matter with him?

A smile tugged at her lips, drawing his interest. He had made the mistake of tarrying at inopportune moments far too many times on this assignment. He could not afford to make the same error again. The grooms who had found them by the lake would undoubtedly still be hunting them. It was only a matter of time before they searched the nearby inns.

Wordlessly, Bram set aside the book and helped her into her petticoats, then assisted her arms into her gown's sleeves, fastening the bodice at her front.

He retrieved the sketchbook. "I'm afraid that we must make haste. I hired a coachman to bring us to London." The coachman had, in fact, requested an absurd amount of money to travel through the night all the way to town. He was, however, the only coachman about and likely the only one within miles, so pay the man's price Bram did.

Rose covered a yawn with the back of her hand before she twisted her hair into a smart knot at her crown.

"Would you care for help with your stockings and half boots?" Bram didn't wait for her answer as he bent to retrieve the worn items.

She sat on one of the two armchairs, and Bram knelt before her.

She placed a hand on his shoulder as he carefully slid her wounded feet into her stockings. Gut clenching, he slid the threadbare fabric up her calf and tied the ribbon into a bow. Despite himself, heat began to warm him beneath his shirt collar as he moved on to the other stocking.

He glanced upward into her eyes before he gently eased her stocking-clad feet into the boots. In another moment, he had them tied.

"Thank you," she said quietly.

He grinned at her. "You are very wel—"

"No," she shook her head. "Not just for this. For *all* of this." She gestured to their surroundings. "For saving me."

A knot settled hard in his stomach, the discomfiting fluttering of nerves confusing and alarming him. He had never felt such an emotion before. He hadn't even a name for it.

"Of course," he forced himself to reply as he rose to his feet.

He held his hand out to her. "Come. Dog and our coach await."

Chapter 21

They had three unexpected fellow travellers on their journey to London. Rose supposed the coachman wished to make the drive worth his while, so he allowed the kindly Mr. and Mrs. Wood and their daughter to pay for their passage as well. It was all the same to Rose, for she hadn't the energy to engage in conversation with Bram.

She had spoken only briefly with the Wood family as they had begun their ride, and had learned very little, and had understood even less. They were travelling to London to visit an elderly aunt and had missed the mail coach's departure. Miss Wood had not yet reached the age of maturity and was excited to see the sights of town.

Rose understood entirely what she must feel; it had been many years since she had been to London. She would have been excited had she not been fleeing for her life.

Dog shifted his curled position on the floor, his ribs expanding as he took a gusty breath. He hadn't enough room to comfortably sleep, for he half rested on the feet of each passenger. They had paid handsomely to include Dog in their number inside the carriage, and not outside with the coachman, but they could not risk his being seen. Rose found it rather comforting to have him close.

Rose's lips tugged in an affectionate smile as her eyelids drooped with exhaustion. The carriage's gentle vibrations lulled her into resting limply against the squabs, her side rubbing against Bram's in their forward-facing seat.

Her body pained her greatly, but the powerful pull of sleep was too strong to mind. She blinked slow and heavy, and every alternate breath was a covered yawn. She wondered how her sister fared.

* * *

A shout rose from outside the carriage, followed by the horses' whinnies as they came to an abrupt stop.

What the devil?

Bram trained his ears to the hollers from outside.

"Stand and deliver!"

He almost groaned. *Damnation!* Highwaymen were common enough in these parts, but Bram had not accounted for that possibility.

Dog rose to a seated position, his hackles up, as he began a frenzy of angry barks.

Mrs. Wood and her daughter screamed in fright, clutching each other, as Mr. Wood tried his best to reassure them. "As long as we hand over our purses, all will be fine," he said in placating tones, though God knew his terrified expression was anything but comforting.

Bram patted Dog on the head and gave him a scratch behind his ear. "Good boy. Now hush, Dog."

The dog whimpered but resumed his position on the carriage's floor, his hackles raised and his ears trained toward the door.

With a glance at the still-sleeping Rose, Bram palmed the knife in his boot and moved to open the door.

"Oh no!" Miss Wood exclaimed. "Do not go out, sir. They will kill you for certain!"

He could hardly tell them that he was trained in all manner of combat. He merely smiled grimly and whispered, "I aim to strike a bargain. I shall not allow him to shoot me."

He pressed the door's handle and quickly disembarked, closing the door behind him on Mrs. Wood's wail.

Only one masked highwayman sat upon a chestnut mare with an ornately designed pistol aimed at the frightened coachman.

"Return to the carriage," the highwayman said from his perch, his voice oddly hitched. Bram recognised it.

He gazed intently at the horse's rider, his eyes narrowed with suspicion.

"I am afraid that I will not do that," he said in a smooth voice.

The highwayman turned his pistol on Bram, his aim unwavering. "Then I shall have to shoot you."

Bram's lips curved up in a grin. "I have a proposition for you, sir, if you would be so good as to give me a moment of your time..."

He knew his offer would be accepted, as the rider's grey-green eyes sharpened on him.

Bram gestured to a point several paces ahead of the coach, just out of earshot of the coachman.

"What are you doing here, Stevens?" The highwayman leaned forward in the horse's saddle, the pistol lowering.

Bram returned his knife to his boot. "I might ask the same of you, Eliza." Bram's grin grew as he gazed at his comrade.

"I am called Lucy now." Her voice grew unaffected but still muffled by the kerchief she wore over the lower half of her face.

He nodded. "You've changed it again, have you?"

"Eliza grew tiresome. I much prefer Lucy."

"Is this your assignment now, Lucy?" he asked.

She lifted one shoulder in a half shrug. "I'm to intercept messages between spies loyal to Bonaparte. I thought I'd be creative with it. I've already given several missives to Hydra."

"Creative, indeed," he murmured.

Her gaze flicked to the carriage a distance behind him. "I thought you were a footman in Willow Hall..."

"I have my evidence," Bram murmured. "I'm on my way to Hydra with one of Hale's nieces."

She nodded. "Would you deliver a message to Hydra for me?"

"Of course."

"I intercepted a missive stating the intention of an attack on Samuels. I am travelling to Eastbourne to warn him."

Bram shook his head. "No need, Lucy. The missive I bring to Hydra is just such a message, as it is Hale and his men who plan an attack. I have already warned Samuels. He stated his intention to travel north."

His fellow agent huffed a sigh, her breath fogging through her kerchief.

"I confess I am relieved," she whispered. "I had feared that I would not reach him in time."

"All is well in that regard." Bram winked at her. "As a matter of interest, I happened upon Amelia…" Bram told her of his meeting with their fellow spy in Willow Hall's gardens and the information she carried.

Lucy sighed. "I miss her. We haven't been on an assignment together for far too long. She's cracking good fun."

Bram turned to glance behind him before he withdrew some coins from his pocket and extended his hand to Lucy.

She knew immediately what he intended, so she bent to accept it with a nod. "I shall return it to you when I reach London."

He shook his head. "It is Hydra's money. Use it for your assignment."

She inclined her head. "Very well, then. Thank you. And good luck, Stevens."

"You as well, Lucy."

With a wink and a grin, he turned back toward the carriage as hoof beats thundered away from him. The coachman gawked as Bram returned.

"What'd ye do?" he asked incredulously.

Bram grinned sardonically in the direction of Lucy and her horse. "I informed him that it was just my sleeping companion and I in the carriage, and I gave him all my remaining coin. He seemed satisfied."

"Cor!" the coachman breathed.

Bram entered the carriage, the family inside trembling as he appeared.

"All is well," he assured them. "The highwayman is gone."

He resumed his seat beside Rose, his mind awhirl while he answered the Wood family's questions.

The carriage rolled into motion once more as they conversed. But Bram's mind was not on the discussion.

They would reach London in mere hours. Until then, he must decide where they were to go once they did. He could not very well bring Rose to her aunt's home at such an inappropriate hour.

He could take her to Hydra's second town house, which was used for the exclusive use of his fellow spies as a safe house or a place for recovery between assignments or injuries. But no. It was not feasible. There were no female spies in residence at the moment, and Bram would not have Rose alone in a house full of men.

There was always the option of… But was it possible? With the exception of Hydra and Christian Samuels, no one knew of that part of his life.

His gaze sought Rose where she slept slumped in the seat beside him. Her eye and neck were purple with bruising, but her expression was peaceful. Bram's heart lurched with some unknown affectionate emotion. He knew he could trust her to keep his secret, but could he trust *himself* with *her*?

* * *

The hack rolled to a stop in front of a nondescript town house in a lesser-travelled part of town. Bram shifted Rose in his arms as he reached his fingertips toward the door's latch. His satchel was already strapped to his back, which made the drive all the more uncomfortable but, short as it was, it mattered naught to him.

The carriage had taken them to the outskirts of town, where Bram had hired a hack and carried Rose to the second equipage, Dog happily joining them. He marvelled at her ability to sleep through each of their movements, but he preferred she get her rest after the events of the past two days, so he let her sleep.

The door swung outward, the chilled night air rushing in and overwhelming him with the acrid scent of coal smoke, lamp oil, stale urine, and too many bodies squeezed into one space. *Home.* How he'd missed this!

The street was lit with oil lamps, their soft glow cutting through the darkness of night. Rose's skin was pale in the low light, and Bram's heart fluttered anxiously in his chest. She looked ill, indeed.

Suddenly he was even more concerned about her exhausted state. Could there be something more to it than fatigue?

With his arms encumbered with Rose's light weight, Bram flipped a shilling to the hack driver, who caught it in the air. The man tipped his wide-brimmed hat and drove off down the cobblestoned street.

Bram turned and strode up the short, narrow steps to the front door of the town house and tapped the door with the tip of his boot. Several moments passed in silence. He knew they were at home, but with only a cook, one footman, and a maid of all work in residence in addition to the family, Bram expected that it would take time for them to answer.

He knocked again.

After a few more moments, footsteps shuffled on the other side of the door, followed by the *snick* of a lock and the *rattle* of a latch.

The door crept open and a small, apprehensive face appeared, the ambient glow of a single candle off to one side. "What is it ye be wantin', sirrah? We ain't got no—"

"It is I, Judith. You needn't fear."

Her eyes widened in disbelief. "Sir Stevens, as I live an' breathe!" the small maid exclaimed as she pulled the door open wide. "What's happened?"

He stepped across the threshold without invitation and turned to whistle sharply at Dog.

"This is my ward. Would you inform Yvette of my arrival?"

A soft gasp rose from the top of the narrow stairs, and he turned his gaze on its source.

"Yvie…"

"Bram!" She tied the sash of her robe about her waist and hurried down the stairs, the lavender of her dressing gown billowing aside to reveal the cream of her nightdress.

"Mama?" The small voice of a child came from the hall, and Yvette deflated.

She turned to the maid. "Judith, would you mind…?"

"But o' course, mistress." Judith glanced warily at Rose's unconscious form in Bram's arms. "The green room was cleaned yesterday morn."

Yvette smiled gratefully at the maid as she turned back to Bram. "Where have you been? You've had me so worried!"

Bram shifted Rose's weight in his arms. As light as she was, standing motionless with her was putting strain on his back, the minor counterbalance of his satchel notwithstanding. "I shall explain everything just as soon as I have Rose safely resting in a bed."

Without waiting for Yvette to respond, Bram carried Rose carefully up the staircase and down the hall toward the bedchambers. The door to the green room stood ajar. Bram bumped it with his hip, walking in sideways.

The bedchamber was of diminutive size and dark as the night. Yvette hurried past him and lit the tapers about the room with a candle from the hall. Soon the room was bright with flickering light, though it still carried a chill.

Bram took the two steps toward the bed and, with the tips of his fingers, pulled back the bedclothes. He laid Rose upon the sheets and slowly and carefully removed her half boots.

The moment he had the bedclothes pulled up to her chin and stepped back, Yvie wrapped her arms about his shoulders.

She pressed a kiss to his cheek. "I have missed you."

Bram turned in her embrace and encircled her with his arms. "I have missed you as well, dear sister."

Chapter 22

The bedchamber had warmed significantly with the lighting of the fire. Bram sat across from his younger sister as they sipped tea at the small table to one side of the green room's bed. Bram had always preferred coffee to tea, but he would not turn Yvette's offer away. He'd not spoken to his sister in many months.

His stomach twisted mercilessly. He continued to sip the tea, relishing the burn down his throat, but it was tasteless, and it sank like a rock in his gut. Each moment that passed in which they awaited the arrival of Dr. Claridge drove another shard of dread in his heart.

Yvette's only footman had departed directly after Rose had been settled, and nearly three quarters of an hour had passed since then. It had given Bram enough time to explain his association with Rose, while leaving out Rose's inability to hear, the intimate details, and, more specifically, his fixated, uncontrollable, and undeniably addictive lust for her.

He took a sip of his scorching tea, his gaze flicking over to Rose, still and supine upon the bed. She would want Dog to be with her, but Bram knew it was for the best for Dog to be belowstairs while the doctor came. If he thought anyone was hurting Rose, he could very well attack.

"Have you told her who you are?" Yvette's soft voice disturbed the silence of the room.

Bram shook his head. He feared that Rose would not take kindly to his falsehoods, honourable though they were.

"You ought to." She sipped her tea, eyeing him over her cup. "A man must be honest with the woman he loves."

Bram's heart lurched alarmingly, but he steadfastly ignored it. "I do not love her," he grunted.

Perhaps he thought about Rose often and felt a mite protective of her—not to mention his burning desire for her—but would not any decent man wish to safeguard a woman in such dire circumstances as she? It was the right thing to do.

A man's voice echoed from the foyer, and heady relief flooded him. The doctor had arrived.

* * *

Terror wound its way around Rose's heart like a vine scaled a lattice as she slowly came awake. Her body ached, her pulse throbbing through every one of her injuries as she was jostled within the warmth and softness of a bed. *Was* it a bed? The air held the scent of dust, burning coals, mint, and the overwhelming stench of ointments.

Hands were touching her. Fear and alarm hit her square in the chest. *Heavens above!* Hands were removing her clothing!

Her eyes snapped open, a scream on her lips, as she came to full consciousness. She began to struggle, slapping at the hands that held her.

A man and a woman stood over her, their lips moving, but Rose could not make sense of what they said.

Instinct that had been beaten into her over the past two years took hold of her, and she turned to her side and pulled her legs to her chest, forming a ball with her body. Pain shrieked through her at the movement. Where had Bramwell gone? Had something happened to him? Where was she? How would she escape?

A finger tapped her shoulder, and a helpless whimper stumbled from her lips. She tightened her grip around her legs, her eyes squeezed shut. The hand gently cupped her shoulder with a light caress, the scent of coffee and sandalwood reaching her nose.

Bram.

She peeked over her shoulder. The man and woman were gone, and only Bram stood over her. He ran a gentle hand over her forehead to smooth away her mussed hair. Then his other hand joined the first as he framed her face with his palms.

Her breath came hard as she strove for calm. *Bram is here.*

"You are safe, Rose," he said, his gaze concerned. "This…Dr. Claridge." He nodded in the direction of the man hovering nearby. "He is here to examine your injuries."

"But I am fine." Her grimace of pain belied her words.

She recalled Bram's mention of a fine doctor in London, but she hadn't thought him entirely genuine on that matter. Doctors frightened her. Since the dreadful fever had claimed her hearing and the lives of Mama, Papa, and Helen, she had reviled the thought of ever seeing another man or woman of healing.

"I am afraid that you must submit." He released her cheeks to beckon a woman to his side.

Her hair was a shimmering chestnut brown, her eyes emerald green, and her skin smooth with a smattering of freckles on the bridge of her nose. She wore a small smile on her full lips as she stared at Rose.

Who is she? Rose's horrid mind began to flit through the many possibilities of Bramwell and a mistress, Bramwell and a lover, or, heaven forbid, Bramwell and a *wife…* Her stomach tightened, threatening to make her sick. *Good gracious!* What if she had unwittingly committed adultery? She'd led him to it! Surely he wasn't so much a cad as that. But the woman could very well be a mistress; he seemed on familiar terms with her, and she was beautiful.

Rose detested the notion of Bram with another woman. Kissing her, touching her…making love to her. Good Lord, she was jealous.

He put an arm around the woman, and Rose clenched her jaw to keep from protesting.

"You will not be alone during your examination, Rose." He grinned at her, and she nearly pouted. Oh, how awful! She'd been reduced to behaving like a child. "This is Yvette, Mrs. Lerwick," he continued, careful to enunciate every word. "My sister."

Relief so strong it nearly made her weep rushed through her, pulling a smile from her lips. *Sister!*

Rose licked her dry lips. "It is a pleasure to make your acquaintance, Mrs. Lerwick."

"Likewise, despite the circumstances," Bram's sister said, returning her smile. "Bram believes that Dr. Claridge is a fine physician, and I am inclined to believe him. If you wish it, I will remain while he examines you."

Rose pulled her bottom lip between her teeth and worried the sensitive flesh. Surely Bram would be just outside the door and would enter should he hear her struggle.

With a hesitant glance at the fine, stoic doctor, Rose nodded.

* * *

The examination was not so horrid as Rose had first feared. Dr. Claridge was a kind man with gentle hands. Having the assurance of another in the room had eased her fears as well.

The doctor had put a soothing, mint-scented cream on her bruises, which lent them a pleasing and somehow cool warmth, if that were even possible.

Bram stood with his sister and the doctor at the foot of the bed, and they listened while the doctor spoke.

"Ravelling only curved to prologue an possibly wore cheese her injuries. They seem to be—" He turned his face to encompass Mrs. Lerwick as he spoke, blocking Rose's view of his lips.

Confusion swamped her as she attempted to make sense of the doctor's words. He simply spoke too fast for her to understand it.

Dash it all.

Rose glanced about the room. She could not see terribly much from this vantage point, but what she saw was agreeable. It was an exceedingly small bedchamber, but it contained the necessary items: a tall, thin wardrobe, two chairs with a petite, round table, a chest of drawers with a washbasin, and pitcher atop it. A rectangular scenic painting hung on the wall adjacent to the bed, and the room was embellished with dark wood and shades of green.

She returned her gaze to the three speaking at the foot of the bed.

"…wish you would have warned me, S—" The doctor halted as Bram clutched his arm.

"Perhaps we…allow Rose to rest." Bramwell appeared oddly stiff as he spoke. "We can resume…conversation in a quieter setting."

Quieter?

He strode to her bedside, his gaze searching. "We will leave you to rest now."

Mrs. Lerwick and Dr. Claridge said their farewells and strode from the room, and Bram retrieved the sketchbook from among his belongings.

"The doctor says that you will recover soon. He admired your strength, but worries that our travels may have worsened your injuries. Rest is the best thing for you, now."

"Thank you."

With one last encouraging smile, Bram departed, leaving Rose feeling unaccountably bereft without his company.

She could not deny her curiosity. What had Bram stopped the doctor from saying? What was it that Bram should have warned him about? Why did he behave so strangely?

She was far too tired, however, to concern herself with those questions just then. Despite her nap in the carriage, Rose could not deny the pull of sleep once more. Her eyelids were heavy and slowly drooped closed on a long blink.

** * **

Mindful of his nieces, nephews, and brother by marriage sleeping in the bedchambers nearby, Bram closed the door quietly behind them as they entered the hall.

"What was that about, Bramwell?" Yvie frowned at him.

"My apologies," he said in an undertone. "Miss Wilkinson does not know my true name and, with the duress she has just endured, I thought it best to save that particular discussion for another time."

Dr. Simon Claridge nodded. "All the same, I would have preferred a word of warning that she had been so sorely abused. I would not have questioned her so."

Bram's jaw clenched as the image of her bruising flashed in his mind's eye. Damn, but he wished he'd bloodied Hale's nose—and a great deal more—before they had left Willow Hall. The man was a right bastard.

Yvette glanced uneasily between the two men before she whispered, "I believe I shall return to my own bedchamber. The children will awaken in a few short hours."

Bram thanked her for her aid then led the doctor to a sitting room belowstairs. He wished to keep watch over Rose while she slept, but first he needed to speak to Dr. Claridge.

He lit the candles about the room with one from the hall and took a seat on a petite understuffed armchair.

"Do tell me the truth, doctor." Bram combed his fingers through his dishevelled hair.

The man sat in an armchair facing him. "I've told you before to address me as Simon." He hesitated. "The truth of what, Stevens?"

"The truth of Rose's condition." Bram's breath stilled as he awaited the doctor's reply.

Simon shook his head. "There is nothing to say, truly. She is badly bruised but has no broken bones, no internal bleeding, nor any serious or lasting injuries...but for emotional and physical scarring, I would imagine." His jaw clenched, and his hands balled into fists. "The way she reacted when we'd entered..." He shook his head in anger. "Who did it?"

Bram knew precisely what the man asked. "Lord Hale."

"The bloody villain who took his fists to her, made her fearful of being touched, who *whipped* her, for—" He broke off with a foul curse, his customary calm and collected demeanour falling apart as he spoke.

"The man will hang," Bram assured him. "He is irrefutably a traitor to the Crown. I will see justice done."

Chapter 23

Hale's fingers tapped indignantly the surface of his large desk, his patience for foolish men all but entirely spent. Yet another night of sleep interrupted.

Bloody Reddington and Piper, along with Hale's hopes for a heavier purse, had already departed to return to London. He needed to find his damned nieces. *Soon.*

Sweat beaded upon, then dripped from, the new head groom's forehead as he stood shaking in Hale's study.

"I thought I said not to lose them this time," Hale said in a dangerously calm voice as he reached inside his desk's drawer.

"Y-yes, milord, b-but they tricked us, ye see."

Hale inclined his head in a deceptively understanding nod. "Of course they did."

He pulled his pistol from the drawer and aimed it at the man's heart. "Tell me again how they managed to get away."

"I-I…"

"I thought so," Hale growled as he pulled the trigger.

Click. Nothing.

The groom's breath rushed from his lungs as he deflated in relief.

Hale snapped, "That was a warning! Fail me again, and the next time I aim a pistol at your heart, it will be loaded." He replaced the gun in the drawer and flicked his hand toward the door. "*Go!* Find them!"

***

Bram sat stiffly in a small chair, gazing through the low, flickering firelight at Rose as she slept peacefully upon the bed. His every muscle was taut with inappropriate desire, and every other part of him was fraught with worry and shame.

How could he think so often of bedding her? She was recovering from injuries, damn it. He should not wish to crawl atop her and awaken her with intimacies that would have them both begging for release.

He clenched his jaw against his stiffening arousal. *Damn!*

He'd remained in her bedchamber with the intention of being nearby should she awaken or require him in the night, not of watching her with fevered images trailing through his lustful mind.

Bram shifted in the seat. He had seen Simon on his way, and he'd found some meat in the larder for Dog and made the beast comfortable before he returned to the green room. This was the only spare bedchamber that his sister and her husband had in their home, but Bram did not care. He would remain here with Rose through the night, he would report to Hydra in the morn, and he would bring Rose to her aunt come afternoon.

Slowly, Rose began to rouse, turning with a mewl and a drowsy grin.

What he wouldn't do to kiss that grin from her lips. He couldn't impose himself on her person in such a way, so instead he remained still, determined not to move from his spot.

* * *

The aroma of coffee and sandalwood swam through Rose's senses the moment she returned to consciousness. *Bramwell.* It was a delightful way to awaken, and she didn't want to leave the cosy nest in which she found herself. She turned, grinning, though her eyes remained closed. The ache in her muscles had greatly improved in the past hours, much to her relief. In fact, the liniment Dr. Claridge had spread upon her bruises had done a remarkable job in relieving her pain. She felt very nearly returned to normal.

She blinked, easily adjusting to the dim light of the room, and her gaze immediately sought out Bram. He sat tilted, his body absurdly large in the small, narrow chair. His elbow rested on one arm, his fingers tapping at his chin, while his other arm draped over the back of the chair and his legs stretched out before him. His coat, cravat, and boots had been removed, and his shirt gaped open at the neck, revealing a smattering of dark chest hairs.

He looked entirely rumpled and delicious. Had the man stayed with her while she slept?

Once he reunited her with Aunt Maureen that afternoon, would Rose ever see him again? She thought not. This could very well be her last opportunity to be with Bram. And if she did not take it, she would regret it for the rest of her life.

Her stomach flipped. Would Bram join her in the bed if she invited him?

She wanted to run her fingers through the hair on his chest, learn if it was coarse or soft. Would he be receptive to her touches?

Her gaze rose to his, and her heart very nearly stopped. His eyes smouldered with desire, his golden irises molten, his eyelids heavy. Lust radiated from him in waves.

The nervous fluttering in her stomach intensified, bringing with it a fresh surge of need…and determination.

She slowly lifted the covers and slid her legs from the bed, rising to a seated position then standing in one fluid motion.

His eyes watched her, alight with interest as she padded the two short steps across the floor to where his legs stretched before him.

The light of the low-burning fire flickered over them, the orange glow waving in ripples through the green room. Bram would be hers tonight. Hers, and no one else's, if only for this one night. But she must be certain.

"Will you permit me to give you pleasure?" she asked, mimicking his earlier words.

She would not squander her only opportunity to touch and taste Bram. He was a remarkable man, a gallant and brave man whom she desired. And she was not a maiden. There would be no repercussions in this union; while she did not have a French letter or a vinegar-soaked sponge, as Vi had suggested, she could ensure that he withdrew from her before he spilled his seed.

Oh heavens. Even the thought of him finding his pleasure with her sent a flood of moisture to her womanly core.

His lips parted, and his chest rose and fell rapidly before he replied. "Christ. Please, yes."

A jolt of desire and eagerness seared through her.

Keeping her gaze locked on his, she knelt to the floor and placed her hands on his decidedly hard calf. Her fingers slowly found the top of his stocking and slid it down. The coarse hair on his legs tickled her palms, but she betrayed nary a twitch of her lips.

She draped the bit of cloth over the second chair and repeated the gesture with his other stocking. It was such an intimate act, removing another's clothing, and his gaze burned ever hotter as he watched her. The responding warmth pooling in her abdomen only fuelled her anticipation.

She stood, positioning herself between his legs. He still had not moved. If it were not for the blatant desire in his eyes and his eager erection, she would have been discouraged.

Bending, she reached for the shiny black buttons of his waistcoat, opening them one at a time and revelling in the movement of his chest. Finally unfastened, Bram allowed her to slide it from his shoulders and aided her in removing it entirely.

Emboldened, Rose gripped his shirtfront and pulled it from the waist of his breeches.

Bram's groan reverberated through her chest as he moved, clutching her hands to halt her.

His sensuous mouth curved in a mirthless grin. "I will not take your innocence."

She tamped down the guilt that threatened. He deserved to know the truth. "I am not innocent. But whatever I have left, I give to you freely."

His eyes lit with a feral possessiveness that both alarmed and thrilled her.

He leaned forward and gripped her hips, pulling her closer to him. With his gaze still locked on hers, he found the hem of her night rail and lifted, running his hot, rough palms up her thighs.

A tremor of excitement rippled through her as he wrapped his hands behind her to cup her buttocks. He gave her a gentle squeeze, his face alight with wild ardour and sensual promise.

He shifted in his seat, bringing himself closer to the edge of the chair before he guided her left leg over his shoulder. She quickly gripped his other shoulder for stability, a baffled frown on her brow.

"Does this pain you?" he asked.

"No," she lied. It didn't pain her nearly enough for her to put a halt to his attentions.

Relief shone in his gaze, before he turned wide eyes to her feminine folds, all but entirely splayed open for him. She quashed the urge to cover herself. This was what she wanted, after all—for them to take this night to explore one another.

He tilted his head up at her, grinning his sinfully charming smile as he spoke. "If tonight is our only night together, sweetheart, then I mean to create a lasting memory."

Dipping his head, he pressed his mouth to her. Her head fell back as she swayed, savouring the sensations. Soon his hand joined his mouth, his fingers delving inside her, bringing her to even greater heights. It was just as it had been by the lake, but far better. His hand and his mouth working in tandem created a tempest of need in her.

Her knee grew weak and began to tremble. She raked her hands through Bram's hair, fisting his dark locks between her fingers and holding on for dear life.

More! her body cried. And he provided it. He flicked and swirled his tongue, and his fingers found her pleasure centre. And abruptly she fell apart.

Her body shook with the force of her completion, stars dancing before her eyes. Then her knee collapsed.

Bram caught her before she fell, his warm, sturdy arms wrapping around her.

Rose gasped for breath as Bram lifted her effortlessly, carrying her to the bed.

He placed her carefully upon the rumpled sheets and removed his shirt, tossing it to the floor behind him.

Rose gaped at the sight. The man was a veritable Adonis, formed as though sculpted from marble. Hard rectangular ridges delineated his abdomen on two sides, and two tempting ridges angled downward in the appearance of a V that disappeared below the band of his breeches…that were impressively tented. *Goodness!*

He made quick work of the buttons at his falls and pushed down his breeches in one swoop.

Rose's eyes widened further. He was impossibly large. Had she truly held that impressive appendage in her hands and brought him to fulfillment? She'd not gotten a decent view of him at the lake, but now, she looked her fill.

She took several long breaths to satisfy her curiosity before her gaze flicked upward to Bram's. His expression held danger, excitement, and a deep, intense longing. If she were a maiden, she was certain he would frighten her. But instead, he thrilled her. She now knew the delights that were possible in lovemaking with Bramwell, and she indecently craved more. Oh, so much more with him.

He stepped out of his breeches, kicking them to one side, then reached for her night rail. He took care with removing it from her, gently lifting it over the bandages around her ribs.

But he wasn't looking at her bandages.

Bram's gaze heated her wherever it touched: her breasts, her navel, her *mons*… His impressive length bobbed before her eyes. It was as though the sleek, stiff, veiny appendage had a mind of its own.

She could not tear her gaze from him, the sight of his body sending a fresh wave of liquid warmth to her centre. She was ready for him.

He climbed atop her, his jutting manhood hot and hard against her thigh.

Then he kissed her. A wealth of meaning and passion went into the kiss, their tongues and breath mingling, the warmth of him engulfing her.

He groaned, the low note vibrating through her.

Rose lifted her hands to touch him, her palms gliding over his muscled chest, waist, and abdomen, and fingers tracing along every one of his ridges. Goodness, but he had a body made for touching!

He returned the touches in kind, his hands flitting over her skin as though he were afraid to hurt her.

His scent engulfed her, the coffee and sandalwood aroma mingling with their passion and causing her heartbeat to falter.

Bram's lips left hers as he pulled back to speak. "Prepare, sweetheart, for I mean to make you come again. But I promise to be inside you when you do."

Chapter 24

Bram could not recall a single time in his life when he'd been so aroused. Something was happening to him. He was a beast, an uncontrollable, lust-mad animal, and only one woman could satisfy such an intense need.

Rose.

Good God, Rose!

She was everything. She was a siren, a goddess, a brave warrior queen… And she was here, in his arms, touching him, wet for him.

Damnation! His mind was in a haze, his thoughts frenzied.

His body begged him to thrust inside her, to pump wildly until he found blissful release, but, God help him, he could not allow this moment to end so quickly.

Breaking their hungry kisses, he slid his lips down the side of her neck, kissing and licking his way down her body. Each flick of his tongue earned him a moan or a sigh of satisfaction from Rose and an almost painful throb from his cock.

Finally, he reached her breasts. They were pert and perfect, just the right size to fill his hands, with one slightly larger than the other. Fuck, he wanted to feast on them for hours. He sucked one flawless, round nipple into his mouth, and Rose arched off the bed.

He groaned, unable to handle another heartbeat without being inside her. "Oh God, I can't wait!" He waited until she looked at his face before whispering hoarsely, "Will you let me inside you?"

Her molten, coffee-brown gaze gleamed with open desire as she spread her legs wider, wrapping her ankles together behind his back and nudging his hips toward hers.

"Yes," she moaned.

His ballocks tightened.

Using one hand to guide himself, he slickened the tip of his cock on her wet folds, preparing her for his entry. Her hips bucked off the bed, another moan on her lips.

"*God*, woman!"

He plunged, filling her to his hilt. Rose's head pressed back against the pillow, and her jaw dropped open on a gasp.

His body moved for him, his hunger for her entirely in control of his motions. His hips pumped hard and fast, his desire begging to be assuaged.

She moved with him, her hips rocking and her legs tightening around him as her hands clung to his back.

He pumped harder, sweat beading at his brow.

He could feel her. *Sodding hell*, he could feel her sheath tighten around him in the first spasm of her release.

Bram quickly pressed his lips to hers and swallowed her scream. Then he came undone. He slammed into her, his body tight against hers as he spent himself deep inside her.

They remained thusly for several long moments, their breath coming fast as their kisses turned subdued in the aftermath of lovemaking.

"You beguile me, Rose," he mumbled against her lips.

He was reluctant to leave her, even though his cock had softened within her sheath. He simply did not want to part from her.

But her injuries were no doubt smarting, so he slowly withdrew and settled himself on the bed beside her, pulling her against his chest in a warm embrace. He reached down to pull the bedclothes over them before he replaced his arm around Rose.

Now that his breath was returning to normal, his mind whirled. *What the devil was that?* What had happened to him? He had always managed to keep control of himself while with a woman, but something about Rose had… Damn it, he did not know what she had done to him.

Bram was certain that he had lost himself. He was not one to be taken in by his insatiable desires. He was always restrained. Always alert.

One thing he did know, however, was that this could not be their only night together. He had entered into this interlude knowing very well that this would likely be only one evening of passion. But it would be a sin to deny such an indescribable experience from happening again.

Rose curled into his warmth, and his arms tightened reflexively around her.

The realisation hit him that he had never spoken so few words to a woman while enjoying the delights of the bedchamber. It was so much more than a quick tupping with Rose. It was not merely an *act* in the bedchamber; this was truly something extraordinary.

His heart still thundered in his chest as his mind circled around that perplexing thought.

Damn it! It was a moment for realisations, he supposed, for neither had he taken precautions to keep her from getting with child. It was another thing that he had never previously done. When he did sleep with a woman, he made sure to have a condom with him. Hell, there was another realisation: he'd never before bedded a woman without the barrier of a condom. Rational thought seemed to leave him entirely when Rose was around. He hoped to hell it didn't turn around and bite him in the arse.

He looked down at her, lying in his arms, her hair tousled, and his gaze caught on her necklace. Releasing his hold with one arm, he lifted the pendant with thumb and forefinger, bringing it closer to examine it. It was a black onyx with white rings through it, the setting topped by small, circular diamonds. It brought to mind another familiar piece of jewellery…

"It was my mother's," Rose murmured, her eyes still closed. "She gave it to me on my twentieth birthday—three years before she perished."

Bram put the pendant down and wrapped his arms around her once more, giving her a gentle squeeze of comfort before pressing his lips to her forehead. She'd endured so much.

The wee hours of the morning were drawing to a close, replaced by the early moments before dawn.

Despite his utter contentment at having Rose in his arms, and his desire to fully understand the impact their lovemaking had had on him, Bram was still on assignment until Hale was in the noose and Hydra deemed the case concluded. But even if he hadn't yet been required to report to Hydra, the news he brought with him needed to be shared.

Bram waited for several long moments until Rose's breathing had slowed and her body had relaxed in sleep. He knew now that she could be a deep sleeper when she was wearied, but as she had slept much of the night, he worried that she might awaken at the slightest movement.

With as much care as he could manage, Bram slid her from the circle of his arms and slipped from the bed. She betrayed nary a twitch as he donned his rumpled clothing.

He moved with stealth and agility as he gathered his things, placed Rose's belongings from his satchel upon the chest of drawers, and stole through his sister's town house. Within minutes he was out the side garden gate in the moments of predawn. He adjusted the satchel on his back as he slunk between the houses in the narrow alley.

A dense fog had rolled in over the past hours, obscuring the vision of anyone fool enough to venture out in it. One could scarcely see a foot before them. It was not so thick as the London particular—nor as hazardous to one's health—but it certainly made it difficult to navigate the streets.

It was an ideal time for footpads to be about in search of a purse or reticule to pilfer. Gratefully, Bram was not the sort of man whom a thief would be successful in attacking. Hydra ensured that each of his spies was extensively trained, and Bram took pride in his aptitude for self-defence.

His confidence waned when it came to Rose, however. He must admit that there were moments in their flight from Willow Hall in which he had doubted his ability to protect her. It was a disturbing thought.

The *click* of his booted heels echoed around him. If someone *were* to attack, he was certainly easily heard.

Hydra's second house in town was only a few streets away. It was a haven for agents in intelligence, a place where they could sleep, rest, hide, or recover from injuries should they require it. He had, himself, resided there on several occasions between assignments.

But for now, it was the ideal spot to meet with his superior.

A shout rose from one of the buildings around him, and a dog barked somewhere off in the distance.

He was blind but for seeing the ground a mere foot in front of him. He knew the path from memory, however, and was, truthfully, grateful for the solitude. Many times had he visited his sister and her family while he was in town between missions, the path long since becoming familiar.

Bram made another turn onto a narrow street, his heels clicking a measured beat.

The clips of footfalls sounded somewhere behind him, and the hairs on the back of Bram's neck stood on end. Was it an innocent Londoner going about their business…or was someone following him?

He sped his steps, deliberately allowing them to be heard. The footfalls behind him matched his pace.

Ah yes. He grinned into the fog. He would enjoy this. His instinct told him that this was not a footpad or pickpocket, but someone interested in *him*. Well, he would find out for whom they worked and for what reason they followed Bram.

He had grown complacent in his role as footman; he would benefit from a jaunt in the fog.

With a narrowing of his eyes and a dark grin on his lips, Bram broke into a run.

* * *

Rose sighed merrily, a smile splitting her mouth, as she carefully stretched. She felt satisfied and rested, though a mite sore. She opened her eyes and gazed through the dimly lit room and out the window.

A thick fog obscured her view, and her smile broadened. She had always adored the fog. She and her sisters used to run about in a game of hide and seek, using the fog as a way to elude their imagined pursuers.

The pleasing memory made her smile deepen.

She had much for which to be thankful. She had escaped her uncle and his men, and she had enjoyed the most memorable and pleasurable experience of her life, her promise to Violet all but forgotten in the moment, though thoroughly fulfilled.

Her stomach rumbled, the bubbling feeling alerting her to her own hunger. Rose lifted her nose to the alluring scent of cooking eggs, ham, and toast as it wafted through the air. Her stomach growled once more. Bram must be famished as well. She turned to wake him, but stopped. The bed beside her was empty.

Mindful of her healing injuries, she rose to a seated position on the bed and looked about the room. Her stomach sank. Bram's items had been removed, and he was nowhere to be found.

She understood, of course, that it would not do to have him discovered in her bedchamber, but she had been hopeful that he would remain.

He must have taken another room to sleep. Or perhaps he was in the morning room breaking his fast or walking Dog in the fog-filled gardens.

On the crest of that happy thought, Rose stood to perform her ablutions. Using a wet cloth, Rose conducted a perfunctory wash of her body. Then she stilled.

Oh goodness! She had entirely forgotten Violet's warnings about the consequences that coupling could bring! And Bramwell had not withdrawn from her to spill his seed. *Oh no, oh no, oh no!* But could one become *enceinte* with just one joining? Surely it took more than one act of lovemaking to produce a child… Yes. Of course. From what Vi had told her, some married couples tried for years to become pregnant—occasionally without success.

She took an unsteady, but calming, breath. Indeed, this one occasion of lovemaking would not have its consequences. She hoped. She simply must ensure that if it were to happen again, she should remain cognizant of that fact.

On that thought, she began to ready herself for the day.

Bramwell had placed her belongings atop the chest of drawers next to the washbasin, while her undamaged black bombazine dress hung in the small wardrobe. She sifted through her things, sudden alarm spiking in her chest.

Her fingers hit the cloth of her reticule and her breath left her in a *whoosh* of relief. Thank goodness! Bram had brought her ridiculous reticule—and within it, her books and her spectacles—inside from the carriage last evening.

Her stomach grumbled again, and she set aside the reticule. When she had a moment of privacy in which she was not famished, she must remember to read the book Vi had purchased for her. As naughty as it was, she was wholly curious about its contents.

Rose laughed at herself as she donned her last clean day dress and slid her sore feet into her half boots. She quickly knotted her hair at her crown and pinched her cheeks.

The ground vibrated beneath her feet, and her eyes widened in alarm. What could be creating such a rumble? Did someone bang on her door?

She took three quick strides to the door and pulled it open to see a petite child running past. Her alarm quickly turned to laughter as a maid chased after the waif.

Curious, Rose stepped out into the corridor, the ghost of her amusement still on her lips.

A hand touched her shoulder, causing her to jump. She spun to see Mrs. Lerwick gazing her with curiosity. *Dash it.* She must have said something.

"I beg your pardon, Mrs. Lerwick," she said apologetically. "I was lost in thought."

"Not…all. I merely inquired…welfare." Bram's sister smiled. "Are…feeling much refreshed…morning?"

"I am sore," Rose admitted, "but very much improved. Thank you."

Mrs. Lerwick inclined her head. "I understand that the…has been prepared. Would you care…join us in breaking our fast? We…not dine on ceremony in our home; our children eat with us." The woman gazed fondly down the corridor where the maid struggled to tie a squirming child's neck cloth.

An unnerving stab of envy bolted though Rose. Despite her best efforts to squelch the feeling, it continued to gnaw at her as she spoke. "I would be pleased to join you, Mrs. Lerwick."

Rose's stomach knotted painfully. She was anxious to see Bramwell and Dog. Bram must already be taking his morning meal. How would he react upon seeing her? How would *she* react upon seeing *him*? Would their rapport be strained after the events of last evening? Or—heaven forefend—would she blush furiously, alerting everyone to the truth?

* * *

Bram breathed deeply of the chilled morning fog as he ran, his swift footsteps outpaced only by the rapid tattoo of his heart.

His pursuer matched him step for step, their footfalls echoing off the nearby buildings of the close, the dense fog around them notwithstanding.

Bram wound through the streets, ensuring that his tail lost familiarity with their surroundings. It would not do to have them somehow escape Bram and report Hydra's second town house location to his superiors.

Finally, Bram stopped, pressing his back against the stone façade of Hydra's second town house, the close narrow enough for him to spread his arms out and touch his palms to either building simultaneously. Instead, he slowed his breathing, his back hard against the wall, as he waited for his shadow to run past.

The running footsteps drew closer, but slowed. Then stopped entirely. *Damn.* They were listening for him.

Bramwell could hear the villain through the fog; the rapid breathing was only a few feet from where Bram stood.

If he moved, the blackguard would hear him. So he held his breath.

* * *

As discreetly as she could, Rose slid three slices of ham from her plate and onto the napkin in her lap. She was certain Dog would be hungry and likely not terribly pleased at having been dragged hither to yon. She hoped this pilfered treat would encourage him to forgive her.

Her fingers found the onyx pendant at her neck, and she toyed with the stone.

Her gaze wandered about the pleasant morning room, not for the first time wondering where Bramwell was. Did he sleep abovestairs? If so, how had his nieces and nephews' boisterous laughter and stomping not woken him? Not that she could hear it.

Turning her fingers to a more productive task, she began to peel an orange while she thought, her gaze still roaming about the room. The walls were painted white and adorned with sunshine yellow wall hangings while accented by white-painted wooden accents in the furniture about the room.

From what Rose had learned about the Lerwick family, they had a maid to help with the five children, as well as a cook, a footman, and another maid of all work who helped with most everything else.

One of the children across the table caught her attention.

"What 'appened to yer face?" a small boy with black hair asked, staring with open curiosity at the bruising still marring her eye and cheek.

Mrs. Lerwick shook her head, drawing Rose's gaze. "Maximus," she chided, "it is rude…questions."

The boy looked down at his plate, contrite, then faced Rose, avoiding her gaze. "I apologise, Miss Wilkinson."

Rose smiled reassuringly. "It is quite all right."

Mrs. Lerwick looked pointedly at the young lad. "Please mind your H."

The boy nodded, and Rose caught his gaze.

"Someone struck me," she informed him. It was not an appropriate topic of conversation, particularly with children, but Rose had always been of the mind that withholding the truth from children was a futile endeavour. They were astute young things and often figured out the truth for themselves. It better served them to have an adult explain matters before they allowed their imaginations to run wild.

"Was…pirate?" A petite girl bounced in her chair beside her brother.

Rose's ears caught on the low rumble as Mr. Lerwick began to laugh. The man was tall and broad…and impossibly large. But Rose was certain that he was all muscle. His hair was the colour of the blackest ink and his eyes the colour of the ocean, not blue nor green, more of a mixture between the two. His laugh was open and unaffected.

"A pirate, indeed, Isabelle." He gazed adoringly at his small daughter.

A hand shot up, drawing Rose's gaze. "…Brigand?" their eldest son offered—Rose assumed him to be six years old. "Or perhaps a highwayman!"

Rose shook her head, a smile on her lips despite the grim nature of the discussion. "I am afraid to disappoint you, but while those are creative scenarios, I was not attacked by a pirate, brigand, or highwayman. Truthfully," she sighed, "it was my uncle who struck me."

The conversation moved too swiftly, then, for Rose to know who spoke, or what they might have said. Mrs. Lerwick rocked an infant girl, not more than two months of age, in her arms as she gazed at her plate, while the toddling child being calmed by the family's maid slammed his palms on the table, wobbling the nearby dishes.

Finally, Rose saw little Isabelle's lips move. "…Was he terribly cross with you?"

Rose smiled soothingly at the little sprite. "My uncle is not a good man. He feels that he does not need a reason to strike out at others." Her smile grew. "But your uncle Bramwell saved me from that life. I am well away from my uncle now, and very much pleased with that fact."

She knew that this line of questioning could become awkward for Bram's sister and her husband, so Rose changed the subject. "Have you children had the opportunity to meet my dog?"

Chapter 25

Bramwell's pursuer took one step closer, waiting for Bram to betray his position. He could not see the villain but knew the person stood mere feet from him. He could not hold his breath any longer. It was time to strike first.

In one quick, circular motion, Bram crouched to the ground and swung one leg around. His foot connected with a pair of ankles, knocking the villain's feet out from beneath them. His pursuer landed on the cobblestoned ground with a winded *oof. Victory!*

With a growl of frustration, a man all in black with a cap pulled low over his brow rolled toward him. Bram leapt atop him just as the cad wielded a blade, the metal dull but deadly in the milky fog. Bram gripped the man's wrist and knocked his hand against the cobblestones.

The cad roared as Bram hit his hand again. Finally, the man let go, the dagger sliding just out of his reach.

Wrists in Bram's grasp, the man bucked, trying to throw Bramwell off him, to no avail.

"For whom do you work?" Bram asked through gritted teeth.

"I ain't never gonna tell *you*," the blackguard spat.

That was fair enough.

Bram released one of the man's wrists, pulled back his fist, and released, his knuckles connecting with a *crunch* with his pursuer's cheek.

"*Argh!*" the man roared, fighting to free himself as Bram hit him again…and again.

At last, he stopped fighting. Bram waited, his arm poised to deliver another blow. When no resistance was forthcoming, Bram knew he had knocked the man unconscious.

With bloodied fingers, Bram quickly untied his cravat and struggled to turn the man over. He swiftly tied the stranger's wrists together as tightly as he could without cutting off the man's circulation. He needed answers, after all.

If the man would not submit to questioning from Bram, perhaps he would answer one of Bram's fellows.

He stood, his breath coming heavy, and took several steps further down the close. He felt along the wall and knocked the edge of his fist against a door hidden in the side of the building.

There was an answering thud. Bram knocked three times more and waited a heartbeat before the door swung inward. He squinted against the sudden light from within.

"Stevens!" Henderson's hushed whisper echoed in the narrow space. "What are you doing here?"

"I was followed," Bram grunted.

His fellow spy stood straighter, instantly alert.

"Rest assured, I confused him in the fog, and he is unconscious on the cobblestones just behind me. I require aid in bringing him in for questioning. Have a runner sent to summon Hydra; he must hear what I have to say."

* * *

Rose wanted to run. Her body itched with the need to *move*, to feel the earth beneath her feet and the wind on her face. Her legs begged to have the freedom to sprint as long and far as they could manage. Not only was that not possible in London society—for she would most assuredly be observed as a hoyden and thus bring shame to Violet—but it was entirely impossible in this intense fog.

It was for that reason that she decided a walk was in order. Bram's nieces and nephews had eagerly charged out into the back gardens with Dog, with Rose following after, but the fog was so dense that Rose could not see the children or Dog as they chased each other about.

Her feet stopped moving in the middle of a patch of grass. Dog's sharp barks, or mayhap the children's squeals of glee, vibrated in her chest, but without the sun to burn away the fog, she was utterly lost.

Perhaps if she were to find a bench on which to sit, she could wait until the fog lifted before she made her way back indoors? She'd seen a wrought-iron bench somewhere along the garden's path; if she could but find it now…

She strode about, bumping into one shrubbery or another, entirely frustrated with herself for choosing to venture out of doors on such a day. Her frustration forced her anxious energy to the foreground as she searched for the bench.

Her anxiety soon gave way to panic, her pulse skittering and her heart lifted to her throat as she stared into the thick white fog with wide eyes. Which way brought her back to Mr. and Mrs. Lerwick's town house? Which way were the children? Were they still out of doors?

She spun in a circle, attempting to see something, *anything*.

Where was Bramwell Smithe? Where had he gone? Had he abandoned her? What of his promise to bring her to Aunt Maureen? Did he expect her to find a way there on her own?

She could feel the terror rising within her breast, her pulse throbbing at her temples, her breaths coming alarmingly quick. Heavens, would she faint?

No. Rose Wilkinson was not a fainting flower, and she would not allow herself to begin now. She *would* find a way out of this mess.

Losing a second of her senses—even for a short while—was disorientating to say the least, but she'd persevered. Just as she would now. She merely needed to think clearly.

Taking a deep, steadying breath, Rose thought. The town house's garden was not terribly large. Logically, if she walked long enough in one direction, she would either find herself at the town house itself or along the garden's wall. If she reached the wall, she could follow alongside it until she reached the town house's terrace.

Indeed. She could do this.

* * *

Bram sat in a midnight-blue velvet-upholstered armchair, exchanging tales with his comrades as he awaited Hydra. His captive sat, tied and unconscious, in an adjoining room. It had been mere minutes since his arrival, but Bram felt as though it had been an hour at least.

"I heard tell that Amelia is tailing Piper," Edward said as the laughter from the last quip had quieted. "She has her hands full with that one."

Thomson extended his legs out toward the fire in the hearth, slouching lower in his seat. "He rides a handsome horse, I grant him. But the man himself is the true beast."

The others mumbled their agreement.

Henderson leaned forward to rest his elbows upon his knees.

"I happened across Eliza—pardon, *Lucy*—on my journey to London," Bram said. "She held up my carriage."

Ed gave a short laugh. "She's posing as a highwayman? She said that she would do it, but I didn't believe her."

"Have you heard of Callum and Harris' assignment?" Henderson asked. "They're to be bloody pirates!"

"Christ," Thomson said. "You know Callum will hold that one over us for years to come."

The other men groaned and grimaced.

The front door to the town house opened, gratefully halting his speech. Bram and his fellow spies stood as the sound of footfalls in the foyer approached.

Hydra and Jones—Hydra's valet and their fellow agent—strode in with purposeful strides.

"Stevens"—Hydra removed his gloves and hat, handing them to Jones—"what news have you? Why have you returned from Eastbourne?"

Sir Charles Bradley and Sir Valentine Jones had gained their knighthoods at the same ceremony in which Bram had gained his. Hydra was accustomed to using his knighthood to his advantage, while Jones and Bram were not. But now was hardly the moment to ruminate on such a topic.

Bram glanced about the room at his fellows. Each man had his eyes trained on Bramwell, expectant. What they saw in him, he knew not. He was ordinarily one with an affinity for laughter, jests, and women—one who was quick to grin. But not today.

Bram hesitated. The agents did not ordinarily conduct their reports in a group setting but rather individually with Hydra. He supposed the others would either get wind of the information or listen at the door, so having them leave would scarcely serve to do more than waste time.

"There are several things, sir, which we need to discuss. But I believe that there are only three that are of the greatest importance at the moment."

"Go on," Hydra urged, shifting his stance.

Bram reached into his pocket and withdrew the crumpled rubbing of Hale's missive. "I have the proof of treason required to incriminate Hale." Hydra accepted the piece of parchment and looked at its contents while Bram continued. "I have already warned Samuels. He aims to travel to the North. He will send his report directly upon his arrival."

Bram put his hands uneasily on his waist, his relaxed stance at odds with the trepidation roiling within him. "Secondly, I aided the Misses Wilkinson in their escape from their uncle, Lord Hale."

Hydra's gaze sharpened on him. "You did *what?*"

He grimaced. "I know it was an ill-conceived course of action, b—"

"But you felt you ought to intervene?" Hydra's voice was ominously calm.

"I did!" Bram stepped forward, anger and outrage stiffening his every muscle. "That bastard not only had them whipped, for Christ's sake, but he took his fists—and his *feet*—to the poor women. Why, Rose has black and purple bruises that cover the entirety of her back and neck—"

"Are you certain this has naught to do with your parents?"

Bram burst. "Of *course* it has to do with my parents! But not just them—with *every* man who deigns to believe that they can abuse women for sport. He was going to sell them to his cronies so they might do more damage to her. They were comparing notes on how well the sisters bruise!" He cursed soundly. "Those sisters needed my help, sir, and I would do it again if I had to."

He could hear a few of the men around them quietly utter, "Hear, hear," while others remained silent and gaped at his having lost control of his emotions.

"Your assignment was to find proof of Hale's traitorous activity, not save his nieces." Hydra's voice lowered a fraction. "Was it worth the risk of your position?

"Unquestionably." Bram's answer was immediate and genuine.

"Very well." Hydra clapped his hands with a loud *crack* that echoed through the still room. "I trust your judgement, Stevens. Now, what is the third item of import?"

Relief rushed through Bram, although the feeling was short-lived. "I know where Hugh is being held prisoner."

* * *

The morning sun had begun to disperse the fog. Rose could now see within a few feet in front of her as she followed the fence around the perimeter of the garden. Her muscles ached, and she grew increasingly tired with each step. The doctor had told her to rest; perhaps she ought to have listened.

She would retire to her guest bedchamber for a nap once she found the rear entrance to the town house.

It was several more minutes of walking before she found the terrace. With a sigh of relief, she strode purposely forward in search of the door.

Mrs. Lerwick appeared in the doorway, concern in her gaze. "Goodness…Wilkinson! We…search…for several… We…quite concerned."

"My apologies, Mrs. Lerwick. I was lost in the fog, and—"

Bramwell's sister waved a hand through the air. "Please…not concern yourself… You are here…quite safe."

"Indeed." Rose smiled half-heartedly.

"Maximus scraped…knee…children…inside, bringing your dog with them. He is in the…room if you…to see him."

That would explain why he had not alerted her to the children's departure.

"Come." She gripped Rose's hand. "Dear me! Your hands…chilled. Would…tea?"

"No, thank you." Rose's smile turned genuine. "I believe I will take a nap."

She quickly took her leave of Mrs. Lerwick and made her way to the green guest bedchamber. The room was just as she had left it. As much as she wished to simply flop upon the bed and sleep, she knew that if she were to stay with Aunt Maureen, she ought to ensure her things were gathered and prepared for departure.

Rose took a few minutes to fold and carefully stack her meagre items.

Downright exhausted and rather sore, she removed her dress and draped it over the foot of her bed before sliding beneath the counterpane in just her chemise and petticoat.

The bed smelled of him. Bram's wonderful coffee-and-sandalwood scent hung on the pillows, the lingering odours of their coupling still on the bedclothes.

Abominable tears stung behind her closed eyelids. She did not bother to stay them, for, as Mama used to say, it was good for the constitution to allow the tears to come.

Why had Bramwell abandoned her? Did he wish to fob her off on his relations?

She shook her head against her pillow, further mussing her hair. She could not allow her mind to think those awful thoughts. Bramwell was, at the very least, her friend. He must have had some errand or another. It was still early in the morning; perhaps he thought to return before she awoke. She smiled to herself. It was also possible that he had gone to purchase her flowers, which he would give to her before they made love for the remainder of the morning.

On that happy thought, Rose settled herself further into her pillow and drifted into sleep.

* * *

Hydra's eyes widened in both relief and dread as Bramwell explained all he had heard in the discussion between Hale, Reddington, and Wycliff. The men around them stood in stony silence.

A string of dark curses fell from Hydra's lips once Bram concluded. He spun to face Jones. "Find Brown, McCully, and Williams. Have them search Reddington's estate in Leicester for a small, concealed outbuilding."

"Right away, sir." Jones bowed and left the room.

"You have my thanks, Stevens," Hydra grunted. "I only hope that the search for the others is swifter than our as-of-yet fruitless search for Hugh."

Bram's stomach clenched. "Others?"

His superior's lips tightened into a thin line. "The Duke of Norshire's daughter has gone missing. She is not an agent, but we have been charged with her safe return. Also, Hermes has gone missing. Seemingly evaporated into thin air. Damn if it hasn't stumped me."

Blazes. Kieran Richards—whom they addressed as Hermes—ran their school for spies at his estate in Brampton. What could have happened to the man?

Hydra ran his fingers through his hair in an oft-repeated gesture. "You have done well, Stevens. Now—"

"I am afraid that is not all, sir," Bramwell interjected.

Hydra clenched his jaw, waiting.

Bram winced. "We were followed from Eastbourne. I took precautions with hiding our trail, but Hale had too many men in pursuit of us." He scratched absently at the back of his neck as Hydra blasphemed. "I encountered one of the men in the fog just moments ago. He sits tied and unconscious in an adjacent room."

Chapter 26

Bramwell paced in the adjoining sitting room, its thick brocade rug muffling the thud of his footfalls. The interrogation had been going on for nearly three quarters of an hour. Several of the men had taken their turn at it, Bram included.

Now, it was Hydra's turn. And damn if he wasn't a frightening interrogator.

Bramwell's pursuer snivelled as Hydra hovered over him. They would get their answers soon enough, he was certain.

Indeed, it was mere minutes later when he finally spoke.

"There ain't no sense in interrogating me," he hissed, his jaw clenched in fear as he gazed daggers at Hydra. "I got no 'ope to live after you 'ear wot I got to say."

"We have no intention of killing you…here," Hydra rumbled. "But regardless of your answers to our questions, you *will* end up in Newgate and, pending trial, possibly hang."

His pursuer's eyes darted about the dimly lit room and at Bram's fellow spies watching with anticipation.

"It ain't gonna make no difference! If'n I make it to Newgate, 'is men will find me an' kill me."

Bram stepped forward eagerly. "*Whose* men?"

The villain's lips pulled back in an ugly snarl, his rotten teeth glistening black in the flickering firelight. "The man wot 'as the rest of 'em goin' to yer purdy sister's 'ouse."

Bram's heart constricted. "*What?*"

The man's gaze was a combination of banked horror and gloating. "Yer lady's gonna *burn*."

Bram spun on a curse, his feet carrying him swiftly across the room and through the door.

He didn't look back. He didn't wait to hear anything more. Damn it, he didn't even pause to request help. He just ran.

His feet pounded rapidly through the hall and onto the street with nary a pause. The fog had begun to clear, making the way far easier to see, but it was damned near impossible to navigate with the other early-morning risers finally venturing out of their homes. Shouts rose up around him as he brushed past one person or another with a mumbled "pardon me."

The fog had cleared far enough ahead of him to see the peaks of his sister's town house…and billowing smoke.

His heart nearly seized in his chest, his eyes wide in alarm. *My God!* His arms pumped as his feet propelled him faster.

He skidded into the alley beside his sister's gardens and jumped, pulling himself effortlessly over the high wall. His feet slammed into the grass-covered earth, sending pinpricks of pain up his ankles and into his calves. But he spared the discomfort not a moment's thought as he sprinted toward the rear door.

The maids and footman ran hither and yon, ushering his nieces and nephews from the town house's smoky interior. One maid held Dog, who barked furiously at the billowing smoke.

Bram hurried to the footman. "Summon the fire brigade!"

The man nodded, and Bram spun to face his nieces and nephews.

"*Yvie!*" Bram called as he neared the children. "Where is Yvette?"

"Here!" Her soft voice came from behind her children as she exited the town house with baby Anne squalling in her arms.

Sharp relief rushed through him. His sister's husband, Roger, exited behind her. Bram grinned, watching the doorway for another familiar face.

One heartbeat passed, then another.

Fear began to replace his short-lived relief as he waited expectantly for Rose to appear. Several moments elapsed in which he stared, his heart in his throat.

He spun to face Yvette. "Where is Rose?"

She frowned. "Is she not yet out?"

"*Do you see her?*" he shouted.

She gazed worriedly at him, guilt written on her features. "Would she not have heard the alarm? The maids and children shouting?"

With a foul curse, Bram spun toward the maid with her arms around Dog. If he were to find Rose among the many rooms of the town house in time to save her life, he would need help. He needed Dog.

"Let him go!" he called to the weary-looking maid.

She did as he bade, and Dog darted headlong through the door.

Immediately, Bram broke into a run once more, following closely on Dog's heels. The smoke in the town house was not as thick as he'd feared, but he was certain it would get worse before the fire brigade could arrive.

He dashed through the halls with Dog's barking ringing in his ears. Where would she be?

"Go to her, Dog," Bram encouraged the small beast. "Find Rose."

The smoke began to burn his lungs. Each gasping breath burned through his chest, but, at the moment, he didn't care. He ran as quickly as he could, following Dog up the main staircase and down another corridor.

Then it came to him. She was in her guest bedchamber.

He pushed himself harder. Faster. Dog hurtled down the hall in front of him then suddenly skidded to a halt. He jumped at Rose's closed bedchamber door, a high-pitched whine escaping him.

Without a falter in his step, Bram pressed the latch to the door and burst in.

* * *

The castle in her dream was burning. And Rose could do nothing to stop it. Fire lapped at the curtains in her circular tower bedchamber and crawled along the floor toward her bed. Terror gnawed at her heart. There was no escape!

The fire grew wilder, the heat more intense. She tried to scream, but nothing came out.

Then, there was a warm presence.

She jolted awake as a heavy, awkward weight landed on her. Her eyes sprang wide, and dread struck her. *Smoke!*

Dog licked her face then began a frenzied barking that reverberated in her chest.

Her panicked gaze flicked upward to Bramwell, who was barrelling toward her, his face a mask of concerned determination. Something inside her flipped over at the sight of him. The last time she had seen him, he had been in this very room, *in the nude*. But now was most certainly not the time for such thoughts.

"There is a fire," he stated baldly. "We must leave. Immediately."

She tossed aside the counterpane and stiffly stood. Bram dispassionately handed her the day dress she had set aside. Rose quickly pulled it over her head.

In unspoken agreement, she preceded Bram to the smoke-filled hall, fastening the front of her dress while she broke into a slow run. As dishevelled as she was, now was not the time for vanity.

Bram drew up beside her while Dog ran ahead. Rose's feet sped faster as they dashed down the corridor. Her fingers worked the last ties of her frock as they raced through the town house. The smoke burned her lungs; her heart drummed a tattoo against her ribs.

Then everything changed. Someone else was there. The low timbre of someone's shout reached her ears, then the low bark of Bram shouting back, though his words were indecipherable. If she turned her head to read his lips, she would surely fall.

She must remember to inquire about it later.

He led her down the main staircase and through several more corridors before they reached the rear door to the gardens.

The midday sun shone brightly in the sky, its brightness nearly blinding in comparison to the dark, smoky interior of the town house.

She breathed deeply of the fresh outdoor air, coughing the acrid smoke from her lungs.

Three new men were in the gardens. Strange, yet fine-looking, men. They bustled about, ushering Bramwell's family and their servants further into the gardens and away from the fire.

Could they be kind neighbours? *They must be*, she concluded.

Bram placed a warm hand on her arm and dipped his head to garner her attention. "You…stay with my sister and her family," he ordered. "There is something that I must do."

With that utterly imperious statement, he was gone, striding across the grass toward a tall, broad, blond man, a gentleman by appearance. Bram's back was to her, but she could see the tension in his stance.

Her stomach fluttered. He was by far the handsomest man she had ever seen. She wished she knew what he thought of her. Did he return her affections? He certainly desired her enough to make love to her, but after his disappearance this morning and his aloof behaviour at the moment, she could only assume… Heavens, was it merely a dalliance for him? Did he mean to spurn her?

The insecurities of earlier came rushing back, and her stomach's fluttering turned to churning.

Another coughing fit wracked her frame.

She looked up at the town house, watching the smoke billowing from the windows. *Goodness…*

Compassion for all Mr. and Mrs. Lerwick had lost felt heavy in her heart. Her own meagre belongings were nothing in comparison to all they were losing. She was a might disappointed at the loss of her books and spectacles, but such things were monetary and could easily be replaced—once she had funds, of course.

Something wet nudged her hand, and she sighed gratefully. Dog always knew when she required a friend to comfort her.

Rose bent to scratch him behind his ears and under his jaw. His white- and grey-spotted fur was long and string-like in its shagginess. Perhaps he could use bathing.

A pair of scuffed boots appeared beside Dog, and her heart gave a *thump*. Bramwell.

He made no effort to garner her attention; he merely stood there.

Pressing her hands to her knees, she pushed herself to stand and face him.

His expression was stony, his eyes expressionless glass orbs. What had happened to him? Where was the charming man with laughing golden eyes and a quick grin?

Her fingers toyed with the pendant at her neck.

It saddened her deeply to see him thusly. Was it something she'd done? Something she'd said? Did he not enjoy their lovemaking as much as she'd thought?

Shame on you, Rose, she chided herself. *Thinking such maudlin thoughts will do you no good. His grouchy moods are hardly your fault. His sister's home is afire; he is most assuredly upset by this new development.*

Still, a quiver of unease tingled down her spine.

* * *

Rose's expression of contentment at patting Dog quickly melted into dejection and self-doubt as Bram watched her.

He wanted to touch her. To reassure her. To tell her that everything would be well. But he could not. Some blackguard had set fire to the town house, endangering Bram's only family as well as Rose. Those whom he had promised to protect.

His family had never been embroiled in his intelligence dealings before. But he had been careless. He had allowed them to be followed. This was *his* damned fault.

Even now, several of his fellow spies were in pursuit of the arsonist responsible for the fire.

The buzz of noise surrounded them. His sister and her husband comforted and hushed their frightened, crying children. The servants murmured frantically, dismayed over the fire. Hydra and two other men stood guard in quiet discussion while the fire brigade worked diligently at putting out the fire at the front of the house.

Bram bit the inside of his cheeks as he stared at Rose. She appeared beautifully discomfited. Her fingers worked the small silver and onyx pendant at her neck, her lip pulled between her teeth and her blonde hair in breathtaking dishevelment as it stuck out over her shoulders and down her back.

He wanted to kiss her. He *burned* to kiss her. But he did not. He kept his expression carefully blank as his anger rode him. He could not kiss her while in such a mood, for it would certainly not be a gentle one. And right now, he sensed she required gentleness.

"We are moving you and the Lerwicks to my town house," he blurted. It was a lie, but he could hardly tell the truth: that he was bringing her to Hydra's refuge for spies.

Hydra had graciously offered his second town house for their salvation until the necessary repairs could be made. The other spies would act as servants until their assignments required them. It would raise questions, undoubtedly, but Bram was skilled at evading such inquiries.

Rose's coffee-coloured eyes lit with curiosity.

"I will have my servants retrieve your belongings and allow you to get yourself settled," he continued, "and this afternoon we shall call on your aunt."

Chapter 27

Rose sniffed mournfully at her belongings. Everything smelled heavily of smoke. Her gowns and underthings were entirely ruined. She could not walk about with smoke-scented attire. She supposed she could request they be cleaned, but goodness knew if it would take the smoke out.

Rose shrugged a shoulder and placed one dress in the small, empty wardrobe of her guest bedchamber in Bram's town house.

How odd for him to have a house in town. He, a servant himself, having servants! Of all the ridiculous things! It was not her place to question him, however; if it were not for his kind offer of aid, she and the Lerwicks would be sleeping in smoky rooms, or, heaven forbid, in an expensive London inn.

His home was warm and tidy, if not welcoming. The furniture was well worn, and the décor was scant. Nary a painting, trinket, or flower adorned the walls and tables. At least not, she amended, in the rooms that she had seen, anyway.

The room she had been given contained only the barest of essentials: a bed large enough for two, a small wardrobe, an armchair, and a table used presumably for writing, eating, and washing, for there was a chipped washbasin and pitcher atop it. And while there was a fireplace in the room, it did not seem to have been cleaned in quite some time, for its blackened streaks spread outward like a terrifyingly large spider crawling out from within.

The drapes were serviceable and sturdy; their deep red colour matched the claret shade of the rug upon which Rose currently paced.

Bram had been distant and reserved as he ushered them to his town house, and then again when he had returned with her belongings. Her heart ached just a little bit more with each passing moment. What could it mean?

Dog uncurled himself from the foot of the bed to pace alongside her.

While Bramwell and a handful of his servants had returned to the Lerwicks' town house to retrieve their things, Rose had scrubbed as much of her sooty skin as she could before she'd donned her smoke-scented frock.

After the excitement of the escape had begun to wane, Rose felt her aches and pains return full force. Her feet burned, her back throbbed and, *goodness*, but her lungs felt all but scorched!

Rose shook her head. She did not know where to focus her thoughts. So many questions ran through her mind that she did not know which to ask first. How had the fire begun? Who was the man Bram had spoken to at his sister's? How was it that a footman could afford a house in town with servants but could not afford to sustain his own living?

She would ask him those questions, but it was gauche for a woman to inquire about such things. Did Mr. and Mrs. Lerwick not find it odd? She supposed not, for they did not behave as though it was such a strange thing.

Sighing, she spun to make another pass by the foot of the bed. But she stopped.

There he stood, the object of her desire, distress, and curiosity, leaning tall and proud against the doorframe.

And he grinned. His golden eyes crinkled at the corners, his demeanour suddenly changed to the man she knew. Rose's heart sang.

He pushed off the doorframe to stride unhurriedly toward her. His gaze sought out the sketchbook, and he quickly retrieved it, scribbling on the first blank page.

"Would you care for a tour of my home?"

Rose's heart flipped over at the warmth in his gaze. "Very much so, thank you."

His grin deepened as she accepted the arm he held out to her. Despite the heavy aroma of smoke, Rose could still detect his coffee-and-sandalwood fragrance. She found it comforting.

The hall was narrow and empty but for a green-and-grey carpet runner that ran down its centre, and dozens of sconces lit the space. Several of the doors remained closed, and Bram did not comment on them. Curious, Rose watched his mouth, but he stayed silent.

Finally, he pointed out a parlour, a sitting room, a family room, and a music room. Then they travelled down a set of stairs to the main floor. Rose frowned. She was certain there was more to the floor than that. She knew the top floor was the servants' wing, but he neglected to mention it as well.

On the bottom floor, they passed through the foyer as Bram pointed out a large drawing room, the great hall, and the dining room.

Rose pointed to a closed door at the end of the short hall. "What is beyond that door?" she asked.

An expressionless mask dropped down over his features, his pencil moving quickly over the sketchbook's page. "You are not to go through that door. The only rooms you may enter are those I have shown to you."

Rose's eyebrows dropped low in a frown as hurt lanced through her. She ducked her head to avoid him noticing the pain written on her face. How could he be so unfeeling? So curt and…and…*rude?*

She stopped walking and released his arm. "Please take me to my aunt."

* * *

He'd hurt her. Bram knew that he'd hurt her. But, damn it, he could not do anything about it! How else was he to react? Under no circumstances was she to be allowed to go through that door and into the realm of spies. It was difficult enough to keep up the charade without his family and Rose taking over the entire town house. Some space must remain for the agents that required aid, sanctuary, or a respite from their activities.

He hadn't thought. He'd simply reacted. It was a mite boorish, but he couldn't bloody well take the words back now.

Bram had only just received word from Hydra that the arsonist had been captured and brought to gaol along with Bramwell's pursuer. Both men needed to be questioned, and Bram intended to be there when they cracked. He was determined to have his answers, to make certain that Rose and Yvie remained safe.

He'd made a promise to Rose, however, and he would see that through.

They rode through the streets of London in strained silence. The carriage rumbled over the cobblestones, the horses' hooves *clip-clopped*, and street vendors called out their wares. Rose sat in stony silence, gazing out the window.

What was she thinking? Did she question the logic of their circumstance? Of Bram *Smithe* owning a house in town? He would not blame her if she did. She was an intelligent woman. But while she might doubt his honesty, she couldn't possibly know the full truth of it.

She had given the direction to Thomson—Bram's fellow spy—before they had embarked on their ride. Her aunt lived across town in a grouping of apartments. It was not a terribly great distance, but with London traffic at midday, it would be several minutes at least until they arrived.

He watched her body move with the motion of the carriage. She held herself stiff, but her body could not help but sway. She tilted her jaw upward to look at something out the window, and his breathing abruptly became shallow and quick.

Even when cross with him, she was beautiful. Her brown eyes were despondent, her lips a soft line of displeasure, and her shoulders rigid. But she was lovely. Fully and completely wonderful.

Bram gritted his teeth against the wave of desire that clenched his cods. He had never been one to take on a lasting lover or a mistress. He'd been eager enough for a tumble or a tup when a clean, willing woman presented herself, but never, *never* had he ever desired a woman after he'd already had her. He had always slaked his lust for each woman with one encounter, tipped his hat, and bid her good night.

But Rose… Rose was different. Something about her compelled him to think about her day and night, to want to be with her even if they weren't making love.

He had become rather fond of Lady Bridget Bradley while he had been on assignment to aid in her protection. He supposed that was the closest to what he felt for Rose, but with Bridget, it had been more sisterly affection than attraction in the physical.

He wished he knew what to make of this.

"Did you ever learn what started the fire?" Rose's soft voice echoed in the cramped carriage.

Bram's response was immediate, his handwriting rushed. "The front drawing room's window was open. A breeze knocked over a candle."

No, his conscience shouted. *It was a man. He threw torches through two windows and then hid in an adjacent alley to watch the mayhem unfold. He likely waited for a moment in which to capture you and return you to Hale.* Damn, even thinking it made his chest hurt.

She nodded and returned her gaze out the window.

Say something! Make amends! He needed to apologise.

The carriage rolled to a gentle stop, halting Bram's thoughts. They had arrived, sooner than he'd expected.

They had no footman to open the door, so Bram pressed the latch and swung it open himself. He leapt to the ground and pulled the step out for Rose before aiding her descent.

She gazed up at the building, anxiousness written plainly on her features.

Bram squeezed her hand lightly, garnering her attention. "Are you ready?"

She smiled half-heartedly. "I am eager to see my aunt. I have not seen her since I was a child."

"Did you send correspondence to alert her of your arrival?"

She nodded once. "I did. Your sister wrote it on my behalf when we arrived."

He would have offered her his arm, but he was stretching the bounds of propriety as it was by not bringing a chaperone.

They entered the building unnoticed. The inside décor was unassuming. The extravagance, Bram assumed, would be reserved for within each set of rooms.

"This is it," Rose murmured as they halted.

Bram rapped on the door, and they waited.

Several moments passed in silence before Bram knocked again. More silence.

"Perhaps she is out," Bram offered.

"Perhaps," Rose returned thoughtfully.

Bram rapped harder, the noise echoing through the corridor.

A door opened nearby, and an elderly man peered cautiously at them, and Bram nudged Rose to garner her attention.

The man grumbled. "What are you two doing? We don't need any trouble around here."

Rose gave the man a smile. "We are looking for my aunt, Miss Maureen Bolton."

The man nodded, stepping out of his doorway. "She left last year. Went travelling overseas. Still pays for the apartment. I can give you a forwarding address, if you'd care to have it."

Rose's lips tightened, but she nodded. "I would. Thank you."

The man retreated into his apartment and returned moments later with a folded piece of parchment. "You look the spitting image of her."

She smiled sadly and thanked the man for his help. With a tug to his forelock, the man returned to his home and shut the door behind himself.

Bram turned to Rose. "Are you well?"

Her eyes swam as she gazed at him, and something tugged at his chest.

He gripped her shoulders in his large hands and pulled her against him. She wrapped her arms around his waist and pressed her face into the crook of his neck, breathing in deep gulps of air.

This obviously hadn't gone as she'd intended. She would be unsure, adrift, not knowing where to go or what to do next. He didn't want that for her. If she had time, she could consider her other options. Mayhap she would decide to journey to Scotland to be with her sister and grandparents, or she could choose to pursue her own interests in London. He would give her the space to choose.

He pulled back and grinned as reassuringly as possible, though he feared it might appear predatory. "Come. Let us return to my town house. I am certain that Dog will be famished and could use a stroll about the gardens." He eased his hands down her slender arms until he gripped her hands, the heat of her nigh burning him through the thin bombazine fabric. "You can send a letter to your aunt and your sister, giving them your direction."

Chapter 28

Rose sipped at her steaming tea, relishing the heat as it slid down her smoke-burned throat. Her gaze was riveted on Bramwell and his niece, nephews, and Dog as they played in the gardens. She sat comfortably alone on the terrace, though anxiousness roiled in her stomach.

The sun shone brightly in the sky, lending warmth to all below. A pleasing breeze blew by, ruffling the ribbons on Rose's black bombazine.

It was a fair day, but she could not enjoy it to its fullest. She fretted. She feared for Violet and was at sixes and sevens about her own future.

Bram had done his best to put her at ease, and, while it had helped, it did not mitigate the difficult choices before her.

Bram's eldest nephew, Oliver, crouched low to the ground, his dark head of hair lowered as he pointed to something in the grass. Rose's heart swelled as Bram crouched beside him, the difference in their sizes adding charm to the gesture.

The Lerwicks' three-year-old daughter, Isabelle, ran toward Rose, her chest heaving and a smile on her lips. "Where…mama?"

Rose returned her smile. "Your mama is abovestairs, putting baby Anne to sleep," she replied.

"Oh." Isabelle nodded. "Where…papa?"

"Your papa is meeting with his solicitor about the fire."

"Very well!" The child bounced brightly before she ran back to join her brothers and Bram.

Dog trotted to Rose, a happy grin on his face. He sat on the terrace beside her and placed his head in her lap.

"You always seem to know, don't you, Dog?" She placed her teacup on the tall table at her elbow and patted Dog's soft fur. He had a knack for knowing when she was in emotional turmoil, and she loved him for that.

She stroked his head and neck affectionately as she watched Bram lift his youngest nephew of one year and a half, Alexander, onto his shoulders. He trotted, laughing, around the garden grass as the other three leapt about him.

Bram would make a superb father one day.

Dangerous thought, Rose, her conscience cautioned. But the thought stayed, despite the warning. How could one look at him play and frolic with his sister's children and *not* think such thoughts?

Her fingers sought the comforting touch of the pendant at her throat as she gazed at Bram.

How was it that he had such a superb sense of fashion? As a footman, one would think that he could ill afford to commission himself a tasteful wardrobe, but it would seem he did. This morning, he wore fawn-coloured breeches with black Hessians reaching high up his calf. His white shirt and cravat stood out against his tan waistcoat and chocolate-brown tailcoat. Why, he was the very image of a gentleman. Her stomach fluttered at the sight of him.

He laughed at something his niece said before he returned Alexander to the ground and turned his attention to chasing Isabelle, the other children squealing with glee and following behind them.

Bramwell was wonderful with children. But would Bram ever settle down with a wife? The thought sent barbs of jealousy careening into her heart.

Silly Rose, she chided. She should not feel jealous of a woman that did not yet exist in his life.

The children surrounded Bram as he feigned fear. They clung to his legs as he attempted to make his escape, dragging the children along with him.

Rose continued to pat Dog, scratching him behind the ears and stroking his soft, spotted fur. But her body was attuned to the man freeing himself and galloping on the grass.

Warmth spread through her, a blush rising up her neck and to her cheeks as memories of the previous evening flooded her mind. Part of her rather wished that she could behave as the children did and climb him like a tree. A deliciously naked Bramwell tree.

* * *

Lord Hale tossed his hat and gloves to a waiting footman as he strode into the foyer of his London house, his boot heels clicking on the reflective marble floor.

"Join me in my study," he clipped to one of his men over his shoulder. "I require a report."

The journey from Eastbourne had felt far longer than it had been, but damn it, the little bitches needed to be found! How dare they run from him? He would ensure that they never did so again, by God!

His study was warmly lit by the fire in the hearth, but Hale still felt an irritable chill in his bones.

"Speak," he grunted as he sat in the chair behind his desk.

"Them wot followed Miss Wilkinson 'aven't returned."

Hale frowned. "Well, where are they?"

The man shrugged. "I saw smoke from across town, so I knows they done their job."

Hale nodded. "Very well, then. Have them report to me once they've returned."

The man bowed. "O' course, yer lordship."

* * *

Bram took another sip of his brandy as he gazed into the roaring fire. Bram and Hydra had taken a hack to gaol and had questioned the arsonist and his pursuer.

The interrogations had come to naught, much to their consternation. It was not wholly unexpected, however. Any spy worth his salt knew how to withstand an interrogation. Bram hoped that their tongues would loosen on the morrow when he returned.

A hand clamped down on his shoulder, gave a friendly squeeze and pat, then disappeared as its owner came around to sit in a neighbouring chair before the fire.

"Overall, a successful day, I daresay," Henderson said before sipping at his own tumbler of brandy.

Bram grinned at the man. "*Successful*, would you call it? I would hate to see what you consider an unsuccessful one, Henderson."

The young man shrugged one shoulder, his gaze on the hearth.

Bram followed his gaze, the flames hungrily lapping at the coals. He wondered how Rose was fairing abovestairs. Had she eaten the evening meal? Was she abed?

Something tugged in his stomach—a visceral pull to the woman who so consumed his thoughts. His blood quickened in his veins and his cock twitched. *Damn.* He clenched his jaw against the surge of desire rising in him.

He must see Rose.

* * *

The fire glowed bright in the hearth, its warmth aiding in the drying of Rose's still-damp hair. She had already concluded her evening ablutions, but she could not sleep for her burning curiosity.

The bedchamber had darkened with the night's sky save for the rippling light from the flames lending pleasing waves to the room.

Before readying herself for bed, she had spent an hour settling Dog with a rope to gnaw and a slab of Cook's roast to eat in a nest of blankets in the drawing room at the front of the town house. Then she had spent another hour writing to Violet and Aunt Maureen. Rose worried for her sister. She dearly wished that Vi's plan had gone how she'd hoped.

It was thoughts of her sister and her burning curiosity that had brought her to this moment in the evening.

She cast a sidelong glance about her to ensure her privacy as she settled herself comfortably on the armchair before the fire. Fixing the spectacles upon her nose, her stomach fluttered with bashful nerves as she read the title.

The Schoole of Venus, or the Ladies Delight, Reduced into Rules of Practice, by Michel Millot.

Her cheeks flamed. With a mutinous tilt to her jaw, she opened the book. If Violet could read—and reread—this book countless times, Rose could do so at least this once. Mayhap it could even teach her a thing or two about the intimacies of making love.

She began to read in earnest, her cheeks glowing brighter with each page she turned. Despite her wish to remain indifferent—but for the purpose of education—toward the writings within Vi's naughty book, Rose found herself growing warm within. Her stomach fluttered in anticipation, as though *she* were doing the lascivious things on the page.

She fanned her cheeks with one hand, then continued reading.

…Their members begin to Itch and Tickle, at last the seed comes through certain straight passages, which makes them shake their Arses faster…

"Good heavens," she mumbled to herself.

…And the pleasure comes more and more upon them, at last the seed comes with that delight unto them, that it puts them in a Trance. The seed of the man is of a thick white clammy substance…

A hand came down on her shoulder, and, with a scream, Rose leapt from her seat and spun. Her eyes were wide behind her spectacles, her breath came in rapid huffs, and her cheeks, she was certain, were as bright as strawberries.

"Bram," she gasped, quickly concealing the naughty book behind her back. "Good evening."

She cast him a shaky smile as his golden gaze bore into her searchingly.

Good gracious, why did he have to be so exquisite? At some point since she had last seen him in the gardens, Bram had removed his cravat and coat, leaving him in his shirtsleeves with his collar opened just enough for her to see his neck and a smattering of chest hair. *Rather like last night.*

His customary scent had a new addition. She inhaled deeply through her nose, taking it in. *Brandy.* Though he was not foxed, he had definitely imbibed.

She swallowed convulsively, and his gaze followed the movement.

"Good evening." His voice low enough to hum in her ears.

Regaining a bit of her nerve, she stood straighter. "May I help you with something?"

His gaze sharpened on her. "What have you hidden behind your back?"

She was behaving like a child caught pilfering a sweet from the kitchens, but she could not help it.

Her chin notched upward. "Nothing," she lied.

She stepped backward, slowly making her way to the low chest of drawers. If she could but make it far enough to hide the book within, she would be free of any scrutiny. *Oh goodness, please don't let him see the book!*

* * *

Bram stifled his irritation at having been lied to while still being unbearably aroused. Rose was very clearly hiding a book behind her back, with the intent of concealing it within the chest of drawers she was slowly creeping toward. But, damn it, it had no bearing on his insatiable lust for her.

He came here to be with her, because Lord knew he could not keep himself away. One look at her, however, curled in that armchair, her head bent low as she read, her spectacles perched upon her oddly stirring straight nose, and her thin night rail all but giving him a complete view of her delectable charms, and he was transfixed.

His fists clenched at his sides, and his jaw tightened. The emotions roiling within him were damned confusing. What did he feel? Lust, he was certain. Frustration, yes. But there was more… He simply could not name them for he was confident that he'd never felt them before.

His heart was hammering like the smithy's on an anvil. He would get the truth from her, and he knew precisely how he would do it.

With slow precision, he rounded the chair. In three quick strides, he had her in his arms in a tight embrace, his lips crashing down on hers.

Rose's gasp of delight and surprise had his lust flaming higher. His mind went blank, his purpose all but forgotten.

Bram ground his hips against hers, pulling a moan from both of them.

He would have her. He would have her right here and now.

Wrapping his hands around her waist, he lifted her until she sat upon the chest of drawers. A dull thud registered somewhere in the back of his mind, but his hunger for this woman forced all rational thought from his head.

Rose's fingernails scraped along his scalp, the pleasure-pain sending gooseflesh along his skin and another surge of blood to his groin.

In a fever of desire, he fisted the material of her night rail and lifted it above her knees. Rose opened her legs willingly for him as he filled his hands with her sweet arse, pulling her closer to the edge of her seat.

His lips captured hers once more, the frenzied kisses adding a spark to his quickly diminishing fuse.

With shaking fingers, Bram fumbled with the falls of his breeches. With the buttons finally open, he sprang free. He touched her cleft with his fingertips, then delved inside. She was wet and ready. Without preamble, he plunged deep into Rose's wet warmth.

Her head fell back, her jaw dropped open on a groan. Her fingers gripped his hair, and her legs came around his waist.

He cupped her arse in his hands, squeezing with the force of his desire as he held her to him.

Bram's movements were uninhibited. He pressed his mouth to her neck as he pumped hard and fast. He could not thrust fast enough.

Rose was the only woman to make him feel such raw, bare emotions. He felt so unrestrained, yet so powerless, in the face of his feelings. He was a tempest. He was the wave helplessly crashing during a storm. He was... *God*, he was hers!

Her gasping moans came fast in his ears, and he matched her pace, each plunge harder than the last.

Finally, she broke. Her keening cry echoed around them as her nails dug deeply into his scalp.

"*Good God, Rose!*" he ground out. "Say you'll be mine...mine...*mine!*"

The words were a litany until he broke off with a curse. He froze, fully sheathed, as he spilled his seed within her.

Chapter 29

Rose slid her hands from Bram's hair, the aftershocks of her release still throbbing through her in wave after wonderful wave.

Bram's hands slowly released her bottom and came up to frame her face, forcing her to look at him.

"You amaze me, Rose. Thank you."

He pressed his lips reverently to hers, the contact sending tingles down her spine and putting a pleasing flutter in her stomach.

Did he feel for her what she did for him? The silly, foolishly optimistic, youthful girl locked somewhere inside her hoped—nay, *dreamed*—that he could come to love her. Marry her. Father children by her.

She sighed. Such flights of fancy could be dangerous for her pride. Though she very much feared that she could be halfway in love with him already. *Dash it all*, she could also be carrying his child, as they had not been cautious in that regard. She supposed that she would deal with that circumstance should it arise. Bramwell would make beautiful children…

Bram slid his flaccid member from within her and fastened his breeches while she straightened her night rail and slid from the chest of drawers. Her legs were shaky after such a lusty interlude, but it was well worth the small sacrifice.

Bramwell bent to retrieve something on the floor, and Rose smiled. She wondered if she could convince him to remain in the bedchamber with her through the night.

She pulled her damp hair into a knot at the base of her neck and smiled again as Bram straightened.

"Would you care to—" She broke off with a gasp as she saw what he held.

"What is this?" he inquired, a curious frown on his perfectly masculine brow.

She reached for the book, but Bram lifted it out of her reach. "It is nothing!" she insisted.

"It is not nothing." He carefully watched her expression. "It is clearly a book."

"Yes." She nodded, reaching for the book once more. "Yes, it is just a book, nothing of true interest."

"Surely if you guard it so fiercely it is of *some* interest." He spun his back to her, bringing the naughty book entirely out of her reach.

"Bram, please!"

She rounded to the front of him, halting his forward step.

Oh Lord, he knows! He held the book open in his palm, his jaw dropped in an expression of absolute shock. *What he must think of me!*

A blush rapidly darkened her already red cheeks, and she clapped her hands to them.

"Oh," she groaned.

His wide golden eyes lifted to gaze at her. "Where in God's name did you get this?"

Rose wanted so badly to disappear. She would have covered her eyes in shame had her spectacles not gotten in the way.

She spun and dashed to the bed, climbing beneath the covers. She removed her spectacles, placing them quickly on the bedside table, then hid her face in her pillow.

Coward! her mind shouted at her. What sort of woman was she that she would quite literally hide from Bram merely to avoid answering a few difficult—and rather embarrassing—questions?

The bed dipped with his weight, and she squeezed her eyes tightly shut, her body tense.

Bram was stronger. He pulled the bedclothes from atop her and turned her, pressing her back to the mattress.

Her eyes sprang open as she realised that he had stripped himself nude. She gazed, dumbfounded, as he hovered above her, his knees straddling her hips while his feet hooked back over her thighs and his hands restrained her wrists to either side of her head.

Rose's gaze slipped downward to the impressive appendage dangling between his splayed thighs. She had the absurd urge to give it a poke to see how it would move. Even while not swelled to its full size, it was a striking thing to behold.

Her chest rumbled, and she looked up at his mouth while he spoke. "Find my cock amusing, do you?" He raised an eyebrow. "Is it anything like what you've read in your wicked book?"

Had she giggled? Oh dear. At least she had not poked him.

She cursed the blush that flared hotter in her cheeks. "On the contrary, I assure you. Your…*cock* is far more imposing than even I could imagine."

His eyebrow rose higher. "And does it make you feel the way your book does?" His eyelids grew heavy as he gazed down at her. "Does it put a quiver in your stomach?" His voice lowered as he spoke, until she could no longer feel the rumble in her chest. "Does it make you throb with want?"

Despite the fresh surge of rouge to her already flaming cheeks, Rose felt her body responding to his words.

"Y-yes," she admitted.

"Say it," he urged.

"Your…" She hesitated.

"Cock," he offered.

She swallowed, and his gaze followed the movement. "Your…*cock* makes me throb with want."

He groaned, then bent to kiss her. With sure movements, he slid her night rail up and over her head, then kissed a path down her body. He paid close attention to her breasts, eliciting groans of delight from deep in her throat. Sliding his lips down further, he reached her hip, and stilled.

Rose waited for several heartbeats before she lifted her head to look down at him.

His heated gaze had cooled, his gaze locked on her hip.

Panic flared in his features, and a responding fear began to well in her chest. Did he hear something?

"I marked you," his lips seemed to say. "My God, I—"

He quickly scrambled off of her, his face aghast.

"What are you—"

He rolled her to her side as he gazed openly and angrily at her bottom.

Her own anger and frustration surged through her, and she batted his hands away and rose to a seated position. "Good heavens, Bramwell Smithe! Will you not tell me what is the matter? I apologise if I've offended you in any way, but to behave…" She trailed off as she watched him.

His expression was stricken. His fingers combed through his hair as he gazed almost fearfully at her.

"Tell me what is the matter." Rose put a hand to his knee, but he pulled away from her as though she'd burned him. "Please."

She clasped her hands in her lap, hurt pounding against her heart. What had she done?

* * *

"Can we not run away, Mama?"

"Oh, Bram, ye sweet dear." She gazed sadly at him while she applied more liniment to her countless bruises, her southeast London accent thick with emotion. "'E is yer father. 'E does not mean te be so ill-tempered."

Bram stood straighter, his chest pushed out. "I'll protect ye, Mama."

She placed a warm hand on his shoulder, though the gesture was hardly comforting. "Ye will let me tend te yer father, dearest. It would pain me far greater te see ye hurt."

He gazed at the tips of his booted toes while Mama returned to dressing her wounds. Baby Yvette toddled about Mama's small bedchamber, entirely unaware of what Papa had just done.

His eyes stung, and he turned his gaze back on Mama. She applied powder to her face to hide the dark blues and reds of what Papa had done. But it would not hide the welts.

Sheer determination dried his eyes as he made a vow. One day he would be strong enough and big enough, and he would protect Mama from Papa. Even if it killed him to do it.

Bramwell stared sightlessly ahead, his mind swimming with images from his past.

"Bram?" Rose's voice sounded far away.

He wished so badly to touch her…but he couldn't. Not any longer. Not after what he'd done to her.

He'd hurt her. *Marked* her. Her neck bore marks from his teeth and lips, where he'd suckled and bit at her soft skin. And her once silky smooth, perfectly rounded buttocks and hips now carried the beginning of bruises from his rough handling.

He groaned, hanging his head in his hands. How could he be such a cad? He was a monster! *Oh God!* What if he turned out like his pater?

A cautious hand touched his shoulder, and he flinched. His heart ached, his stomach roiled. Rose was a good woman. How could he have done this? He'd never been taken out of himself with a woman before. He'd always been in control. Always courteous, but always distant. They had their pleasure and parted ways amicably. But Rose… Rose made him *feel*.

"Bram?" Her soft voice pained him.

He pulled his hands away and faced her, but could not meet her eyes. "My most humble apologies, Rose. I mustn't be in your company at present."

He scrambled from the bed in search of his clothes.

"Wait!"

Bram kept his back to her, afraid that if he saw her sitting there, tousled and beautiful, he would not be able to keep from returning to the bed and taking her again.

He found his breeches and tugged them on.

"Bram. Do not go," she pleaded. "Tell me what is wrong."

He shook his head as he found his lawn shirt and pulled it over his head.

"Could you—" Her voice cracked, and the ache in his heart grew stronger. "Could you tell me what I've done to displease you?" She hesitated, raw, stark pain in her voice. "So that I might learn?"

What was the matter with him? By trying not to hurt her, he was hurting her. She had a right to know why he mustn't touch her again. He wouldn't—*couldn't*—allow himself to be like his pater.

She will hate you, his conscience warned. *She will never speak to you again, and you will have to live the remainder of your life knowing that you frightened away the one woman able to make you feel alive…*

As much as it hurt to realise the truth, he had no choice in the matter.

He spun on his heel to face her, difficult though it was, and spoke.

His spine was stiff as he watched her for her reaction. "My father murdered my mother," he blurted.

Rose gasped, her hands covering her mouth.

"And I killed my father for it."

Chapter 30

Rose watched him in shock and dismay, her heart tripping over her stomach. He stood, expressionless in the small space between the bed and wardrobe, his hands fisted at his sides. The orange glow from the fire rippled over his still form, part of him shrouded in grim shadow.

"P-pardon?" Her hands lowered to the pendant at her throat. She could not *possibly* have heard him correctly.

His jaw clenched and his muscles bunched, his eyes staring sightlessly somewhere to her right. "My father…an abusive man. From my earliest memory, I recall seeing Mama covered in bruises…recovering from broken bones." He shrugged his shoulders, but his impossibly rigid posture belied the casual gesture. "He would drink directly from the snifter in his study…"

Rose listened as Bram stood shaking, revealing the sordid details of his father's despicable behaviour. Her heart ached with each word he spoke, and broke piece by piece for all he had witnessed, all he and his mother had suffered. He'd made such an effort to shelter his sister from the truth while taking on such burdens for himself.

"He beat her so severely…day that I feared…her life," he continued. "I…my father and punched him. I punched him so hard in his jaw that his neck snapped, killing him instantly." The muscles in his jaw tightened as his eyes darkened with sadness. "Mother died only hours later from her injuries."

"Oh Bram…" she whispered, her heart in her throat. "I'm so sorry. How old were you?"

His throat bobbed as he swallowed. "Sixteen."

"You were but a boy!"

"Man enough to understand what I did."

His eyes misted, and Rose's chest ached for him.

"You punched your father, Bram. You did not intend to kill him."

He waved his arms in the air. "Do you think he intended to kill Mama? No! He wanted to continue using her as an outlet for his rage!"

"What he did and what you did are very different things."

He shook his head, tears quivering on the surface of his eyelids. "I should have taken Yvette and Mama away long before that happened. I should have—"

"And where would you have gone with a mother and sister and no funds to support them at the age of sixteen?"

"What does that matter now?" He gestured toward her. "I'm becoming my father, for Christ's sake!"

He rubbed furiously at the tears that spilled over his eyelids, his eyes red and pained.

This time Rose frowned. "How in heaven's name are you becoming your father, Bram?"

"I…marked you."

She touched the tips of her fingers to her neck and felt the raised skin there, then gave him a bashful grin. "You *pleasured* me."

He shook his head again. "I can see the marks, Rose. I have hurt you. I—" His throat bobbed once more. "I do not deserve to touch you."

"Stuff and nonsense." She placed her hands upon her hips. "Have you ever raised a hand to a woman in anger, Bram?"

"*No!* I would never intentionally hurt—" He halted, awareness dawning on his features. "I see what you are doing. But if I have done it by accident, what is to say that I wouldn't—"

"You *wouldn't*." Rose slid from the bed and strode toward him.

He stood stiff and unmoving as she clasped his cold hands in her warm ones. "I am sorry for your loss and all that you have suffered. Those are truly horrific things for a young boy to witness." She squeezed his hands, stepping closer to him. "But I shan't allow you to punish yourself for your father's sins. You are not your father, Bramwell Smithe."

Guilt washed his features. "Rose, I have to tell you—"

"No." She shook her head, refusing to watch his lips. "You are *not* your father. And you did not hurt me."

His face turned mulish, and Rose squared her shoulders. He was hurting, and she was sorry for that, but she simply could not allow him to believe himself an abuser of women when he most decidedly was not. If this was a battle of wills, she would win it. Only then would she provide him the comfort he needed.

She lifted up on her toes to nip his neck. He reared back, his eyes questioning…and aroused.

"Did that hurt you?"

"No."

She lifted on her toes to nip him again, then she smoothed it with a light suckle. The rumble of his groan vibrated through her chest, and she grinned.

"Did *that* hurt you?" she asked.

He returned her grin, warmth lighting his golden eyes once more. "You know it did not."

She touched his neck with the tips of her fingers. "But I have marked you," she noted. "Surely that makes me an abuser of men."

Reaching behind him, Rose filled her hands with his muscular bottom and squeezed, pressing the hardening ridge in his breeches against the apex of her thighs, and a tingle of desire bubbled in her abdomen. He placed his hands tentatively on her shoulders.

"Does this hurt?" Her voice had lowered a fraction as she squeezed him again.

He bent until his lips were inches from hers, and she watched them move. "No."

"Do you believe that I would stop if you asked me to?"

"Yes."

She nodded. "Just as I trust *you* to stop should I ask you."

She squeezed his bottom again. "Am I abusing you?"

"No."

She ran her hands up his chest, over his shoulders, and into his hair as his slid around her waist.

"In fact," he continued, "I would very much enjoy it if you did that again."

So she did. The next hour was consumed with exploration. Rose made sure to nip and suck at each available piece of skin on his person, exulting in his quivers and groans as they rumbled through her chest.

By the time she took him inside her and rode him zealously, he had been begging her to take him. She was eager to comply, for touching and kissing him had fuelled *her* desire as well.

She rode him, her breasts filling Bram's hands, until she found her release; then he gripped her thighs and pumped frantically until he gained his own.

Soon their breathing and heart rates slowed to normal, their kisses turning languid and relaxed as they slipped into sleep.

* * *

There was a jostle to the bed, pulling Rose from her light slumber. A smile touched her lips as she stretched; she was pleasantly sore from their *activities* of last evening.

She cracked open her eyelids to see Bram pulling his shirt over his head. He already wore his fawn-coloured breeches, the light material stretching tightly over his muscular thighs.

Rose glanced through the dimness of the bedchamber toward the window. The hour must be early. The fire had died out sometime during the night, leaving the air cool over her skin.

"Slinking away like a thief in the night?" She rose to a seated position on the bed, keeping the covers clutched tightly to her breasts.

Bram turned at her voice, his lips curved in a humourless smile. He tucked his shirt into his breeches and slid his arms into his waistcoat. "I must leave. I have somewhere to be."

He fastened his buttons and started tying his cravat. Rose steadfastly squelched the disappointment that weighed on her heart and forced her interest to take the fore.

"Where must you be?"

His frown was fleeting in the dimness of the room, but it was impossible to miss. "I shouldn't think that is any of your concern, Rose."

Hurt lanced through her. What was it that he wished to hide from her? She supposed she had no true right to inquire, for they were not wed. Nor was she even his mistress. She was nothing to him but pleasure in the night. The realisation was lowering.

She braced herself for further pain, but her curiosity demanded she ask. "Might I be able to join you?"

"No."

It was absolute. Irrefutable. And it hurt.

He clearly had no desire to discuss his daily activities, which made her wish to question him all the more.

He forced a grin as he slipped on his coat and ran his fingers through his mussed hair. He quickly strode to the bed and pressed a passionless kiss to her forehead.

"I will return to you this evening." He winked as he spoke, adding heart-sinking punctuation to the horribly insulting presumption. Though she supposed that he had her wanton behaviour to base his assumption upon.

He turned and quit the room without another word, impertinent or otherwise.

Was that all she was to him? A means to satisfy his desires and nothing more?

Oh good Lord! Her heart stalled in her chest. *I have become a harlot!*

Thoughts and fears flooded her mind while panic settled heavily in her chest.

No. No, Rose. Do not do this. Their interludes were pleasurable, to be sure. Indeed, she had created many a fine memory with Bramwell Smithe. But that was all. It *had to be*. She could not be a lightskirt. The position of mistress she could accept, if he were to offer, but not that of a lightskirt.

Could Bram be one to take on a mistress? As she sat upon the bed, thinking of him, she realised how very little she knew. She knew of his parents and the unfortunate circumstances of their horrid demise, and she knew that Bram had been a footman with her uncle, that he had a sister and nieces and nephews, and that he favoured coffee over tea.

She frowned into the dim light of the bedchamber.

Rose also knew that he was gallant, intelligent, resourceful, affable, a supremely talented lover, and countless other pleasing things. But what of his ability to ride a horse? How had he learned? How could he afford a town house in London on a footman's salary? How had he learned to shoot a pistol so expertly? Why did his servants not wear livery? How was it that he enunciated so clearly, and in perfect English? How had he learned to drive a team of horses?

Goodness, there were so many questions, and none had plausible answers for a footman working out of Eastbourne. How had she not seen how impossible he was?

Who is *Bramwell Smithe?*

Chapter 31

Bram strode stiffly toward the waiting hack, pausing only long enough for Hydra to enter before he followed, taking his rear-facing seat.

"*Damn it!*" He punched the side of the carriage, the *thunk* echoing through the small space.

"They will speak eventually, Stevens. They always do."

"Unless Hale's men get to them first." Bram cursed.

Hydra shrugged one shoulder. "Yes, there is the possibility they will be murdered before we are able to glean any information from them, but that is a risk we consistently take."

"But where is Hale now? What does he plan to do? Does he know where Rose is being kept? Does he know the location of your town house? Bloody hell, Hydra, there could be an attack at any moment!"

"Calm yourself, Stevens."

"I will *not* be calm!" He punched the thinly cushioned seat beside his thigh. "That woman has done nothing wrong, but she has been inadvertently embroiled in Hale's traitorous activity and endured his bloody fists! We already have our proof of his guilt, so why not follow through? We could take down their entire network of traitorous spies!"

"We need Hale to lead us to their superior. There are other traitors among the gentry, and I mean to find out who they are. Gabe and Mary saw other traitors the night of their rendezvous. There was one man, their leader, whom they had not seen clearly. He is at large and very dangerous. He murdered two of his own spies in cold blood, leaving their bodies to float down the Thames. We cannot allow the danger to our men, and to our king and country, to pass."

Bram hated the logic in Hydra's thinking. But it was sound. He gazed out the window as the hack drove them through the streets of London. Men, women, and children strode along the cobblestone, each one a possible traitor.

"You love her." Hydra's soft, low voice cut through his thoughts.

Bram bristled. "Love? No." Rose was a fine woman; she was beautiful, caring, alluringly curious, and strong. Immensely strong, though he was almost certain that she did not know it. Had he truly ever thought her a mouse of a woman? It was ludicrous.

He felt passionate feelings of affection for her, but not love. He could not afford to fall in love with anyone.

"Most often," Hydra continued thoughtfully, "those who are in love do not see it right away. Only those looking in from the outside are able to see how strong their connection is." He smiled openly at Bram. "And you, sir, are in love."

* * *

Perhaps Bram had sprung from the loins of a gentleman farmer, Rose mused. Once his parents passed, if the estate was entailed, it would have gone to…Bram. *Drat.* That did not work, either. Although, perhaps the town house was what was entailed, and Bram could not afford to keep an estate afloat, so he sold it and became a footman. It explained his ability to ride a horse, his speech, and this house in town.

It was as plausible a tale as any other. Could that be what he was hiding from her? Did he go to visit a solicitor? But why would he feel the need to hide such a thing from her? There were still so many questions.

She wanted to give him the benefit of the doubt, to put her faith in him. But something was shouting at the back of her mind. This was not right.

Perhaps if she peeked behind one of Bram's many closed doors, she could assuage these persistent feelings of insecurity and mistrust.

She nodded to herself, her decision made.

Dog required a morning walk in the gardens; it was the perfect excuse to venture belowstairs so early in the morn.

* * *

Bram leaned forward with the movement of the carriage as it rolled to a stop in the rear close, between house garden walls, his ears ringing with Hydra's words. *You, sir, are in love.* He couldn't possibly be.

He had the urge to shake the thought, to pass it off as merely a fleeting bit of foolishness. But something in him would not let the notion go. *In love.* With Rose.

He shook his head. *Impossible!*

With his mind focused on that entirely disquieting thought, Bram preceded Hydra down the carriage step. The close was shadowed, the two buildings blocking out most of the daylight. But that wasn't why Bram was suddenly alert.

The hair on the back of his neck stood on end, and a frission of awareness tingled down his spine.

They were not alone.

"*Smithe!*" A voice whispered to his left, and he spun toward it.

Hydra reacted as well. His pistol was withdrawn and aimed toward the dark figure slinking against the wall only a few paces from them.

Bram held a hand toward his superior. He recognised that voice…

"Davies?" Bram whispered back.

The young footman tentatively stepped from the shadows, his hands lifted in submissive trepidation.

"Don't shoot!" he whispered emphatically. "I was waiting for you to arrive. I 'ave come bearing a warning."

Hydra released the hammer on his pistol and returned it to the hidden pocket in his coat.

"What warning?" Bram asked.

His former fellow footman hesitated. "Perhaps we 'ad best go inside…"

Hydra stepped forward stiffly, a menacing calm steeling over him. "You will give us the warning *now*."

Davies' words rushed out. "Hale has men searching London for you. He is desperate to find you and the Misses Wilkinson. He—"

"You mean to say that he has not yet found Miss Violet Wilkinson?" Bram held his breath, awaiting Davies' answer.

"He 'as not." The man shook his head, a frown on his brow. "In fact, 'is lordship believes that she accompanied you and Miss Rose Wilkinson to London." He shifted his feet on the damp cobblestone, true fear darkening his eyes. "'Is lordship is mighty angry that he 'asn't found the twins yet. Frightfully so. 'E's…'e's killed men in cold blood… 'Is own servants!"

Ballocks.

Bram placed a calming hand on Davies' shoulder. "I thank you for informing me, Davies."

"I don't know wha's going on beyond the misses rightfully escaping, but—"

"Why do you not join us inside, Mr. Davies, where we can discuss this further?" Hydra stepped forward and motioned toward the hidden door in a conciliatory gesture. "I imagine you would not wish to return to Lord Hale after speaking with Smithe…" He left the rest unsaid, but Bram knew that his meaning hit its mark.

Davies' eyes were wide with panic as he allowed Hydra to lead him inside.

* * *

Hale ground his teeth as he glared daggers at Reddington. The light in his study was bright, but he could feel the darkness surrounding him.

"I have received a portion of my stipend," Reddington groused. "You said that you would have the girl for me by now—"

"You have said as much already, Reddington," Hale growled. "There is no need for you to repeat yourself. I have informed you that this matter has taken more time than I had anticipated. I have men searching for them at this very moment."

Reddington scoffed. "You've claimed as much before, but I have yet to see the results! *Where is my bride?*"

Hale rose slowly from the ornately carved armchair behind his matching desk. He bit back the steady flow of curses that begged to be released and took a steadying breath.

"I assure you, Reddington, I will find her directly," he ground out. "My men are on their trail; I expect them to return with a report by the noon hour."

The man nodded with visible reluctance. "Very well, then." He pulled on his kid gloves as he spoke. "I will take my leave of you. I shall await your summons…once my future wife has been located."

* * *

Bram watched as Hydra led Davies down the hall and into a secluded room. He undoubtedly wished to speak with Hale's footman privately, and Bram would give him the time he required.

He turned into the intelligence agents' drawing room, his mind buzzing with information and mystifying emotion.

"Stevens!" A familiar feminine voice cut through his musings, bringing a grin to his lips.

"Mary!"

He looked up to see his good friend, Mary Wright, gliding toward him. She was a supremely talented actress on Drury Lane. She was also a gifted spy and unparalleled at gathering intelligence.

She returned his smile, the gesture pulling at her split lip. *Good God*, she looked a fright. Thank Christ that their assignment had concluded as well as it had, or Mary's injuries would be a sight worse than they were now.

Her arms spread for an embrace, and Bram swooped down to oblige. It was pleasing to have her here again, for her assignment with Gabe had taken her out of reach for some time.

"What brings you to the town house today, my dear?" Bram asked as he released her.

Mary shrugged one shoulder. "With Gabriel acquiring the title of Baron of Winning, much is required of him from his solicitors. He is here to discuss his plans with Hydra. I believe he intends to remain in town for another fortnight or more before he must submit to his duties in Cumberland."

Bram's grin deepened. "And might you travel with the baron?"

If Mary was one to blush any longer, he was certain she would have. "I believe I might."

"You caught him, did you?" He affectionately squeezed her shoulders.

Mary dipped her head, her striking red hair slipping slightly from her chignon. "He has confessed his love for me, and I him. I am ever so happy, Bram."

Something in his chest constricted as his friend spoke. He was happy for her, to be sure, but her admission struck a chord with him.

"I am pleased for you, Mary."

She linked her arm through his and led him into the drawing room. Several of their fellows sat in the brightly lit chamber, some in deep discussion, others completing paperwork at writing tables set about the perimeter of the space. The draperies were shut so they would not be seen from without, but fire and candlelight lit the room.

"Tell me, Bram"—Mary sat on a settee, pulling him down close beside her—"about this pretty Miss Wilkinson I have heard so much about."

* * *

"Milord!" the young groom gasped as he tripped into Hale's study uninvited.

Hale frowned fiercely at the impertinent wretch. "This had better be important for you to behave so insolently."

Despite the beads of sweat appearing on his brow, the man continued. "It is, your lordship."

Hale waved his hand dispassionately through the air. "Go on."

"I saw the footman, Smithe, enter a house across town."

Instantly alert, Hale sat forward. "Did he have the girl?"

"No, milord, but she might have been within. I did not remain to see, for I came to report to you."

Hale stood, pointing a finger at the footman nearest the door of his study. "You, have my carriage prepared." The man bowed and fled.

If he found the bitch, he damned well wasn't going to waste time putting her on a horse.

"Sh-shall I return to the town house to keep watch, milord?" the groom snivelled.

"No," Hale grunted. "You will lead me to it, and then you will aid me in getting the girl and killing Smithe—and anyone who gets in our way."

* * *

Rose crept from her bedchamber, having washed, dressed, and mentally prepared herself for whatever she might find in her sleuthing. She burned to know what Bram might be hiding, though her conscience warned that this could very well lead to heartache. And perhaps the wrath of the man she spied upon.

She mentally cringed at the thought. But now was not the time to retreat. She had already made her decision, and she would follow through.

The hallway appeared deserted, but she kept her footsteps light in an effort not to be heard. She came upon a closed bedchamber door—one of several that Bram had not allowed her through on her tour of the building.

She pressed her hand to the latch and slowly and cautiously pushed. *Unlocked.* She dearly hoped the door did not creak as she eased it open enough to glance within.

It was a bedchamber, much like her own, though the décor differed slightly. Her gaze travelled over the room, toward the bed. And there her gaze stopped.

A man was sleeping in the bed! *Oh heavens!* Rose quickly closed the door and darted away. Who was that man? Why had Rose never seen him about the town house?

Perhaps searching the bedchambers was an ill-conceived plan, for one never knew what one would find behind a bedchamber door. The belowstairs rooms were far safer.

The halls were illumined with candlelight, though no servants were about. Mr. and Mrs. Lerwick and their children were likely still abed or in the gardens, depending on when the children awoke. But

Rose saw nary a soul while she traversed the halls and stairs to the foyer.

She made her way to the *forbidden* section of the town house. A number of doors remained shut, and Rose gazed at them with narrowed eyes. Her answers could lie just beyond.

Pressing the latch to one door, she entered the first room. A study. It was a masculine room, dark with wooden panels and shelves upon the walls, a large desk, and leather wingback chairs. A tantalus stood against the wall beside the grand desk chair, and the deep-red drapes hanging on either side of the wall blocked out most of the daylight.

Determined to learn more, Rose moved toward the desk. It was neat, yet disorderly. Piles of paper lined each side while pens, inkwells, blotters, and other writing implements graced the top edge of the desk.

Her gaze scanned the papers. Oddly, the letters were either not addressed, or they were written to someone called *Hydra*. Such an odd name. What mother would name her child after the mythological Greek many-headed serpent? Could it be a pseudonym of some sort? It was a logical assumption, but what would they be doing in Bramwell's study?

The letters themselves made no sense. The words were scrambled as though in a code or riddle. Who would write in such a manner? The question frightened her, for she knew she did not wish to know the answer.

She stepped away from the desk, more questions warring in her mind. It was time to venture into another room.

* * *

Mary's smile grew as Bram spoke, the details of his mission spilling from his lips like a waterfall, far too powerful to be controlled. He concluded with the events of the fire and Rose's miraculous strength in recovery.

The others in the room continued in their business while Bram spoke to Mary. Gabe and Hydra had retreated to another, more private, room for discussion, and other men had come and gone on various assignments. The hour was still early for the average denizens of England, but a spy's work was rarely complete.

Finally, he fell silent, the last words still hovering in the air around them.

"You love her." Mary's soft whisper drifted across the air to him, slapping him full on the face. And somewhere disconcertingly lower.

He shook his head, ready to deny the presumptuous statement again, but the words did not come.

"Why does everyone insist on that?" he asked instead.

Mary's warm grey gaze bore into him. "Perhaps because it is true?"

"It couldn't be." He frowned, his body tight.

Mary placed her arm upon his shoulders in a comforting gesture. "What will it take for you to realise it?"

* * *

Rose continued down the hall, stopping before a large set of double doors. It must be a ballroom. *A grand house, indeed.* Though why Bramwell would deny her entry into his ballroom was beyond her.

She pressed the latch on the dominant door and swung it wide.

Unbidden, a gasp escaped her. It had, indeed, been a ballroom at one time. Now, however, the walls were lined with all manner of weaponry. Firearms of all shapes and sizes—some entirely foreign to her—lined the far wall. To the right were spears, clubs, and knives. To the left hung bows and arrows. Chandeliers and sconces brightly lit the room, the flickering candles reflecting in the blades on the wall.

Rose's heart tripled its pace, the hammering in her chest all but making her feel faint.

It wasn't just the walls that had her attention: the expansive space was filled with other accoutrement. Toward the bows and arrows there were targets made of straw with circles painted upon them, presumably for target practice. In the centre of the room were, what appeared to be, two enormous, thin straw mattresses, the purpose of which eluded her. But to the right, nearest the knives and spears, were straw and wood figures shaped like humans. They bore gashes and deep gouges from attackers.

Her breath came in gasps as she struggled to garner control of her body.

My God! she cursed internally. *Who is Bramwell Smithe?*

While she gazed numbly at the practice forms, a door in the corner of the room suddenly opened. Her heart halted in her chest and her breath stalled as a shirtless man entered. Rose did not recognise him. His muscles bunched and rippled as he strode nonchalantly toward the wall of knives.

For some unknown reason, her feet would not move. It was as though she were fastened to the spot, her being entirely frozen.

The man selected a series of knives then stood with his back to the figures. He took several deep breaths before he spun, flinging the blades with deadly precision into the form's wooden head.

She must have made a sound, for the man's dark gaze flew upward to meet hers across the room.

That freed her. With a terrified gasp, Rose fled.

* * *

"Where is it, precisely, that you saw him, Jon?" Hale strode down the narrow alley between the buildings, leaving the carriage at the alley's entrance on the neighbouring street. He needed to ensure an easy escape.

Rain fell on them in sheets, and water dripped off Hale's tall black hat.

"He entered through the side door of a town house just three down from this 'un, milord."

Hale nodded. "Good."

He motioned to the other men with him to keep their eyes on that town house. If there was any movement, they would know it.

Chapter 32

Rose glanced over her shoulder as she darted down the corridor. The man was following her!

She increased her pace past the closed doors. She was running further into unknown territory! Dash it, she should have returned to the foyer. But it was too late now. She had a pursuer!

Who was Bramwell Smithe to have coded letters in his study and an armoury and target practice in his ballroom?

The answer frightened her nearly as much as the question.

The door at the end of the hall drew closer. It was her escape; somehow, she knew it.

She reached for the door's handle, but just as her fingers touched the metal, the shirtless man grabbed her from behind.

* * *

What will it take for you to realise it? Mary's words hovered in the air around his head. He did not know. He did not *think* he was missing anything.

The low rumble of footsteps came from the hall beyond the far door to the room, and he tilted his ear toward the sound.

"What is that?" Mary whispered, her posture suddenly alert.

It could not be Dog, for the tread did not match. It was one…*no*, decidedly two sets of footfalls. One light, one heavy. Had Amelia come bearing news?

A scream rent the air, and Bram tore from his seat. He was across the room in a heartbeat, pulling the door wide.

His chest tightened. Rose struggled for freedom, kicking and flailing from the circle of Thomson's arms.

"She walked in on me practising with knives," Thomson called over her struggles.

She must have felt him speak, for she caught sight of Bram and halted.

"Bram!"

His heart ached for her. For her fear. But most of all, it ached because he knew… This façade of Bramwell Smithe was about to end, and she would see him for his true self. And it frightened him. *God damn it*, it scared the devil out of him.

"Thomson, you may release her."

His fellow spy and comrade opened his arms, and Rose scrambled to gather herself.

The others followed Bram out of the drawing room, gathering at his back to see what had happened.

Hydra's voice sounded at his left shoulder. "What is happening, Stevens?"

Bram's gut clenched. *No, no, no…* His gaze darted to Rose. Had she seen it? Had she seen his name on his superior's lips?

Her cheeks drained of all colour, and Bram's heart sank. *She saw.*

"Stevens?" she whispered. One glance at his face, and her gaze turned accusing and distrustful…and hurt by betrayal.

His heart sputtered, and he stepped forward pleadingly. "It is not what it might seem, Rose."

She retreated a step, and Thomson slid out of her way. "Then what is it?" she asked, her voice unnaturally loud. "Who are you?"

His lips thinned to a grim line. "My name is Bramwell Stevens." He left out the fact of his knighthood, for it did little good to him now.

She nodded once, her lips pulled between her teeth to keep them from trembling as her eyes began to swim with tears. She blinked rapidly to clear them.

"And all this…?" She gestured to the walls of the narrow corridor.

"Not mine," he admitted.

She made a sound like a wounded animal, and the pain in his heart threatened to undo him.

"How could you?" she whispered through distressed gasps.

He strode forward, reaching for her. She flinched, stepping out of his reach. Pain lanced through his chest. It hurt, her rejection. But he understood it.

"I did not mean to deceive you—"

"Did you not?" Her lip trembled. "You live a life of lies, Mr. Stevens."

He grimaced at her formal address and the painful truth behind her words.

"Tell me something, sir…"

"Anything," he interjected.

She toyed with the pendant at her throat. Her gaze briefly darted at the others standing behind him before it returned to him.

"For which side do you spy?" she asked hesitantly. "England or France?"

He recoiled, her accusation and clear distrust in him acting like a dagger through his heart.

"For England." His voice had turned to gravel.

She took a shaky breath, and his heart wept for her. He wanted to touch her. To hold her. To tell her how much he loved her. And damn it, he did, if this persistent ache in his chest and the gut-wrenching fear of losing her were any indication.

Rose nodded. "That is something, at least."

He stepped forward again, desperate to make a connection with her once more.

"*No!*" She nearly screeched it, the shrill fear in her voice very real. "You mustn't touch me. You mustn't *ever* touch me again!" Her lip trembled as more tears sprang to her eyes. "I don't know who you are. I have never known who you truly are, Mr. Stevens." She began to hyperventilate, her sorrow written plainly on her features. A sob wrenched from her throat. "The man I loved does not exist."

He stilled, his eyes wide as her words sank in.

On another heart-wrenching sob, she spun on her heel and ran.

His fellows' muttered curses barely permeated his awareness as he broke into a run behind Rose. He could not allow her to leave. He must make her see! He could not lose her!

* * *

Tears blurred Rose's vision. She held one hand out to the wall beside her to guide her way as she ran through the corridors.

Bram is a spy. Oh God! How could she have been so fooled? He used her for his own purposes, for pleasure. Oh, how could she have fallen for his machinations? She had let herself believe his lies. She thought he'd cared for her. Oh Lord, she had even begun to fantasise about wedding the blackguard!

Was her judgement so poor as to believe anything flattering? Even his friendship was a ruse!

Her feet propelled her faster, pain fuelling her retreat.

What a horrid time to learn her feelings for the man. *Love!* What a grand joke at her expense.

Rose reached the bright foyer and spared not a word for the gaping man at the door as he held it open for her.

Rain had begun at some time that morn, and now it came down in sheets. The rain hit her hard, soaking into her worn black bombazine day dress, but she just kept running. She wished Dog were at her side while she ran like a hoyden down the street in the heart of Cheapside. At least she could place her trust in her pet's loyalty and devotion. She would return for him later. But for now, she must run. Must put as much distance between her and Mr. Bramwell *Stevens* as possible.

She darted between the few occupants of the walk. She could not hear the complaints and murmured objections she was certain were uttered by those she passed. But she could not bring herself to care.

Alarm prickled the back of her neck. She chanced a glance over her shoulder and spotted Mr. Stevens barrelling down the walk behind her.

His ashen skin was tinted with the green hues of a turbulent cloud.

Then she hit something—some*one*. With a mumbled apology, she moved to sidestep the man and continue on her way. But she couldn't. Thick arms came around her, holding her in place.

The smell of tallow wax and stale liquor washed over her, instilling dread—nay, *terror*—in her heart.

No. No, it could not be!

The man gripping her began to drag her into a close between two buildings. Then she struggled in earnest. She pleaded with a passerby to come to her aid, but while he gazed curiously at her, he did not help.

Darkness slowly surrounded her as they ventured deeper into the close. The coal-filled, humid air became stale and scented of urine and rotted animals.

She screamed. She kicked. She clawed, bared her teeth, and flailed. But it was to no avail.

Hale had her.

Chapter 33

Bram's shout carried through the street. The few denizens of Cheapside daring enough to be about on such a day stared in open curiosity and disgust at the outburst. But all cleared his path.

Losing Rose was a fear unlike any he had ever known.

She and Hale disappeared into the close while Rose fought valiantly—but fruitlessly—for her freedom.

"*Rose!*"

Bram continued to run, chasing after the woman he loved in the hope of saving her.

Three rough men at the mouth of the close blocked his path; he tried to push through them, but they held firm.

"You ain't goin' nowhere, mister. 'Is lordship got what he wanted, an' 'e's got us to make sure you don't follow."

Another scream echoed in the close as Hale roughly tossed Rose into a waiting carriage at the other end.

"Get out of my way," Bram ground out.

One man withdrew a dagger from his stocking while the other men withdrew their own weapons.

Before Bram could withdraw his own blade, the *clop* of a horse's hooves were upon them.

The *click* of a pistol being cocked garnered Hale's brutes' attention.

"Stand down," Hydra called from atop his mount.

"Ain't no pistol gonna work in the rain," one of the men spat.

"Shall we test that assumption?" Hydra said smoothly, a deadly undertone to his voice.

Bang! He fired the gun directly into the ruffian's shoulder, knocking him to the filthy, wet cobblestone. The brute howled, holding his rapidly reddening shoulder.

Hydra drew another pistol from his coat, aimed it at another man, and cocked it. "Shall we conduct another test?"

Bram watched as Hale's coachman flicked the reins, pressing the horses into a gallop at the other end of the close. His heart plummeted.

Ignoring Hale's other two men blocking the path, Bram started at a run down the close.

"Hold!" Hydra's voice called through the pelting rain.

Despite his intense desire to follow Rose, Bram halted, facing his superior.

"Take the spare horse. I thought you'd have need of it."

With a nod of thanks, Bram accepted the reins Hydra held in his hand. The persistently ill feeling in his gut would not abate as he mounted the horse and flicked the reins.

* * *

Rose wilted, pressing her back firmly and painfully to the corner of her uncle's carriage. Fear seeped through every pore of her body from the centre of her being.

"…Thought you…get away…fleeing from me…girl?" the madman sneered. "Mark…words…gladly kill you…"

The man spoke too quickly for her to understand all of what he said, but what she did understand told her plenty. Rose pushed her bruised back further against the squabs, pulling her legs up until she formed an oddly shaped ball. Her familiar veil of fear fell firmly into place as she attempted to hide within herself.

"You…essential…plans, girl. If not for…alliances…would have done away with you long ago. If everything goes…plan—and it *shall,* damn it—I will…very powerful man. I…not have you jeopardising…"

Rose's view of her uncle's lips was blocked as he turned to look out the window.

And suddenly, it all became clear.

Her uncle, Lord Hale, was a traitor to the Crown. That must have been why Bramwell had been an acting footman in Willow Hall. He was a spy simply doing his duty. Had she caused him to neglect his mission? Had he garnered whatever information was required of him?

Regret hit her full force. Despite his falsehoods, she should not have been so distrustful of Bram. He was likely following orders by keeping his identity a secret. In aiding her and Violet in their escapes, in protecting her from harm when her uncle's men came after her, he had acted valiantly.

His life as a spy certainly explained his curious abilities with pistols and horses. It also explained why he had fled her bedchamber before dawn each morning. *Goodness*. How foolish she was!

He'd protected her from villains, from the fire…and she had no other response upon learning of his secret than to accuse him of being a villain himself. She shook herself internally. His secret was his livelihood. Surely revealing it to her could have meant a very real threat to both of their lives.

Now, here, she cowered. Curled up in the corner of her uncle's carriage bound for heaven knew what place Hale deemed appropriate for her murder…or her wedding. She only wished to have the opportunity to apologise to Bram first.

* * *

Bram's mount snorted and huffed as he spurred it to a gallop. The beast would only last a few minutes at such a speed, but, with luck, he would catch up to Hale and Rose before his horse tired.

The clamour of horses' hooves thundering behind him roared over the din of the rain. His comrades and Hydra followed. He was grateful for their aid, though he hadn't the time to show it. He was focused solely on saving Rose.

Bram wove his mount around the thin traffic. In moments, they would be out of London and onto the dirt roads of the town's outskirts. On muddy roads, the risk of injury to horses and damage to carriages increased with the rate of speed.

The coachman glanced back at the approaching riders, the movement causing the team to swerve.

Bram's heart faltered as the carriage rose on two wheels before righting itself. The coachman was driving the team dangerously fast. And many people perished in carriage accidents…

* * *

Rose's stomach swooped with fear as the carriage tilted. She gripped the seat's cushion, pressing herself hard against the squabs, before the wheels touched cobblestones once more.

Her entire body vibrated with tense energy: the horses' hooves rumbling, the wheels trundling over cobblestones at a breakneck pace, and her uncle's shouting.

"…Do not care…fast…must go!" Hale bellowed at the coachman, his features a mask of fury, and the low timbre of his voice barely reaching her ears. "I…not be beaten! Outrun the riders…whatever means necessary!" His face turned purple as he spat the last few words.

Terror pierced her heart. Would she survive the carriage ride?

The equipage careened through the streets of London, swerving around other travellers and rattling over the wet cobblestones. Rose squeezed her eyes shut, unwilling to witness her own demise, and turned her thoughts to a more pleasing subject.

Bram. Their last moments together were not happy ones, but she hoped he would interpret her overreaction as shock at such a discovery and the pain of having her heart broken, brief though the moment was. For she knew now that the Bram she had come to love was his true self.

Stars appeared before her eyes as the blow of a hard slap knocked her senseless.

She blinked and tried to see what Hale was saying.

"…little bitch! This…your fault! If you…not left Willow Hall—"

Rose missed the last of what he said as he gripped her arm painfully and shook her.

* * *

Bram urged his mount to run faster, his face drenched in sweat and rain, his clothes all but entirely soaked through. Hale's coachman struggled to keep the carriage steady while swerving around other conveyances and riders. He was mad, Bram was certain.

Screams and shouted profanities whizzed past, cursing the carriage and mob of riders in its wake.

The unlikely convoy reached the outskirts of town as the rain steadily fell, the roads turning to mud. Bram's mount was tiring; its coat was slick with a mixture of perspiration and rainwater.

The coach's horses were labouring with the weight of the carriage, but as they slowed, so did Bram and his fellows' mounts. The coach swerved in a turn, the wheels sliding on the slippery road. The horses whinnied as the coachman cracked his whip.

Damn it, Rose!

An idea formed in his mind, and he turned to shout at Thomson, for he was the best with horses. "Thomson! We're going to overtake them. Prepare to gain control of the horses' lead!"

With a low—but audible—apology to his horse, Thomson pushed the beast faster until he came abreast of the carriage horses.

The coachman shouted, pulling a pistol from beneath his perch. Controlled by only one of the driver's hands, the horses veered violently to one side. But it did not stop the coachman. He aimed the pistol at Thomson and foolishly pulled the trigger.

With a hoarse shout, Thomson gripped the driver's arm as his own horse shied. The carriage horses whinnied in fear, and the coachman struggled to regain control of them.

"*Ho!*" Colin Greene—another of their men—shouted.

Abruptly, the coachman cried out and slumped forward, the hilt of a throwing knife jutting from his back.

"Damn it!" Thomson cursed as he reached for the horses' reins.

Bram's breath halted as the reins slipped from Thomson's grasp and the horses galloped wildly out of control. Their eyes were wide with panic, their teeth bared, and their sides heaving.

"*Rose!*" Bram called helplessly as the carriage began to tip on two wheels.

The horses attempted a turn, pulling themselves further out of Thomson's reach and sending the carriage rolling. It fell to its side in the mud before settling on its roof.

Bram leapt from his mount, his heart caught in his throat as he sprinted toward the carriage. The muffled cock of a pistol stopped him.

"Do not move." Hale's dangerous voice emanated from within the upside-down equipage.

With a grunt, the man kicked at the carriage door, knocking it off its hinges. Rose cried out as Hale gripped a fistful of her hair and pushed her out before him as he would a shield.

A small trickle of blood seeped from the edge of her left brow, and her frock was slightly torn in places, but she wasn't limping or carrying her arms in a way to suggest a more serious injury. Relief rushed through Bram before dread took its place once more. Hale aimed his cocked pistol at her beautiful temple, and Bram's pulse spiked with his ire.

Hale bled from a cut above his ear, the blood seeping down his cheek to his jaw, dripping upon his rumpled white cravat.

Bram waited until he had Rose's attention before he spoke, his stomach knotted beyond comprehension. "Are you well, Rose?"

* * *

The earnest trepidation in Bram's gaze eased the ache in Rose's heart. But before she perished, she must speak her mind.

She mustered her strength as she shakily answered. "No."

He winced. "We will have the doctor examine you just as soon—"

"No," she repeated. "I was wrong. I am sorry for—"

She broke off as Hale's grip on her hair tightened. He shook her, his voice rumbling at her back.

Bram put his hands out in a placating gesture. "Here now, Hale. Let her go, and we can discuss this."

The rain had already soaked through her layers of clothing, chilling her skin. A shiver wracked her frame as her uncle's pistol pressed harder into her temple.

"Thank you, Bram," she said, her voice stronger as she pushed on. "I understand now that you were doing your duty. That you—"

Hale's grip tightened painfully, and she grimaced, hissing a breath between her teeth.

"I never meant to hurt you, Rose." Bram kept a wary eye on Hale.

"I know that now."

Hale's voice boomed at her back as he shouted.

"You…never get away with it, Hale." Bram turned his attention to her villainous uncle, his expression dark with fury. "I…proof of…treachery. You will hang…the gallows for treason, your name…disgraced…family forced to flee…in shame."

Hale's roar of anger reverberated in Rose's ears. His fingers tightened ever further in her hair before he pointed his pistol unwaveringly at Bram.

Her heart stalled. *No!* She could withstand the threat to her own mortality, but not Bramwell's.

"Do not hurt him!" She struggled against her uncle's hold, but he was far stronger than she and easily kept control.

Hale said something, his hand tightening on the pistol.

Surely Bramwell must have a plan. He was a spy! Would he not have experience in such matters? Had he no weapon of his own?

Bram's despondent gaze locked on Rose, full of regret. "I love you, Rose."

Hale bellowed once more. She could see his finger tightening on the trigger, and her instinct took over, to the devil with the consequences.

She flung her arm upward, knocking Hale's arm with it.

Bang!

Chapter 34

Bram howled in pain as the ball grazed his neck. He pressed his hand up to cover it, the searing heat of it bringing him to his knees.

Mud soaked his breeches, squelching as he fell.

Rose's scream pierced his ears and echoed around them. Bram's startled gaze rose as the men behind him dismounted and held their own weapons on Hale.

With the shout of a warrior queen, Rose wrestled the discharged pistol from her uncle's hand. Bram ought to have protested; the pistol was likely hot enough to burn her hands! But oddly, no sound emerged when he opened his mouth.

Now armed with the spent pistol, Rose spun, apparently ignoring Hale's grip on her sopping hair, and began knocking the blackguard repeatedly in the head.

The man's hand slackened, releasing Rose. But she did not stop. Swing after swing, and *thunk* after sickening *thunk*, she hit him. Lord Hale grunted and cried out with each strike as blood began to trickle from his mouth and nose.

"Whoa-ho!" Hydra eased up behind Rose and clasped her hand just as Hale slumped to the mud-covered road. "I will take that," he said soothingly, relieving Rose of the weapon.

Seeing that the danger had passed, several other men hurried forward and tied Hale's wrists.

Someone bumped Bram…or touched him—he was uncertain. He merely became cognizant of the fact that he lay upon his back, falling rain beating upon his face.

Rose's lovely face appeared above him, blocking the flow of rain, worry marring her brow and fear darkening her coffee-brown eyes.

"So beautiful," he heard himself mutter.

Her eyes widened as she gazed at his neck, and she began frantically tugging at his cravat. Her lips began to quiver, and tears flooded her eyes.

"Don't die, Bram. Please don't die…"

He would be fine. It was merely a graze. He was unsure why it weakened him so.

"I wouldn't dream of it, sweetheart." With a grin, Bram reached his hand up to cup her cheek. Then he frowned. Blood smeared on her cheek and dripped from his hand.

"Good God, is that mine?" he heard himself ask.

Rose gazed up at one of the men moving nearby. "Bramwell requires a surgeon!"

Hydra appeared, his expression grim. "This is beyond my abilities." He turned to one of the others. "Ride back to the house and summon Dr. Claridge. Quickly!"

Keeping his grin firmly in place, Bram continued to stroke Rose's cheek.

"Do not fear," he urged, his voice turned to gravel. "Be strong, my lovely Rose."

Her lip trembled. "I am not strong."

Then he frowned, forcing himself to speak through his pain. "But of course you are. Do you…not see? You are capable of so much. Persevered through extreme loss, abuse, heartbreak… You are daily…living proof of your strength. Be proud of all you have…accomplished."

"That's enough, Lord Byron," Colin Greene grunted as he bent to lift Bram beneath his arms. "If your legs work, you had best use them. We must get you to my horse."

* * *

Rose's throat all but closed and her heart hammered painfully in her breast. She watched Bram sag against Mr. Greene's chest as they

244

galloped toward the house. Mr. Greene held his hand to Bram's neck as they rode, using Bram's cravat to stem the flow of blood.

Fright clutched her as she followed on Thomson's horse. The man's arm wrapped around her middle, far gentler than when he had held her at the town house. But she spared it not a moment's thought, for while they were riding, Bram could be dying.

Please don't let him die. The thought repeated in her mind.

Time passed slowly as rain pelted them. The horses tired quickly with the added weight upon their backs. Two men had remained at the site of the carriage accident to begin cleaning. Two others had taken her uncle to gaol to recover from the accident and the thrashing she had given him.

The moment they halted before what she'd come to learn was Hydra's town house, Rose slid gracelessly to the ground, her sopping skirts sticking to her legs. Pinpricks rippled up her feet and into her calves at the contact.

The men worked at aiding Bram into the building. Within, mayhem ensued.

Mrs. Lerwick screamed at the sight of him, the children cried before being ushered to their guest chambers, Dog barked fearfully, and other men and women hurriedly prepared to attend to Bram.

With Dog at her heels, Rose followed Mr. Greene and Bramwell up the stairs, poised to assist them should Bram lose his balance. They laid him down, unconscious, in a bedchamber abovestairs. Rose held his cravat to the side of his neck while the other men began to remove his coat and waistcoat.

The room had evidently been readied for their arrival, for the bed had been turned down, a fire started, and candles lit about the room.

Dog sat alert near the hearth, watching them carefully.

A low rumble alerted her to someone speaking. She spun to see the attractive tall, blond gentleman speaking.

"…These men address me as Hydra," he was saying.

She nodded her understanding. "And this is your town house."

"Very astute, Miss Wilkinson." He suddenly appeared discomfited. "Perhaps…be best…you waited in…corridor while we…" He left the rest unsaid, but she could not mistake his meaning.

"It is nothing I have not seen before, sir," she said, impassioned. "And if you think for one moment that I will leave Bram here, possibly to die, on his own, you are grossly mistaken."

She'd just openly admitted before an audience that she and Bram had been intimate, and, while it should have embarrassed her, she couldn't bring herself to care.

A blinding smile lit Hydra's features. "I like you. And I can see why Stevens loves you so."

His words warmed her despite the direness of their circumstances. She inclined her head. "Thank you."

Rose adjusted her hand upon Bram's neck as Mr. Greene removed Bram's shirt. *Good heavens!* His side, chest, and arm were smeared with his blood.

Mr. Green greeted someone beyond her, and she turned to look over her shoulder. Dr. Claridge entered, his professional demeanour marred by the concern in his gaze.

The three men had said something, but she missed what it was. They watched her expectantly, and, suddenly, her fear of judgement of her impairment did not matter. Humiliation paled in comparison to the threat to Bram's life. And she would do anything to ensure that he lived.

"I am afraid you will have to repeat yourselves," she admitted. "I am deaf. Reading lips is not a skill at which I excel, but if you speak slowly and clearly, I should be able to grasp your meaning. Written word, however, works best for communication with me."

The shock in their gazes was gratefully brief, but warm with compassion.

Dr. Claridge stepped forward and was careful to enunciate. "You may release Stevens now."

With a nod, Rose stepped back, allowing the doctor to examine Bram's wound.

Her hand found the onyx pendant hanging from the silver chain around her neck. The ordinarily comforting gesture could not soothe the deep ache in her chest.

A painful amount of time passed while Dr. Claridge cleaned Bram's neck. The implements in his large black bag came in useful as he prepared to stitch Bram's wound.

Mr. Greene, ignoring the mud and blood caked to his front, climbed on the other side of the bed and opened Bram's mouth, placing a thick strap of leather between Bram's teeth. Mr. Hydra clambered over Bram's legs and firmly held them down.

Good gracious, this would be difficult to watch. But Rose would not leave him.

Dr. Claridge carefully inserted thick thread into the eye of a needle, and Rose's heart stuttered. She could not stand helplessly by while Bram endured such pain.

Uncaring what the others said, Rose rounded the bed and perched herself on the pillow beside Bram's head. In as soothing a gesture as she could manage, she tenderly stroked the wet hair from his forehead.

The doctor uttered a warning to the men as he pressed the needle to the skin of Bram's neck.

Instantly awakened, Bram arched alarmingly from the bed, a harsh growl grinding from his chest. The men scrambled to hold him down while Dr. Claridge stitched him.

Rose ached for him.

She bent until her forehead touched his.

"Shh-shh. Easy now, my love," she whispered in his ear. "The doctor must stitch your wound."

She continued to stroke his hair, and he calmed, his rapid breaths brushing past her hair.

"I am here, Bram," she reassured him. "I am here…"

With Bramwell calmed, Dr. Claridge quickly stitched his wound. Mr. Hydra and Mr. Greene were able to release Bram while the doctor added a poultice and bandaging, but Rose remained at his side.

Several minutes passed in which Rose spoke in Bram's ear, her gaze cut off from all around them.

A hand gently touched the back of her neck, and she raised her head. Bram gazed at her, his golden eyes clouded with banked pain and relief.

"Thank you." He attempted a grin.

She shook her head, an answering smile on her own lips. "You do not need to thank me."

His grin deepened despite how it must have pained his neck. "Then I shall kiss you instead."

He pulled her head down to his, his lips pressing hers in an achingly tender kiss. Her heart soared. His lips moved lightly over hers, his tongue dipped once, touching hers and sending warmth rippling through her.

Good heavens, this was hardly the time for such feelings! She pulled away with a laugh.

"Naughty man," she scolded playfully.

A hand lightly gripped her shoulder, and she turned her gaze upward to Mr. Hydra.

"You had best change before…catch the ague," he said.

Embarrassment heated her cheeks. "This is my last good dress."

Shock lined his features. "Good gracious! Well…afraid that we cannot have that." He winked audaciously at her. "One of…many perks of being…spymaster is that I have a…talented modiste…my disposal. I shall summon her directly."

"Oh." Rose shook her head in protest. "I haven't the funds to—"

"Nonsense!" Mr. Hydra crossed his arms over his chest.

Bram's hand slid within hers and squeezed.

"You aided in the capture of one of several dangerous, treasonous spies working…Napoleon Bonaparte," Mr. Hydra continued. "It would…remiss of me not to handsomely reward such assistance."

Squeeze. Bram's thumb caressed the back of her hand.

Mr. Greene stepped forward, a ghost of a smile on his lips. "It would seem that you are now a spy, Miss Wilkinson. I must say it has been a fascinating initiation."

Chapter 35

Two days later, Rose balanced a tray in her hands as she pushed Bram's bedchamber door open with her bottom.

Bram sat upon the bed in his shirtsleeves, his cravat left untied to allow his neck to heal. His green waistcoat brought out the gold in his eyes.

She beamed at him as she thrust the door closed with one foot. "Your meal, *Sir* Bramwell Stevens."

She could not stop that thought from whizzing through her mind. Bram had been knighted! But of course he had—he was the best man she knew. He most certainly deserved it.

Dog perked his ears up and sniffed the air as the scent of food reached him. Bram scratched the canine behind the ear as he sat grinning at the little beastie while Rose approached. Bram had braced his back comfortably with pillows. The room had been cleaned and the sheets and counterpane washed since he had arrived, injured, two days past.

He was well enough to move about with minimal discomfort, but Rose quite enjoyed this time pampering him. He was still not permitted to return to his duties as a spy, though he did his utmost to glean any information he could about his fellows.

Rose kept herself out of it, for goodness knew she had been through enough excitement for the time being. Though…perhaps one day she might wish to go on another adventure.

She put the tray on the table beside the bed, retrieved the sketchbook, slid off her golden slippers—which matched her borrowed, yet perfectly fitted, yellow day dress—and settled herself beside Bram beneath the counterpane. Dog moved to sit between their legs, his anticipation of a meal evident in the drool gathering at the corners of his mouth.

Rose laughed and reached to toss a slice of roasted beef onto the floor.

Dog pounced, picked up his prize, and trotted about the room in search of a place to enjoy it.

With one last grin at Dog's antics, Rose retrieved the tray and laid it across their thighs as they squeezed closely together.

"While Cook prepared this tray, I had a thought." Rose selected a grape from the tray and popped it in her mouth.

Bram's utterly sensual lips curved in a breathtaking smile, and wrote in the sketchbook. "And what was that?"

"Even though I have not yet received a letter from Violet, I know she is safe. Hale will be hung for treason, and his men have all but disappeared. My aunt and cousins will very likely flee from society… Violet will not be pursued." She smiled at the man she loved more with each passing moment. "We are free."

"Indeed, you are." He raised an eyebrow at her. "Although…" He paused, tapping the sketchbook.

"Although what?"

"I received this while you were belowstairs." He handed her a folded missive. "It's for you."

"From Violet?" She accepted it eagerly and read the direction. "This is not Vi's handwriting."

Curious, she broke the stamped seal at the back and read the first sentence.

"Oh, gracious," she breathed.

Bram sat straighter, showing her the sketchbook page. "What is it?"

"It's from my father's solicitor." She scanned the letter, her breath coming fast and her fingers trembling. "My God, Bram. Violet and I inherited our father's estate!"

"*What?*"

She handed the parchment to him, and he read through it. "My father never told us that his estate was not entailed. Perhaps he thought he had more time."

Bram's head swung to face her, before he scribbled in the book. "This would explain Hale's animosity toward you. He wanted your father's estate for himself: more land, more power."

Rose nodded, placing the letter on the bedside table. "I must write a letter to Vi."

Bram tossed Dog another slice of beef before taking one for himself. "Tell me, Rose." He gazed thoughtfully at her, then wrote again. "What was it that your sister had planned for her escape?"

Rose contemplated the question for a moment. She supposed it would do no harm to tell Bramwell now. It had already been perpetrated, after all.

"While you and Hale were gone, we pilfered one of our cousin's duelling pistols. Vi planned to go to the neighbouring estate to—"

Bram gripped her hand with his free one, anticipation and mirth lighting his eyes as he waited for her to read his writing. "Do not tell me, Rose… My God, she didn't…"

"Goodness, Bram, she did not shoot the man, I am certain. The pistol was not even loaded, for heaven's sake. She merely meant to *coerce* the man into escorting her north to Scotland, to our grandparents."

Bram threw his head back, a deep bark of laughter emanating from his chest and rumbling in hers. He winced, holding one hand to the bandage at his neck, as he continued to laugh. Tears began to seep from the corners of his eyes, and he swiped at them with the back of his hand.

"Bloody hell, Rose."

"What?" she asked, feeling very nearly affronted.

"The landowner of the neighbouring estate is Christian Samuels, the Viscount Leeds."

She expectantly raised her eyebrows. "Yes…"

Another laugh escaped him. Goodness, but he was striking when he laughed!

His shoulders shook as he wrote. "Samuels taught me everything I know about cryptology, which, admittedly, is very little, for I rarely paid attention in that particular class. He is only one year my senior, but he has been a spy for the Crown since he was able to walk. His father taught my superiors. He is currently our lead cryptologist and works out of his estate. And that is only because he was injured in the line of duty." He laughed again. "Your sister will most assuredly have a safe journey to Scotland."

Rose blinked. "But Vi said that he was elderly and walked with a limp."

"His hair went grey prematurely, and his limp is from his injury. The man's one-and-thirty."

Rose's hands came up to cover her lips as she began to laugh. "You're bamming me!"

"Indeed, I am not!" His eyes misted with amusement. "And I daresay Samuels will have his hands full with your fierce sister."

Rose guffawed in an unladylike manner, but she simply could not help it. If Lord Leeds was anything like Bramwell, Vi was in for a fascinating journey. *Perhaps her naughty book will come in handy after all.*

The thought had her laughing harder, her stomach aching with the force of it. Her sister was safe. It was a wonderfully freeing bit of knowledge.

There were several moments of liberating laughter before she calmed herself enough to press a kiss to Bram's lips.

"Thank you, my love." Her eyes warmed as she gazed into his strikingly golden eyes. "I needed that."

"Marry me."

Startled out of her mirth, Rose's eyes widened. "Pardon?"

"I love you, Rose. You inspire me to be a better man; you are strong, beautiful, amusing, fascinating…and you drive me mad with desire. I cannot imagine a better woman for me than you. Will you do me the honour of becoming my wife?"

He pulled a ring from his waistcoat pocket. It was a black onyx with white rings surrounded by small, circular diamonds. Warmth spread through her chest; it matched her pendant. When had he found the time to commission it?

Her eyes stung with the threat of tears, and she pressed her lips together to keep from weeping as she nodded vigorously. "Oh yes,

Bramwell! Yes, I will!" She wished to embrace him but did not want to aggravate his injury. She settled on an ardent kiss.

When they were both lightheaded and gasping for breath, she pulled back to accept the ring. It suited her to perfection.

Bram tipped up her chin with his crooked index finger. "It was my mother's. It means everything to me. And so do you."

"I love it, Bram," she said earnestly. She pressed another kiss to his lips, her heart full of light and joy. "And I love you, my charming spy."

www.ingramcontent.com/pod-product-compliance
Lightning Source LLC
Chambersburg PA
CBHW021127190726

48288CB00008B/2543